The Gin Trap

The O's are dead. Beautiful Olivia MacIntyre died when her twin daughters Charlotte and Iona were two. Ormonde, the girls' glamorous young uncle, was killed in WWII in mysterious circumstances. The children, born in 1943, are brought up in the wilds of Scotland by puritanical, war-damaged Fardie, who controls them with a dog whistle, imposes an unrealistically harsh regime and draws a veil of silence over their own background, his brother's death, his war and his shame.

With only her portrait and a pair of sparkly slippers to go by, the twins, united in their longing for their mother, succeed in inventing *'almost a whole person'*. But, as Charlotte reflects later:
It's like doing a jigsaw puzzle. If you're missing a piece of sky you can make a bit out of cardboard and colour it blue. The trouble is you can never be absolutely sure there wasn't a bird flying past at that very moment.

As the protagonists' lives and loves proceed along very different lines in America and England, Charlotte and Iona find it harder to colour the missing parts of their lives blue. The sky darkens and the birds flying past prove unsettling, as their curious story unfolds.

Sarah Paton Wiseman was born in Scotland at the start of WWII. In 1969 she moved to Mexico with her husband and children where she worked as editor and writer, creating some of the first books for Mexican children drawing on their native myths and legends. During those years she developed her interest in fiction and joined the Tramontane Poetry Group, publishing poems and short stories for American magazines. Presently living in Somerset, Ms Wiseman returns in her imagination to childhood holidays in Argyllshire for the background of her first novel, The Gin Trap.

The Gin Trap

Sarah Paton Wiseman

Kennedy & Boyd

Published by
Kennedy and Boyd
an imprint of
Zeticula
57 St Vincent Crescent
Glasgow
G3 8NQ

http://www.kennedyandboyd.co.uk
admin@kennedyandboyd.co.uk

This novel is entirely a work of fiction. The names, characters and incidents portrayed in it are the work of the author's imagination. Any resemblance to actual persons, living or dead, is entirely coincidental.

ISBN 1-904999-15-8 Paperback
ISBN 1-904999-16-6 Hardback

for John

Acknowledgements

I would like to thank my agent Caroline Dawnay for her constant support and encouragement, my husband who has helped me with the research and my daughter Octavia, whose advice has been invaluable.

I am grateful to Jennifer Clement, poet, novelist and teacher, whose ardent belief in 'the individual voice' spurred me on the road towards discovering my own.

I also want to thank many wonderful friends for their comments and enthusiasm.

Prologue

1985

CHARLOTTE

Today they'd call it abuse.

I didn't need to go to Los Angeles to learn that. He fucked us up! Not physically, you understand, he never raised his one hand against us. Our father hated that sort of violence.

But mentally John Calvin had nothing on Fardie. From the age of three we were controlled with a dog whistle. We were indoctrinated with God (his version), honour, duty, frugality, the Morse code, how to be a good loser, how to behave in a boat, how to put tar on a sheep's foot, how to use a compass – psalms, punishments ... guilt.

You spend your life trying to throw it off. You put God on hold, or rather reinterpret Him to suit yourself. You create other gods: lovers, therapists, homeopathic drops from Chinese bark. You go in for Vipassana meditation – I was grappling with precept number four of the eightfold path when I lived in Manhattan. You're free of it, almost entirely, but bits of it stick. It's like scraping black paint off a walnut fireplace. However hard you rub there are traces of it for years.

Our father made me ashamed of my body. I was fourteen, I think. Very tall. You know that angular look young, young girls have when their legs go on forever and they are behindhand with breasts? The feminine thing is just beginning, wavering like a match flame. I mean the girl has probably got a crush on someone. She may be in love with a dead poet ... or a schoolmistress. It's a delicate time. Especially if that girl has no mother.

Once, I remember, he was taking us somewhere for lunch. I'd made a pair of trousers from odds and ends I'd found in the attic. They were tight and long. I loved them. And I liked the feel of my short hair under a big French cap. It might have been Ormonde's, we were always wearing Ormonde's things. I ran down the stairs at Craigmannoch ...

'Charlotte!'

'What?'

'Go and change immediately.'

'But I am changed, Fardie.'

'What the devil ... those... ? They're too tight. Disgusting!'

'But ...'

'Give the wrong impression. Make you look like an actress, damn it ...'

I can see him now standing at the bottom of the staircase, thumping his stick. Our father lost his left arm in the Second World War. His neck is shorter that side. You get the overall impression of a tall bird tucking its head under one wing. I used to wonder if it wasn't just a good acting job, an excuse for avoiding looking into other people's eyes. Vivian says his were once North Sea blue like hers; ringed by thick black MacIntyre lashes. But I remember them always as faded, blue seen from a distance, like the haze you get behind our island where sea meets sky.

'Make you look like an actress, damn it ... !' Actress from him meant whore. I was sensitive about being likened to a whore at fourteen, although I could take it later.

He lost his arm in battle - someone must have told us that. Anyway, it's what one would presume. His younger brother Ormonde was killed that day. They were in the same Highland regiment so it seems obvious that it was the same battle. When I was little I imagined our father stumbling through a hail of bullets, hoisting his younger brother aloft with his remaining arm, crying out *Undaunted go we forth* ... or *Their's not to reason why* ... two of my favourites.

I say *we* not *I* because everything has to do with my twin sister Iona, or Puff as she's often called. We don't have those weird twin things, like matching halves of a pineapple on opposite buttocks. We're fraternal, not identical. Anyway no birthmark would make a difference. Toby used to steer me away from the word love. He said it was 'too Hollywood'. I find it's too small, when you're trying to encompass everything.

They say that the firstborn twin is more aggressive – more complex if you like. I'm not sure who the *they* that says this is, but I suppose they do have a point.

From the only available accounts, those of Forrie, our dear

housekeeper, and Elsie Campbell, her niece, I was born first – fighting my way fiercely out into the cold March air. Iona, the more placid child, sailed easily down the path I'd forged. It was the year 1943. Our father was fighting the Germans in Africa. Apparently our mother had *a right time of it*. She never fully recovered her health and died of ovarian cancer when we were two.

We were brought up with a certain amount of brutality. Brutality and beauty. Lambing is an example. Usually it's easy to get them out, just a gentle pull on the forelegs, but sometimes one is stuck. Our aunt Vivian was the only one who could turn a lamb. She'd reach right in up to her elbow. If it lived and the sheep died we were allowed to keep the woolly baby in a corner of the kitchen and feed it from a jar with a teat. If it came out dead it was flung on the midden heap and left to rot. We were used to that sort of thing.

Harder to bear were gin traps. They're illegal now, but they were used all around us then. Grey mouths with steel jaws which bit down when something triggered one off. They hardly ever caught the whole animal. It was usually a single paw – or a leg. Foxes, hares, rabbits, otters, cats. If they managed to free themselves it was by biting through their own limb.

Once, when we were very small, we were walking down the gully, first Fardie, then me, then Iona – when suddenly we heard a scream, then another ... round the corner we came on the pitiful sight of a hare with its hind leg caught in a gin trap. The leg and thigh were almost severed. The beast was trying to haul itself free.

'What'll we do, Fardie?'

'What'll we do?'

'Walk on, children!'

'Fardie?'

The hare screamed again. There was blood all over the heather. He lifted his stick. I wrestled with him, trying to get it away. Iona was sobbing, kissing the hare. There was blood on my sister's face.

Then I noticed our father – a shudder was bolting through him like an electric current. I didn't understand that. Scottish men find it easy to finish off wounded creatures. They're good at killing things.

'Walk on!' he roared. His voice was tremendous.

His brother Ormonde was our hero. We only knew him through

the meticulous wash of silver nitrate in soft sepia tints, but we felt we knew him well: Ormonde at four in velvet knickerbockers ducking for apples. Ormonde, cheeky and engaging, driving the tractor at twelve. Ormonde at school leaning against a pillar, long and lethargic in Oxford bags. But the photograph we loved the most included our mother.

In it Olivia is sitting at the garden table shelling peas. On the table are her gardening gloves, the yellow secateurs, the brown kitchen bowl and the flat basket. It used to amaze us that she should be touching these familiar objects. Except for the gloves they are all still here today. She is wearing a large-brimmed summer hat. Across from her Ormonde is sitting, smoking a thin cigarette in a cigarette holder. He must have just said something funny because she is looking up and laughing. The gauzy part of the hat shades her eyes, but you can see her tossed back head and her wide, pretty mouth. We admired Ormonde all the more for making our mother laugh.

We even admired him for getting killed. It seemed to us a more glamorous resolution than limping back from the war like our own father, as bitter as a green plum.

The difficulty we had was that our father would tell us nothing about his past or our own. Even Vivian told us nothing. When you don't know things you tend to fill in the best you can. It's like doing a jigsaw puzzle. If you're missing a piece of sky you can make a bit out of cardboard and colour it blue. The trouble is you can never be absolutely sure there wasn't a bird flying past at that very moment.

Puff and I were good at filling in. In the case of our mother we invented almost a whole person. We had few facts to go on, just some sparkly slippers she'd given to Elsie and her portrait which hung in the hall. Olivia was beautiful. In the painting little slivers of gold and silver play in her hair and light up her skin, like evening sun catching on loose hay as it jolts back to the farm on a cart. She looks very like Iona, except for her dark eyes, which are like mine. For years I thought she could see us through her painted eyes.

We blessed her with favourite foods, favourite books, favourite flowers. We gave her a kind voice and an all-abiding love for the twin daughters, from whom she'd been so cruelly snatched. When one of us was frightened or lonely our mother would say, *Hush, child*. Or rather the other twin would reassure her frightened sister that that was what she was saying.

Even today, at the age of forty-two, I have to remind myself that she never said 'Hush, child' in her life. And that, from the disturbing reports we have of her short and dazzling life, it was not the sort of thing she would have said.

We longed to hear about her, so long as it completed our perfect picture. We didn't want anything else. Iona didn't deserve to hear what smirking Elsie blurted out years later on her sofa. My sister had babies of her own by then and she wasn't well at the time, not well at all. And when I was in California living with Toby, my cousin Morgan accidentally let slip Vivian's jaundiced view of Olivia. It was wrong of him. We needed our mother as she was ... as we thought she was. I wonder if this needing ever stops.

Vivian, our father's sister, was what we actually had – the only one that wasn't dead, or almost dead like Fardie. On the surface she was gruff, not at all motherly. But we loved her madly and, in her abrupt way, she loved us. She was never out of trousers, boots and a smelly old jacket and there was usually a hat thumped low on her head so you couldn't see her dense blue eyes. She'd buried herself in neatsfoot jelly, goslings, planting and sheep. As children this didn't strike us as odd. We didn't expect her to have friends. Although, now that I think about it, she was in her twenties.

One thing we couldn't help noticing was the whispering. When you walked through the village with Vivian you could feel it around you. She'd toss back her head, her skin tightening like a sheet on the washing line. 'Bugger off,' she'd mumble under her breath.

We lived in a wild part of Scotland. Craigmannoch is a dour, shabby house built of grey stone. Behind lie moor and hill. In front the house looks out onto a sea loch. There's a little island – just rock and heather – but it's a wheel of wings: gulls, puffins, cormorants and gannets nest there and seals flip on and off the rocks. The house has a drowsy, overgrown garden going down to the water. The air is saturated with rain, sea and the smell of bog myrtle. It is sweet with it. When the sky isn't an angry grey or blank with snow the sun can surprise you, suddenly lighting everything up like a stage set, clowning around, showing off the mad purple beauty around you.

It can't have been easy bringing up motherless twins. Looking at it now from the perspective of someone who has inherited a child through painful circumstance, I do see that it can't have been easy.

But if only he'd talked to us. The irony is that he's talking now; now that he's dying he can't stop. Last night, our first night back at Craigmannoch, he whispered Ormonde's name. We held our breath. We bent our heads close to his mouth, but my hair must have touched his face and startled him for it set him off.

'Down! Down!' He cries, over and over, as if something were jumping up on him, tearing at him with teeth ...

PROLOGUE

1985

IONA

My psychiatrist would love to know what I packed for coming back to Craigmannoch! My feather pillow (the ones here are definitely horsehair), my hot water bottle with its dear cover which Hughie made in handwork class – it gets cold at night, even in July – a proper bath towel, my cashmere shawl, a Thermos that works, a large box of truffles and, most important, a torch. Gareth would consider it very revealing that his forty-two year old patient whose father wouldn't allow a light in the passage should take a torch back to her childhood home, although the father that forbade that light is too ill to stir from his bed.

Call it self-indulgent if you like but how can you be supportive to a raving father if you're miserably uncomfortable? That's where Fardie's God and I part company. If, as he relives the march from Bebra to Colditz – folding and refolding the sheet between his emaciated, shaking fingers – I'm depressed, will it help either of us?

Yet I felt bad about packing the pillow.

Our poor father had his left arm amputated in the war. His younger brother Ormonde was killed by his side. At least that's what we think. We're still confused about what actually happened and why our father will never say his name. Our aunt Vivian has always considered him 'a frugal old sod'. Although I suppose you could say there's a peculiar unspoken affection between them, the kind that allowed Fardie to kiss the air about a yard from our hopeful cheeks when he shipped us off to boarding school aged eleven.

The strange thing was that when he got back after the war to us – my twin sister Charlotte and me – he chose to perpetuate the violence. Not physically, you understand, but from the point of view of imposing the most rigorous, loveless regime. Never a hug, no sweetness of any kind. And I was the sort of pudgy, loving child that craved sweetness, the emotional and the purely carnal. Rationing was officially over by the time we were eight, but our father was a manic puritan. We were hardly ever allowed butter, although we churned it at the farm. The top was taken off the milk and sold in the village. No sugar, no jam, one sweet a day. Worst of all were the strawberries. They were shipped off to some other nation – I can't remember which – and we were forbidden to pick them.

One of my earliest memories is of kicking my heels into the soft mud, inching my way under a strawberry net and closing my lips around the soft fruit – one wiggle and it dropped whole into my mouth. Oh, the swampy, scarlet spread of pleasure! I also licked the top off the milk in the dairy pail before it was skimmed, and I stole cocoa.

When I was caught our father called me deceitful and I was punished. It shamed me, but I didn't stop. In my opinion you shouldn't use words like *deceitful* with little children. Mark and I wouldn't dream of doing anything so horrid with ours. From the perspective of a forty-two year old mother trying to get it right, I'd say he got that absolutely wrong.

But maybe he was on to something? Maybe. Because later, when I was fourteen, I did do something blatantly dishonest to someone I dearly loved. I read part of my Aunt Vivian's diary. It was the beginning of finding out what she was concealing and a punishment inflicted on her worse than anything we could imagine. I little realized then that her secret would become mine many, many years later. It's no longer a secret. I've told Mark and Charlotte. I've said sorry to Vivi over and over. I've been forgiven ... although Gareth says it's really about being able to forgive oneself.

Not long after I'd told my darling husband, sobbed it out in a Heathrow telephone kiosk, I actually went to confession. We were on holiday in France and I went up to one of those slatted boxes and knelt down. I put my hand up to the curtain and said: 'Father?' 'Yes, child.' (He answered in English). I told him the whole thing. Mark said it was a greater sin posing as a Catholic when you've been brought up as a strict Presbyterian and don't believe in God anyway. It's true that I don't. But in times of need Catholicism is so much more sympathetic than all the roaring and rebuking we were subjected to.

Vivian wasn't like our father, her brother Harry. She thought sin and punishment were bollocks. If she'd given anyone half a chance I think they'd have found her very handsome. She had dark hair then, like Char, good cheek bones and a fabulous figure which nobody ever saw as it was perpetually enveloped in dungarees. She was tough on the outside but she loved us, no doubt about it. Fardie once asked her to give us a 'facts of life' talk when we were about nine. Her way of dealing with it was absolutely typical, no intimate woman-to-woman gentleness, nothing like that.

'Look kiddos, we're women right ... ? Egg machines ... ? Stunted eunuchs at the end of the day but, in your cases, let's just say plain female.'

'Yes, Vivi.' We couldn't imagine what was coming.

'Have you any idea what goes on inside us?'

'Not much.'

'I thought not. Right, there's a womb floating abou ...'

'We know about wombs,' interjected Charlotte, 'because of Mary's.'

'That's a point. But it's not just Mary, it's the lot of us. Do you know what happens when you're about twelve?'

We didn't.

'It starts up a rhythm of bleeding once a month – when we are far too young to take it on board.'

'Where?'

'From our vagina ... the little hole placed incongruously between ...'

'Moira's big sister showed us one in the Encyclopaedia Britannica,' I told her politely.

'But why?' Charlotte wanted to know. 'Why does it do it?'

'It means your body can make a baby, provided you've got a man, that is.'

'What's the man for?'

'Christ!' Vivian said under her breath. 'Look, blighters, you don't need to know that bit yet. It all hangs together in the end.'

'Does Fardie know about this?' my sister asked sternly.

'Everyone knows! It's all part of God's perverse little plan.'

It makes me laugh now but I found it shocking then. I longed for a cosier approach. There was a minimum of cosiness at Craigmannoch and what there was came from Mrs Forrester and her niece, Elsie Campbell.

The truth is I loved Elsie then. Her plump pink arms are the first thing I remember. 'Whose Elsie's wee gurl?' she'd say to us in turn, when she picked us up from our prams, kissing our wind-scorched cheeks, jouncing us about in her sixteen year old arms. Later on, when one of us had been shut up for an afternoon learning a psalm, she'd say, 'Come to Elsie-Pelsie for a wee kiss an' a cuddle ... '

Ours was a strange childhood. My earliest memories are of blood: Vivian up to her elbows in it pulling out a lamb, Jimmy wringing hen's necks, the abattoir where they killed the tups, dead deer slung over Minnie the pony's back. We got used to it in a sense. Although we never got used to gin traps.

I remember, when we were very young, walking in the gully with our father. It was a lovely day. He didn't like us touching him but he let me put my hand in the pocket of his jacket. Suddenly we came across a hare struggling in a gin trap. It screamed and screamed. Our father raised his stick to kill it. I tried to pull it out of his hand. There was blood everywhere. There was blood on my sister's face. I can't forget that even now.

Char has led a more dramatic life than I have. Closer to the edge. Although when I did go off the tracks I certainly did it in style! It was wrong of me, I know. But could I have missed it, I wonder? I still feel his eyes on my body, perilous, passionate ... deeply anxious eyes.

Our father really meant well. He believed that God was our only salvation. My sister was fascinated by religion. Still is. But she was a rebellious child and she challenged him on every point. The night after we'd seen the hare we were kneeling at our beds, saying our prayers. I must have rattled mine off agreeably. I was an agreeable child, eager to please. But Charlotte confronted our father - and God - on the hare business.

'Jesustendameekanmildlookuponalittlechilpitymysimplicity ...' she used to run the words together which infuriated Fardie. 'Thank you, God, for curing Minnie's worms. Tell our mother in heaven about it and about how Jimmy shoved the medicine up her bum. Bless IonaFardieViviForrie and Elsie and, God, can't you even save hares?'

'No! Charlotte.'

'No, what?'

'You can't say bum to God. It's a nasty word ... and you must stop challenging him.'

'You said prayers are private.'

'They are.'

'Then?'

When our father was agitated he would put his one hand in his breast pocket to steady it. His face was crimson with distress.

'You must understand. God is great. You mustn't question Him ... He could save hares - if He wanted to. His ways are mysterious ... '

'Well, I think he's mean to hares!'

'So do I,' I agreed, in a cowardly voice that was almost a whisper.

'That's enough!' He roared. 'Now go to sleep. D'you hear?'

For a few minutes we lay rigidly between the cold sheets, then Charlotte started us off.

'Bumbumbumbumbum ... !'

'Bumbumbumbumbumbumbumbum!' I said from my bed under the window.

We were snorting, hiccupping – giggling helplessly. We put pillows over our faces but Char only had to say 'bu ...' and we were off again.

Our mother died when we were babies. There's no way I could remember Olivia, logically speaking. But when I think back it seems she was with us every day. Now that I'm a mother myself our behaviour does seem strange. We picked flowers for her, knitted scarves for her birthday and somehow engaged her in long conversations. I'm not sure how we managed it, but there was a magical sense of being listened to. I haven't told Gareth. He'd take all that away, calling it sublimation or something deflating like that.

The nights were different. I still dream that I'm searching for the light switch in the passage, running my fingers over a blank wall, not finding it, feeling a tingle in my bladder like the tines of a fork, crying out for my mother.

Not allowing us a light in the passage was the one really wicked thing Fardie did. Why? Why, when he'd known such darkness himself?

Now that he's dying he lets me touch him. I stroke his hand and he talks to me at last. Only it still isn't me. He thinks I'm Olivia. He tells her about their children. But they aren't us either, not anymore, not the women we've become.

'Lovely girls, Livla. Good children,' he said last night. 'Charlotte's brave y'know and little Iona ... just like you, dearest. Did m'best. They know their prayers, I think. I'll hear them tonight ... go over it all.'

It's our second night back at Craigmannoch. I haven't told Char the last thing he said, after she'd gone to bed.

'Don't tell the children!' he cried out suddenly in anguish. 'Don't let them know ... '

Don't tell us what?

Chapter 1

CHARLOTTE

One minute our father had us in training for the commandos then, out of the blue, we were shipped off to Westfield, an archaic girls' school in the south of England – a flower arranging hell-hole. Our geography books still have the British Empire intact, if you can believe it! Miss Whitely doesn't want to clutter her girls' heads with the ungrateful little countries that have separated themselves from England's green and pleasant land.

Now that I'm fifteen I can laugh about it. Well, sometimes. But it wasn't easy at eleven.

I say *I* not *we* for Iona took to it right away. In no time at all she was surrounded by a cluster of Arabellas and Melissas. She picked up the *jolly d, soo-pah* language in a jiffy and dropped her Scottish accent. It's what she'd always wanted really, to be warm and popular and tell secrets after lights out. She loved changing into the frocks Fardie had bought us. The teachers liked her too. She made beautiful maps with India ink and bright, well-sharpened colours, without questioning what was pink and what was not.

But I missed the moors, the sea, the vastness. I yearned for rains that drench and the scream of the sea birds. I'd never thought about Vivi properly before but I ached for the tufty sheep-smell of her jacket. Under my school blouse and house tie, homesickness scorched through my breast like acid.

The worst of it was everything conspired to separate us: the teachers, Iona's friends, me not having any friends … but most of all it was our bodies. By the time we were thirteen Iona's plumpness had simply vanished. Real breasts appeared and her tummy dropped to her bottom, leaving a sleek shape behind like the neck of a wine bottle. Her skin was the colour of peaches, with the same surprised flush. I was proud of her … very. But I just got thinner and thinner, a string bean if anything, light years from a peach. We didn't look like the same species, let alone twins.

When half-term came that Spring, Puff got invited to Melissa's house. Mel's older brother came to collect them. I watched from an upstairs window. They were dressed to the nines, as Elsie would say. I hardly recognized my own sister. She'd taken her skirt up and borrowed a suspender belt and breathtaking silk stockings. The seams slithered up and down her legs like water snakes.

It had never happened before. Division! Like the pressure of water, like water itself heavy between us. Yet we'd shared water once, drifting silently together in the amniotic fluid. That day, the day Iona climbed into Jamie Phipps-Corbett's Mini with his seventeen year old eyes on her thirteen year old legs, I thought I'd lost her forever.

For consolation I looked us up in the medical dictionary. The diagrams show two almost featureless heads and a tangle of froglike limbs indistinguishable from one another, yet curiously compatible. The womb wall curves around them both, like a shawl or a cupped hand. Iona *must* understand. Olivia made us like this. It was what she wanted.

Later that year I developed a passion which changed my life – although it separated us even further. One stifling July day our literature teacher took us outside to work under the giant cedar tree. Miss Glazebrook wasn't like the other teachers. Mostly they were spinsters with blouses clamped shut at the neck with cameo brooches. Miss G. was utterly beautiful. She wore Greek dresses and her voice had a deep underwater tone. She said your name as if you mattered, as if you were a line in a poem yourself. That day she introduced us to the First World War poets:

What passing-bells for these who die as cattle?

'These who die as cattle?' It struck home. I'd seen our neighbour's bullocks in the abattoir – a fearful pile of rigid legs and staring eyes.

Only the monstrous anger of the guns,
Only the stuttering rifle's rapid rattle

Only it wasn't cows she was talking about. It was beautiful young men like Ormonde.

Can patter out their hasty orisons.

'Can I read please?'

She must have sensed something in me, a breaking love, a yearning beyond anything I'd known. She handed me her book. The words! The music inside the words. As I read I thought of Ormonde buried in Italy. When I reached the end:

And each slow dusk a drawing-down of blinds.

I was lost in the dark, mournful d's. It was a different war, but the same ... surely the same. The blinds were eyelids, I imagined, hiding eyes that couldn't bear to see. Perhaps that was why Fardie never would let the morning light into the library.

That morning I fell in love with poetry – and from there prose and then acting. For a while Audrey – Miss Glazebrook – was part of it all, with her shining black hair and bare, narrow feet in Greek sandals. Oh, I did love her so! She lent me books and guided me like a star towards Yeats and Auden. But my passion for her was only a stage, before I came to understand sex properly, and its political significance. I was thirteen then. There *is* a difference! At fifteen you're out in the world. Well, if you're not actually out in it, you're on the brink, planning your escape.

***

Only in the holidays was everything the same again. We swam in the freezing loch, careened over the moor on farm horses, painted our nails and practiced jiving. Then suddenly, last summer, something happened which brought the 'O's' into closer perspective. A torch momentarily flicked onto Ormonde's pale face – a day when Olivia almost literally danced into my arms. I was invited to stay with my maternal grandmother Eva in Ireland. Poor Puff! Eva specified it should be me – the dark one. We hadn't seen her since we were four. Elsie says she sent us home early because of Iona – because she looks so like Olivia did.

I was met off the ferry by a gloomy old fellow called Brian.

"She'll tire of you quickly," he warned me ominously on the way to the house, a pale streaky stucco with a beech avenue leading up to it.

"For she's not got the strength of a sparrow and I'm worrying myself blind with the cooking and my lady hardly touching a morsel."

I didn't listen. I was so excited. He left me in the drawing room for what seemed an age. Such a pretty, pretty room – so unlike home. Long Italian mirrors gazed across the room at each other and a pair of cherubs clasped china hands on the mantelpiece. Plum coloured silk curtains swept down to the floor, ending in vermillion pools. I went round touching everything, half expecting to catch my mother's reflection in one of the mirrors. Then he was back,

"Come along now! And don't be wasting my precious time."

My first sight of Eva! She was standing very still and quiet in her sewing room. I got the feeling that she'd stopped in time. Her face was like one of her teacups – glazed white with a web of infinitesimally fine lines. I was afraid she might shatter before I had a chance to talk to her.

"Charlotte, dear girl ..."

She stretched out her hand, but I wanted to kiss my mother's mother. I avoided the hand and laid my cheek against hers. Her skin was crinkled, like fallen leaves, almost gone.

"You must be tired after your journey."

"Oh, no! I'm pleased to be here."

"You will have some tea?" she said, sitting down, pouring me a cup and looking a little wistfully at her sewing.

"Thank you."

"I hope you will not be bored. There are lovely walks ..."

"I'm never bored, Grandmother. I just wanted to come here ... to meet you. To see where my mother ..."

"I live very quietly now," she interrupted. "There are tennis racquets," she added vaguely, "and lovely walks."

"I've been longing to see where Olivia ..."

"I'm afraid you must find your own amusement, my dear, I go out very seldom."

After we had drunk our tea she changed chairs, slipped a silver thimble onto her finger, and picked up her material. I realized she only felt safe with little things: the small sips she took from her Limoges cup, her tiny repetitious stitches.

"I will see you later at dinner, Charlotte."

As the days passed I despaired of getting her to talk to me. Yet I found myself growing fond of her and one evening we had a curious conversation which included Ormonde.

"Richard MacIntyre was a friend of ours," she told me. "He had two sons. The elder one, your father, married my daughter. The younger boy was not ... all was not well with him I believe. Like Hugo, like my own beloved son, Hugo."

"Not well with him?"

I tried to make my voice as unobtrusive as possible, to meld it with the ticks of her carriage clock.

"You see some of our young men were too gentle for the war, Charlotte. Cressida Glyn sent back Hugo's ring wrapped in a handkerchief. I found it amongst his things. They were secretly engaged to be married, but she left him for somebody else. They send back a soldier's personal belongings, did you know that? Many families did not have their son's body – but they always received his possessions."

She sat very straight, looking out into the dusk. Her eyes were like porcelain too, laced with faint cracks.

"How awful!"

"I knew it was her handkerchief because CKG was embroidered in the corner," she went on, "that would have been Cressida Kiloran Glyn. We'd known the family for a long time. It must have been most distressing to Hugo, most hurtful."

"But Ormonde? What about Ormonde MacIntyre?"

"I didn't know him, my dear. I believe your grandfather was disappointed in him. Richard had fought in the First World War and wished his sons to follow in his footsteps. He was a forceful man. I seem to remember he sent the boy back after he tried to desert. There was very little understanding of nervous illness in those days. Later the poor young man was killed, like my Hugo."

It was not until my second last evening, when I'd tried for the umpteenth time to get her to talk about Olivia that she suddenly spoke to me directly about my mother.

"I'm sorry; it is too painful for me to bring Olivia back into this house. Young death, you see Charlotte, never loses any small part of its vitality. It runs, as the young person used to run, into a room. It has the same freshness. An old person can be folded away, that's what is meant to happen. But your child still comes running into the room ..."

I put my arms around her.

"You may try Bridie, dear," she said after a while. "She lives in the village. The country people find it easier than we do." The next day I got it out of Brian where Bridie lived, although he couldn't have been less helpful.

"Ah, and there's no point in talking to her," he said dismally, "for isn't she as daft as they come and forever drinking the whiskey." I ignored him and bicycled off to the second cottage on the hill, where a tiny woman was muttering to herself feeding a handful of hens.

***

"Bridie! I'm Charlotte MacIn ..."

But I didn't have to explain myself for she ran up to me and clasped my hands.

"Well now, what a wonder!" she cried. "For didn't I hear that Olivia's child was to pay a visit at the big house? And wasn't I hoping you'd be down here to seek out old Bridie." She pulled me into her kitchen and sat me down.

"Let me see you now," she said fiercely, standing back and gazing at me in an embarrassing way. "No! You're not like her at all, save for your eyes. Aren't those Olivia's eyes staring back at me out of her own girlie's face?"

She made us tea, splashing a dollop of Irish whiskey into hers, and sat opposite me with a fat grey cat on her lap.

"Tell me about my mother, Bridie?" I asked straight away.

My time in Ireland was running out. I wanted her memories encapsulated. I wanted to take Olivia home with me, like essence of roses in a little bottle with a cork.

"There was never a more beautiful child," she mused, "as wild as wild ... racing after her brothers from the age of seven. 'Hold still there!' I'd tell her when I was brushing her hair - but she'd not stop for a living soul."

Bridie cried a little, mopping her eyes with a dishtowel, then staring into the fire, remembering. I interrupted her thoughts.

"And when she was older - my age - what was she like then?"

"Ah, well, she could charm the life out of the boys that's for certain!" Bridie cackled, sploshing more tea into our cups and giving herself another swig of whiskey.

"Do you remember my father, Harold MacIntyre?"

"Indeed I do. He was a sweet shy boy, poor soul."

"Poor? Why poor?"

"The war, child. Didn't you know there's a war raging out there? And isn't he dead like the rest of them?"

"Dead! No, Bridie, he's not dead ... well not really. And the war's over now."

"Well, well. It wasn't long after it started that my darling lost her heart. It was the night of the dance up at Drumtorragh and I was fastening her dress. It was shot silk - the colour of farm cream. 'You've found me out, Bridie!' she said, and wasn't that the truth of it?"

"You'd found her out? What did she mean?"

"And why wouldn't I? For she'd never loved a living soul before. There was a fire in her that night, alright! Hadn't I known her since the hour she was born?"

"You must be talking about my father."

"There's fighting and slaughter going on. Didn't they tell you that, child? They leave on the boat and that's the last you see of them."

"That dance must have been before the war started." I said.

"And what would you know about it? I remember that day as if it was in front of me for it was the last time I saw her. She was weeping when she got back from the dance - weeping and weeping. Then she left on the boat too, for there's no stopping them. May the blessed Virgin watch over their souls!"

I'd had enough. "I have to go, Bridie. I have to say goodbye to my grandmother."

"Let me look into your face, child!" her breath smelled of milk and whiskey, soft white hairs brushed my cheek. "For soon enough you'll be leaving on the boat too - just like the rest of them."

***

"Mad!" was Iona's response, when I'd repeated it all for the hundredth time. "Bonkers!"

"Bridie must have got mixed up," I said.

"Old girls like that go batty. She'd have been weeping because Fardie was leaving."

"Yes," I agreed, a little hesitantly.

"Char! Our mother would never ..."

"Of course she wouldn't."

But we were filled with renewed longing to know more about Olivia and it led to a terrible scene with Fardie. We cornered him. But it was like trying to get close to a red stag, the way they scent your presence, start, stare at you for one liquid moment, then with two red leaps are gone.

"Do you remember a dance at Drumtorragh?" I asked. "Before the war?"

"What ... ? What's that?"

"Olivia! We want to know ..."

"Know what?"

"Everything!" said Iona, piteously. "How you met ... about us ... about her wanting us."

"It's over, d'you hear? No going back! You've got to learn ..."

"But she's ours too!" I shouted

His hand shook violently. He took off his glasses and laid them on the table with a jerk, searching his breast pocket for a handkerchief to demist them. Without his glasses on he was vulnerable, his movements uncoordinated.

"It's not to reason why, not for us to reason ..."

"Why? Why is it not for us?" Iona cried, bursting into tears.

"You're mad!" I cried. "The war made you mad - and mean - and you're hiding something from us. I hate you!"

Our father stood stock-still for a moment, then he squared his shoulders, put on his glasses and bashed his way blindly to the door with his stick. For some time the only noise was Iona's sobs, my gulping tears and a low moaning sound ... it must have been the sea.

***

I've got to get out of here! I've got to leave Westfield. Important things are happening in the world. Chairman Mao is launching his Great Leap Forward. Apartheid is destroying South Africa - and the subject for our debate this week is HATS!

Should it be compulsory for young women to wear hats in church or should they, given the changing times, be accountable for their own attire.

I want to study drama more than anything on earth. If Fardie won't pay I'll take my chances in rep. Needless to say, he disapproves of acting, thinks it's frivolous, thinks it's sordid, thinks I'm frivolous, thinks I'm susceptible to becoming sordid. I've tried to explain it's a voice that matters, but he's stuck in the mire of the Old Testament and doesn't hear a thing.

Breasts at last and does it change things! Superficially, I mean. When you're flat-chested and seething with passion nobody knows or cares. Now I see sex is everywhere. I'd say Miss Botsworth's in love with Janice, the new matron. And there's a strong undercurrent of it on trains. I let a man kiss me between Crewe and Glasgow - just experimenting.

I could fall in love now. A jazz player, perhaps? Or somebody black. It would be ideal if the person were black. But what are my chances of meeting anyone worthwhile in this bleak white ghetto?

I'd love to have someone to ask about things. Puff is out of the question, I'm afraid. She's got sex confused with dances and Sinatra songs. She has been to smooch parties, but that's just upper-class fumbling with boys in suits respecting the fact she's a virgin - not the real thing. I've read up on it, of course, but a mother would know. She'd help with crucial issues, such as whether fornication is still a sin and about how far to go ... ? And French letters? All that.

My dream of her is more physical since Ireland. I feel she is only a breath away, a colour beyond the colours I know. She's water that has flowed past the place where I am. I drink where she drank and hold the cool in my throat for as long as I can.

CHAPTER 2

IONA

I loved Westfield right away! It's more of a house than a school: a rose garden, pretty grass tennis courts, piano music filtering along the passages, cocoa for elevenses, church only once on Sundays and sewing counted as a lesson. One of the first things that struck me (we were only eleven then) were the older girls. They were allowed to wear suspender belts and nylon stockings. I'd never seen anything so glossy, so utterly lovely! And my new friends had mothers that called them *darling* and smelled of fur coats.

Now that I'm fifteen and life is so complicated ... sex, I mean, and being in love with someone older, someone of nearly nineteen, I realize all that was quite normal and we were the ones who were peculiar.

At the beginning I worried about Char. She was terribly homesick and angry. She antagonized everyone right away by trying to impose Fardie's rules – like never going for a walk without a compass. Things which simply don't apply here where the country consists of peaceful orchards, as opposed to vast hunks of moor and hill perpetually shrouded in mist. They put us in different dormitories. I didn't like it either, but Charlotte felt threatened and kept dragging me off to the library to look at diagrams of the gestation period of twins. They were revolting! A mishmash of tubes and guts. I didn't need that to know how much I love her.

It got easier when Charlotte discovered poetry. We were about thirteen at the time. She joys in words, tastes them and eats them alive like oysters. At Craigmannoch she recites in the boat - stands in the bow and shouts out The Fiddler of Dooney against the wind. At night she reads war poems, curled on her bed, hugging a pillow.

Now all that has changed. Char's become elegant! Immensely tall and slender. Her sloping eyes are as dark as coffee with chips of Demerara sugar in it. Most boys find her daunting. But that's the impression she wants to create.

School is marvellous but the holidays are a trial. Fardie is getting worse. He's troubled by the fact that we're growing up. I think he sent us to Westfield hoping that it would delay the process indefinitely. All we get is preach, preach, preach: smoking is vulgar in young women, foreign travel is extravagant, all men are dangerous ... he keeps us on such a tight shoestring we can hardly afford knickers. And now that we are fifteen there are scenes - terrible scenes. You see, we don't know a thing about who we are. He won't tell us. Char found out a bit about Olivia in Ireland, her beauty and love of life. She sounds like me, fond of dancing and clothes. Elsie says: 'If it cost money she wanted it, and why not for them as has it!' But as to how they met, their romance, our birth, her feelings about us ... he won't tell us a thing.

Vivian too has her silences, a point beyond which she retreats. She shrugs herself back into her smelly jacket, stalks out of the house, lifting her eyes to the hills, screwing them up as the sun dashes burgundy glances over the heather. 'Bugger off, sweeties!' she says, not unpleasantly, when we ask too many questions.

***

Last Christmas, however, I uncovered the most astonishing secret about Vivian. Fardie took me up to Loch Cottage to look after her when she had bronchitis. It was a ferocious night, cold winds sweeping across the hill spewing out mouthfuls of snow, the sea slapping up against the rocks. I was happy. I love taking care of people. Vivi was lumped in bed looking dishevelled and feverish, but in no time at all I had stoked the fires, poached eggs and made her a honey and lemon drink. 'Thanks, Puff,' she said weakly. 'Sling a little whisky in that lemony thing, won't you?' That put her to sleep right away.

I was going to write a letter but sometimes I just sprawl. Outside, the wind whirled round the house, biting at the window panes, snuffling under the door. Inside, the light from the coals turned everything the colour of roses. Malcolm, the dog, was a pink raggedy toy, the sagging sofa glowed and Vivian's desk was as ruddy as hips and haws in the firelight. It's always chaotic, her desk, the cubby-holes bulge with letters and farm bills. Years ago she showed us how the vertical pillars are really secret drawers ... one of them was half open. I noticed a green suede book was sticking out of it. The more I looked at it the more it looked like a diary, thumbed soft and intimate. What could Vivian possibly have that was private? I went over to the desk. For a while I just stroked the cover of the book with my middle finger as if it were a small woodland animal. Then I gave the drawer a nudge and it fell out - open! I didn't open it. It just opened itself, so I read the part that showed.

I'm being kept here. – I read in Vivi's younger handwriting – *Today I tried to walk out of the garden but Antoine was there again. He asked me politely what I wanted. I'm beginning to realize they must know - all of them. And Cecile ... I'm not sure, but I think she's like me. Poor little Ceci, and she's only fourteen. I've got to post my letter. I've got to let O know where I am. I cried all weekend. Madame made me ...*

I shut it quickly and shoved it back into the pillar, but not before I'd seen the heading: *Normandie 1938* - 1938! Vivian must have been sixteen.

"How could you have?" Charlotte asked me, shocked and fascinated. "It's wicked to read people's diaries."

"Wicked?" I hadn't thought of it as wicked exactly.

"You must confess."

"I don't see why I should."

We argued about it and came to the conclusion that the best thing was to get Vivian to tell us about it herself.

***

"Have you ever been to France, Vivi?" I asked her when she was convalescing, wrapped in a tartan rug in the porch, supposedly catching a few rays of sun as the snow thawed around the house, creating rivers, hurtling down to the sea in ecstatic leaps.

"Yes, I have."

Perhaps she was weakened by her illness because she reached for a forbidden cigarette and began to talk.

"It was a punishment." she said bitterly. "I was sixteen at the time. My father found out that I was in love with a boy called Oran. He was apoplectic with rage. He sent me away ..."

"Oran?" Another O! "Who was Oran?"

Bit by bit the magical story evolved of a boy whose job it had been to haul her father's two ton boat over the stones into the ice-cold water. 'One, two, three - heave! One, two ...' We could imagine Oran, his bare feet curved like a rib over the shells and stones, navy sweater rolled up to the elbows, flecked hazel eyes fixed on her blue ones as she stood on the beach with the picnic basket.

"Gosh!" we breathed together.

They'd been fourteen when it started, she told us. (When what started exactly? We longed to ask, but didn't dare) Children, in her father's opinion. Old enough to be left on the point to collect mussels while he fished the upper loch, It hadn't crossed his mind that his daughter might be lonely with her brothers off at school in England and the nearest town over twenty miles away. It hadn't occurred to him that she was growing up, that her eyes were the deep delphinium blue that arrests other eyes. Besides, he didn't even know the boy's name, he was just one of the keeper's sons.

"Oh Vivi!" Charlotte said, admiringly. "And Fardie - I mean your father - didn't like him?"

"Like him! What's wrong with you two?" Vivian lit another cigarette, in between coughs. "Father didn't not like him, he didn't consider he existed. Class! You know, bloody class ... Oran might have been an animal so far as he was concerned - no, sorry, Father was fond of animals."

We'd never seen her like this, her voice scraped with scorn. She got up and paced around.

"But Fardie wouldn't ..."

"Don't confuse them! My father was evil. Yours is ... well, Harry's different. Don't forget he and Ormonde were punished too, often. But my sin was venal in the eyes of Father's class-conscious God." She sat with her head in her hands, only just holding on.

"Why France, Vivian?"

"It was far away. It gave my father a chance to dispose of Oran."

"Sounds like Macbeth ..." Char ventured.

"It was. I imagine he sent the whole family to Australia or somewhere, as an alternative to a dagger."

"You mean you don't know? You never found out where he was?"

"I tried. Ormonde tried too. Our father was very powerful ..."

"But, what abo ..."

"Look, you two," Vivian said abruptly. "That's it! No more questions. Buzz off and leave me in peace."

"God again!" I said that night when we were going to bed. "God was the trouble."

"Can't you see our grandfather got God wrong?"

"Like Fardie, you mean?"

"No, Iona! Fardie's different. He's humble ... he wouldn't have ... Anyway there's something odd about the whole thing. The punishment is out of proportion, the house in France? What was going on?"

"Well, I don't believe in all that gloomy, obsessive guilt. I don't believe in punishments or God, and I don't think you should either."

"I couldn't not." she said quietly.

"Why, Char?"

"Because He's here. I feel Him – emanating."

"What does that mean?"

"Letting off little bursts of love, I think. Anyway, I feel love emanating from Him!"

That's the thing about Charlotte. There are parts of her even I can't reach. She's cleverer than I am. She's more inspired, minds more, rages more ... and sometimes there's a light inside her that's so bright I feel she may break into bits, like the chimney of a hurricane lamp when it gets too hot.

***

I want her so badly. I wanted her when I was little but now that I'm fifteen it's worse. All my friends have mothers. Mel has Tessa. She tells her pretty well everything. Mrs P.C. sits on her bed and really listens. She gives her opinion, not fanatic unyielding advice like Fardie. Arabella's mother says: 'Don't be silly!' without going into what being silly really means. When there's a party she's adamant about Bella being home by midnight - as if being silly could only happen between midnight and breakfast? Tawda's mother says: 'Men are only after one thing and the worst you can do is behave like a tramp.' She's on her third husband, so she must have behaved like one somewhere along the line.

I don't know what to do. Jamie, Mel's brother, had his nineteenth birthday party six months ago. God, it was heaven! Tessa and Old Smackers went to bed after dinner and we danced for hours. Anyway, I met a friend of Jamie's - Alastair Graham. He's miles older than me, nearly nineteen, and terribly, terribly attractive. I pretended I was seventeen - anyone would have. But now I'm in a bind. I've seen him again twice. It's getting pretty intense.

Tessa has been sweet to me. I've told her about Fardie being so hung up and she understands completely. But when it comes to boys I'm basically too shy to ask her advice. I mean about going too far and if it's true about men not respecting you if you do? And what if it's a much older person and you're on the verge of getting carried away, although you're trying your best not to?

Olivia would know what to do.

Mrs. Phipps-Corbett lets Mel call her Tessa. It's a joke between them. But if I had Olivia I wouldn't want to. I love the word mother. Charlotte would probably go for mum, being a socialist, but I never would. Sometimes I dream she's alive. In my dream she's wearing the sparkly shoes she passed on to Elsie. We are chatting and laughing and I'm making tea for her. Then I wake up hot and ashamed. You see, I don't even know if she'd want sugar in it.

Chapter 3

CHARLOTTE

"I'm going out!"

He'd been standing watching me put on my make-up. I was doing it at home, giving myself more time with Gil, hoping he might talk about last night, bring it up himself. He was wearing black suede trousers and his Indian shirt. He was looking petulant - petulant, and utterly beautiful.

"Oh ... where?"

"Drinks with Beach and the others."

"Oh?"

"Just for a couple of hours ..."

"Could you pick me up at the theatre afterwards?"

"Shall we leave it that I might?"

"Gilly, it was weird not having you at home last night when I got back."

I tried to keep my voice light and unthreatening, knowing that when one person is working and the other isn't, it's much harder for the one that isn't. But it was depressing, coming back to the flat alone after the performance for the second night running and finding the fridge empty and him still not there. I'd eaten nothing all day. I couldn't find any cash, although I was sure I'd left some in my bag. I waited for an hour, then I cut the mould off an old loaf with scissors, ate the remains with some stale cheese and went to bed ... but it wasn't so much the food that upset me.

"Home ... ! Home?" he said, widening his beautiful eyes like he did in *The Lover*.

"It's where we live, Gilly."

"Darling Charles, you can hardly expect me to wait around in this dazzling home of ours like some fucking nanny to unlace Madame's stays when she comes back from the theatre. Anyway, I was here this morning, wasn't I?"

"So what ... ? Isn't that the general idea?"

"You refer to the bonds of holy matrimony?"

"No, Gil ... I meant when people choose each other, as it happens, choose to live together, they're supposed to like living in the same place."

I took off my dressing gown and started to get ready. Gil watched me. When I was slotting my belt through the loops on my jeans he reached out and grabbed it, pulling me towards him. It's the sort of thing he used to do before this new cruelty crept in, the sort of thing that was irresistible before - me coiling into the belt, Gil pretending to be bringing in an errant horse - that sort of thing. We'd been on such a high then ... so mad about each other. And mad about ourselves together.

"Fuck off, Gil!" I said, pulling my belt back and buckling it.

"On that devastating note," he said, his voice ridiculously melodramatic, "the slighted lover leaves the young couple's cosy home never to ..."

That's the trouble. He still makes me laugh. In amongst this new degradation I suddenly see how young he is, and laugh.

"So what about picking me up after the show?"

"I promised to spend the evening with Beach and the others."

"But mightn't I join you? Or why not bring them back here?" I felt a carping, dependent note creep into my voice, a soap opera 'I-am-your-wife-after-all' whine. The sort of thing we promised we'd never do. Gil sensed it immediately.

"Back here? My dear Charlie the day you pick your knickers up off that revolting pile and pay an unprecedented call to the launderette with all our stuff and do a little, little-woman act around here I might bring Beach and ... "

"Who the hell or what is Beach, anyway?"

"Americans are often called names like River and Lane and Beach, Charlie dear," he answered sarcastically. "There's lots you don't know on earth and lots you'll never know!" he misquoted, bounding downstairs laughing demoniacally.

I'm not sure if it was then or earlier - when I woke up that morning to find Gil beside me asleep, naked, with his long, clean hair and his ridiculously long lashes splashed like dusky grass across his pale cheeks - that I began to suspect that something was absolutely wrong.

There was nothing wrong with my husband lying naked beside

me, nothing really wrong with him having come in late two nights in a row ... but I leant over and smelt him and he didn't smell like a man who'd been out with the boys, not a whiff of beer or smoke. He didn't smell like a man who'd been making love to a girl, either. No stickiness or girl smell. He smelled fresh, like June buds. I couldn't help finding that unusual.

***

Pinter is light years ahead of any other English playwright. Osborne started the whole kitchen sink thing but he stuck there. Pinter has such dimension. He's absorbed working class theatre and gone far beyond it. He's writing about silence, about what people don't say, about how we lose each other using the wrong words. God, how I love Pinter! I'm so lucky to be acting now. With his sort of theatre it doesn't matter if you're tall. Physical attributes are simply not the issue. It's understanding what he's trying to do, the incredible significance behind a Pinter pause.

Two years ago I was just getting on my feet. I'd had a great break with Private Lives and had the luck to play Hilde in Ibsen's *The Lady from the Sea* in the Chichester summer festival. Anyway, I was on the loose for a while and suddenly got a chance to play Sarah in Pinter's *The Lover*.

I was playing opposite Gil Grey. He'd caused quite a stir the year before in his Picture of Dorian Gray, although they'd had a hard time making him look ugly at the end. He has the sort of liquid beauty that is hard to disguise. We started out, like one does in theatre, very cool and professional. Both, I suppose, trying to show how we were there to act, and perfectly capable of playing lovers without being remotely interested in each other.

I remember Jonathan, our director, leading us through it. 'This piece is like being on a swing,' he explained. 'Grey starts off the rhythm between you and, Charlotte, you are carried into it here ... you take over and swing back on this line, only since Richard is both your husband and the lover who visits you in secret in the afternoons you must remember there are ostensibly four parts in this play, and immerse yourselves in Pinter's little game.

We understood. We were inside our parts, relating well on stage. At the end of each rehearsal Grey used to rush off somewhere with a 'Bye, darlings!' to Jonathan and me, or I left first with a 'Bye, darlings!' to them. Occasionally we all had a glass of wine in the pub and talked shop.

So it was completely unexpected. One day, at the end of the play, when I say:

'Mmmnn? Would you like me to change? Would you like me to change my clothes? I'll change for you, darling. Shall I? Would you like that?'

Silence. She is very close to him.

And Richard, or rather Grey, says:

'Yes.'

Pause.

'Change.'

Pause.

'Change.'

Pause.

'Change your clothes.'

Pause.

'You lovely whore.'

I suddenly noticed his eyes were really looking into mine. They were like a storm coming in from the Irish Sea ... disturbed, tumultuous, passionate. And I realized, in that instant, how attractive he was, how I'd been attracted to him all along but never acknowledged it. For the first time we lost our rhythm and just stood there, like amateurs who didn't know how to improvise.

"What's wrong?" Jonathan called up to us. "You're losing pace! Do that last bit again."

We started again. Gil was wearing a frayed jersey. When he stood close to me, as directed, I felt out of control, longing to put my fingers into the holes of his jersey, longing to be pressed up against it, to feel the length of him along the length of me.

"We'd better call it a day," Jonathan said in the distance.

Then we just walked out of the rehearsal together. 'Bye, darling.' Grey said to Jonathan, as though our leaving together were the most natural thing in the world.

Thinking you've found the one and only person for you is the ultimate Pinter pause. You know, in that instant, that you'll be giving so much away - parts of your childhood, thoughts, words that move you. And getting, too - things that you don't know about yet, his childhood, his words. You know there will be the slow unwrapping of your bodies, the gradual unwrapping of all that you will become to each other.

I thought those things then, and I truly believe that Grey, off stage for once in his life, thought them too. How can I accept that we got it wrong?

***

Iona's so happy! You can see it in every dear strand of her fair hair. The gauzy lightness in her eyes is like thyme or sage, or any one of those blueish herbs that holds summer in its silvery smell. I shouldn't think she's read anything except the back of the cornflakes packet for months. It has completely passed her by that this is the sixties and all that we stand for. She's not for or against anything ... just sailing along oblivious, in love with her husband and son.

And Mark is the same, clever, lots of integrity, but bathing in domesticity, rolled up in a thermal blanket of love. He accepts me 100 percent. Realizes, I suppose, that I'm part of the packet. When I go there they both encircle me with their sweetness. Mark cooks fantastic meals. Puff wants everything to be as it was between us. Sometimes we lie in their big bed talking, just like we used to at Craigmannoch. Mark unobtrusively slips in on his side in his stripy schoolboy pyjamas. If we go on for too long he puts out his lamp and falls asleep.

Finn, their son, is a bit on the fat side, not really like anything except a baby, but I do love him. Iona and Mark might easily have put me off. They are absolutely blinded. Iona has become quite vindictive about other children. She's always dragging on about how advanced Finn is and hurling insults at perfectly harmless babies. I've seen her take a cloth book out of a little girl's hand and give it to her darling, who was perfectly content doing his double roll.

She thinks, in all her happiness, that I must feel envious of her or sad because I haven't got a baby. I've told her I don't think about it. What I really mean is that it's unthinkable at this moment. I am sad, but the sadness is so much bigger. Perhaps it encompasses not having a baby. I don't even know.

When Iona got married Fardie gave her Olivia's portrait. I thought I understood. You can't cut a painting in two and she did get married first. In his eyes she's the only one of us that got married, since he doesn't count my marriage to Gil because it wasn't in church. On the other hand, Olivia is *my* mother too. When Iona told me about it I remained silent for as long as I could hold my breath. That usually helps. But when I surfaced nothing had changed. Fardie has betrayed me. He has given my mother away.

When I was small, and convinced she could see me, I would go to the hall and skip around under her portrait, singing out whatever I had to tell. Sometimes I'd catch her eyes following me with an amused expression. If I was in trouble I'd sit cross-legged on the cold flagstones under the painting just to be close. On these occasions her face was full of compassion.

I know a picture is only a thing, a worldly possession, an earthly trapping: Set not your treasures up on earth where rust and moth doth corrupt and thieves break through and steal. I believe it absolutely. I go along with it. But my mother's portrait is the one treasure I dearly love. I'd risk a fair amount of God's wrath to see those eyes every day, to have her on my wall - now, when I need her most.

***

When I was seventeen I met a boy called Daniel on a demonstration march in York. It was in support of the ANC. Mandela was standing out bravely against the pass laws and the way the government was denigrating the coloured people. The South African police had just killed sixty-nine peaceful demonstrators in Sharpeville. We were urging people to boycott British companies that were doing business there. Daniel was one of the organizers. It was a desultory sort of day without much action or reaction, so we talked as we meandered along with our banners. I saw such tranquillity and goodness in his round, earnest face all I wanted was to be with him - to follow him wherever he went. At that point Fardie was refusing to let me act, cutting me off without a penny - so I was on the loose. We just hooked-up together. I was very fond of Daniel, I really was. But I see now I mistook idealism for love.

We set out to prove that we didn't need material things. We rented a tiny cottage on the west coast of Ireland and grew everything we ate - at least that was the idea. But grinding flour was quite beyond us and there was a shortage of fish. Daniel never gave up, but I used to go and stay with my grandmother and smuggle in baking powder and proper flour. Our peat was damp and slugs ate the beans we'd planted in nine rows. The only real argument we had was when I bought tangerines. I thought we'd get scurvy if we didn't have vitamin C.

I'm afraid there's something indolent in my nature because one day I woke up and couldn't bear the thought of another cabbage. We'd been working at it for three years but I was tired of Daniel's patience and the bloody rain. I went off to London on the pretext of finding a publisher for our journal *No Earthly Trappings*. In fact I did find someone, but it never came off. I don't want to go into it, but it never did get published in the end.

***

Back in Scotland Fardie and I made it up. We didn't talk about it - you can't with him. But he more or less forgave me in his dysfunctional way and welcomed me home. Iona came up for a few days and that was when we found out about our money. I still think he only told us because he absolutely had to. We were twenty years old at the time.

"Time you knew," he said one day at breakfast, "because of your mother's death ... there's some money. Yours."

"How lovely," Iona said, enthusiastically. "I thought we didn't have any!"

"That's just it. That's why I haven't told you before. It's not for spending. Capital! It's capital. You can never, never touch capital." He said the word with reverence, in the tone he normally uses for God.

Nonetheless we looked at each other hopefully - there might be a way of getting our hands on it and I was longing to study drama. Now I realize that nothing on earth is harder than being able to spend your own money. Fardie had surrounded our inheritance with a wall of conservative trustees, the worst of them being James Craig of Craig,

Creary, Calquhoun & Sons Ltd. Craig was in charge of our investments. He was the giant we had to face before getting anywhere near the golden egg.

On a dreadful day, with the rain lashing down, we waited expectantly in Mr Craig's cold Glasgow office. The windows were long and smeared with soot. Metal heating pipes, painted a thick cheerless brown, were clearly not working and let off clammy condensation. The carpet was a greenish brown with scrubbed areas, where I imagined previous clients must have vomited from a surfeit of Mr Craig's despondent caution and gloom.

We had hoped he would be brief. But Craig was not brief. A moralist and dramatist by nature, it took us over an hour to begin to break him down.

"In view of the fact your mother, Olivia Adaire Dermot MacIntyre, had left no will at the time of her demise ... been agreed by her trustees, namely ... the following adverse circumstances ... two surviving daughters ... in the case of their espousal ... at the age of ... should each inherit ... eighteen thousand pounds ster ... "

"Crikey!" said Puff. "How absolutely super!"

"Now, young ladies, do not, I emphasize not, make the grave mistake of looking upon this inheritance as money. No! This sum is CAPITAL and your father has given me the pleasurable task of explaining to you the nature, the noble – if I may say so - nature of capital.

He paused for dramatic effect.

"Oh, do go on, Mr Craig," Iona said politely. He got up from his chair to better deliver his soliloquy.

"Miss Charlotte, Miss Iona, you must think of this capital as a dwelling place - a place that will shield you from the storms of life, a shelter that will protect you from the cruel rays of the sun."

There was a rumble of thunder outside and tea was brought in on a trolley in a brown teapot with a knitted brown tea cosy and three plain biscuits. We tried to control our giggles.

"Now, gur ... young ladies, it would never do to start chipping away at your dwelling place, would it? To remove one honest brick?"

"What about the income?" I asked.

"Aha, Miss Charlotte, now there's a clever question from a young person who knows that every lamp well trimmed..."

"Sheds forth some generous light?" interjected Iona hopefully.
"Indeed, indeed - but ..."

And on it went. At the end of it all we got some sort of limited access. My drama college was considered educational and that September I took up the place that I'd been offered before I went off with Daniel. Iona managed to siphon off some of hers for further education, which consisted of a short course in French conversation from an attractive tutor, a luxurious holiday in the south of France, and two stunning Parisian dresses.

***

Just as I was about to leave Murray arrived. Murray is Fardie's oldest and, as far as we can see, only friend. And a very odd ball he is too. He's the thinnest man I've ever seen, with a head like a weasel and bright little hazel eyes which miss nothing. He has a neatly trimmed moustache and always wears a regimental tie and well-pressed shiny blue suit, while Fardie hobbles around in his father's ancient corduroy jacket with patches on it and a pair of his grandfather's plus-fours which hang loosely over his darned socks.

Murray's voice is not what you'd expect to come out of a neat, weaselly body. It's a low, even burble. When he's with you it's like living beside a millstream. 'Well now, Mrs Forrester, you've done us proud today, hasn't she, Harold? This is the best stuffing it's been my pleasure to sample in a long, long time!' A little smile, a little wipe of his tidy ferret mouth, and on he goes. 'You gurls are lucky, 'though I say it myself, for you've a fine man for a daddy and there's many a lass that doesn't get treacle pudding on a Sunday.' A little laugh, a little smile in our direction. 'Kippers, now there's a treat! We'd have been happy to see a kipper in Anzio, is that not right, Harold?'

He chews very slowly, a fact that annoys me now but as children we were not annoyed. Murray was virtually our only guest and we were fascinated by the extraordinary effect he had on Fardie. He forgot to hear our psalms and hurried Murray off to the library to smoke and play chess. Once or twice we even heard him laugh. It was an odd sound, something between a cock's crow and a hiccup. It impressed us deeply. We didn't know how to make our father laugh.

Anyway, I was determined to see what I could get out of Murray and I got my chance when Fardie had to go to Edinburgh for a day, leaving us alone. I must admit that I courted him ... talked about my love for war poetry and brought up the subject of Fardie's medals. I pretended I knew more than I did. It was deceitful, perhaps, but it worked. I now know the battle was in Anzio and it took place in January 1944. The moment I got back to London I went to the Public Records Office in Chancery Lane. I looked it up and there he was:

Harold McIntyre, Major, Gordon Highlanders. D.S.O.

The citation described how he'd run a quarter of a mile through enemy fire to warn his troops of a hidden enemy encampment near the Anzio-Albano road, receiving severe shrapnel wounds. It reported that three weeks after that he was taken prisoner with most of his regiment and transported by train to Bebra POW camp in Germany. Then came the inexplicable part. Ormonde's name isn't listed amongst the soldiers killed that day ... there's no mention of him at all. Yet Vivian, who never lies, has told us that Ormonde was killed the day Fardie lost his arm. Why isn't his death listed with the others?

***

At first Gil and I did everything together. We were together when we were apart, so wrapped up in each other that our reactions, voices and moods were interchangeable. It was like having another twin. We rented a little attic flat in Islington. We always planned to do it up, to paint the steel beams black and the walls red. I was going to make a patchwork quilt illustrating bits of our lives. I did the first three patches - a map of Wales where Gil comes from, a black bike helmet against a red sky background and the orange tomcat that had adopted us. But somehow I never got any further.

We heard each others' lines, went dancing and dressed up. Gilly liked me dressing for the bike. The shorter my skirt the better. He liked me sitting sideways in my leathers with long black stockings and my wedge-heeled shoes. When one of my shoes fell off he did a wheelie and scorched round while I picked it up with one hand. We wasted a lot of money on clothes. It amused us. Well, it amused Gil and I loved seeing him amused, silver sandals, black jackets, velvet trousers - there was nothing over for paint.

On a good day, if one of us wasn't working, we'd take off on Gil's bike in any direction and just keep going until we found the right patch of field. We'd lie there all day, playing around and reading poetry. We talked and talked. Gil was born Gilbert Stokes. He'd had a grim childhood. His mother was very violent, manic about cleanliness and tidiness. When he left anything out of place or failed her in any way she'd lock him up for hours. The father cleared out when he was about three. I don't think he'd told anyone about it before. I have to remember that now. I have to keep it in mind when I think I'm going mad.

The change in Gil came during the second year of our marriage. I hardly noticed it at first ... the same jokes with a drop of acid in them. Then they got worse. He used to call Fardie 'The Marquis' after Bosie's father. I hated that. Then he began to make snide remarks about Iona, veiled in humour, but snide. 'How is everything in the nirvana of domesticity?' sort of thing. I let that pass. But one day he referred to her as Mother Milk and I almost killed him.

Last summer we only went out on the bike once and it didn't work. Love-making was never the major thing with us. But it happened less and less. I began to feel that I was taking up too much space in our own attic. The minute you're with someone who doesn't find you attractive you become less so, your skin loses light and you don't walk with the lift you had when you knew you were being watched with adoring eyes.

But the worst part was Gilly himself. I sensed how unhappy he was. Behind the cleverness and cruelty there was so much pain. He was like a captured beast hating his cage but frightened, in some baffling way, of leaving it. I would have simply cleared out, buggered off ... if I hadn't seen how afraid he was.

***

In the middle of all this Iona came and dug me out. She asked me to go up to Scotland with her. I didn't want to, but I felt too exhausted to argue. Going home is like a rerun of a familiar movie. Nothing changes. The bleating on the hill, the bath taking twenty-five minutes to fill, the towels which still have our school name tapes on them, carrots and shepherd's pie for lunch, a lump of bready pudding ...

Only this time it wasn't the same. There was an unprecedented, unbelievable change. Vivian wasn't there! Fardie hadn't mentioned a thing about it in the car, but the minute I went into the house a feeling of absence came over me, as if I were running my tongue over the place where there used to be a tooth.

"Where is she?" we asked him.

He gave us some cock and bull story about her having gone to Montana for a holiday, which I don't think he believed and we certainly didn't. Then he grudgingly admitted she'd left us a letter. Puff almost dropped the baby onto Fardie's lap and we belted upstairs, knowing instinctively she'd have left it in our old nursery. And there it was:

Dear Char and Puff,

Sorry not to be here when you bring Finn. Look! I think you must have guessed - that time in France - I was sent there because I was pregnant. I'll be brief. My son was born on September the 18th, 1938. Father had set the whole thing up so that he would be adopted ... I only saw him for eight hours. Oran never saw him at all.

I've had a letter from a peculiar organization in California. Suddenly came. It's called, 'Louise Leroy's Lost and Found Loved Ones.' They purport to be able to link up lost people. Sounds batty, but they say there's a man - a man of nearly thirty, trying to find his mother. They've traced his birth certificate back to France. Paid people, I suppose. It's probably wrong, the date of the certificate is wrong, but my father could have fixed that. It could be a freak who just wants any old mother - or could be some criminal ploy on the part of the producers? God knows what sort of a mother I'd make anyway. It's not really my bag, but I have to find out.

Harry doesn't know about my boy. He's had enough sorrow so stick to the 'cattle in Montana' story. Don't worry about me. I have to have a go; you'll understand that, kiddos. I have to see for myself, even if it is a red herring.

Vivian

It's the most thrilling news. To think that all the years we were growing up she must have known that somewhere out there was a child like her - a son who might have the same blue eyes and loping stride - and now this man wants to find her. Naturally she left immediately, anyone would have. The only disconcerting thing is she didn't leave an address. Now that she's so far away, in peril in a sense, I want to tell her that she doesn't need lessons in being a mother. She's alright. She had us.

***

I'm back in London and everything has changed. It's clear now - as clear and unblinking as loch water on a summer evening when the trail of every stuttering heron is reflected in its surface. Today we were walking along Camden Passage. (We still do that on Saturdays, walk to the book stalls, mosey around and have a cheap lunch) An old Riley drew up at the corner with the top down and a voice called out:

"Hey, Grey . . !"

I'd never met Beach. He is tall and graceful with short hair - an ingenuous, rather naughty face. He was wearing a rumpled linen shirt with the top buttons undone, so you could see his collar bone and part of his long narrow chest. There was nothing extraordinary about Beach. It was Gil that caught my attention ... I saw him, for a fraction of a second, destabilize, flush, glance at me with a world of apprehension in his face, then lock back into his charming, relaxed self.

"Beach! You haven't met Charles. Charlie, this is the dreaded American with the back-to-nature name!"

But in that instant I'd seen that my husband loved him. Seen it, and understood at last.

We still live together. Gil can leave tomorrow if he wants. He knows that, but he isn't ready yet. What holds him back? It's not his mother, I'm sure of that. He hates her neat, pretentious life. It can't be the theatre, his chosen profession, hardly anyone *isn't* homosexual. It isn't me. I know he's genuinely fond of me and I'd still be his friend, which is what he really wants.

"Charlie," he whispered last night, "don't make me leave quite yet."

"Is coming out of the closet such a jump?" I asked him. "Wouldn't being what you really are be easier?"

"It's not what it seems."

"Explain!"

"It's tied up with little things, Charles."

"Like what?"

"Like walking into a restaurant with you - being the man."

"But you'd still be the man with someone like Beach."

"It's a different sort of entry."

"Entry?"

"Causes a different sort of a stir. Anyway, I love watching women brushing their hair and I loathe being the passenger on a bike."

"Gil, darling, you're beginning to sound superficial."

"Alright then," he said. "If you must know, I like being a husband ..."

"Look at me! Are you sure you are queer?"

"Absolutely. I hate all those bits and pieces women have. They're so hard to memorize."

"Gilly!"

One day it will just happen. He'll go off and I'll be alone. There's nothing to divide. We haven't even built shelves. Our paperback plays are piled on the floor - we could split them 50-50. The music is his and the mattress is mine. The ginger cat senses Armageddon and doesn't come round anymore. I feel such a failure. I thought Gilly loved me. Now I understand he was only trying to prove a point.

***

I think back to being a small child in Scotland when the right and wrong of things was crystal clear. I remember a particular incident when the children in my class at school turned against my best friend Moira because she had lice. We had lice too, everyone did. But Moira's parents had shaved her head and one Monday morning I arrived to find my entire class gathered round her chanting:

Bare heid, bare heid whose got the lice?
Moira MacGinty 'an that's not nice
The Germans'll get you wait 'an see
Wi yon shining pate they'll be coming after ye!

I stood there traumatized, but didn't intervene. Then Jean Cameron ran into the middle of the circle and spat on Moira's shaven head. I wanted to fly in and kick Jean's shins, but I didn't dare. She was a magnetic leader, all-powerful. My feet were rooted to the cement playground.

Finally, another girl grabbed Moira's elevenses apple and threw it into the cow's field. I watched in tears, but still didn't have the courage to take them all on.

That night I poured it out to Fardie. He listened carefully, then reminded me of the story of Peter denying Jesus thrice. It related exactly - the chant, the spitting, the stealing of the apple and my dreadful silence. I empathized with Peter. I loved him desperately and prayed for forgiveness. Temptation, sin, repentance ... life was simpler then.

Gil is another matter altogether, a multi-coloured butterfly with transparent wings, my husband, yet not my husband, loving me, yet hating himself for being with me. I'm twenty-five already! Where have I gone wrong?

I concentrate on the fact that I'm doing what I most want to do - theatre! I think to myself there's nothing on earth like the fact I can hold an audience. They are there, sitting in darkness ... then the curtain goes up. At first they are simply aware. But then I get the sensation that I am drawing them, like an indrawn breath, like hill air sucked into lungs. I have that power. It's not only the words. It is movement, silence, sorrow or joy conveyed through the manner in which one turns aside or the intensity of a glance. I love those people in the dark. I love the stillness between us ... the shared breath.

Chapter 4

IONA

Just being in love as opposed to falling into it is so ordinary it's easy to miss.

"Do you wish we were being interesting?" Mark asks me sometimes, knowing I don't. "Writing a book about India or doing a survey on the sociological impact of rock 'n roll music on our generation?"

"No, I adore our life," I answer, as he knows I will. It's peace! It's what I've always wanted. It's been such a hassle with Fardie and Char storming at each other and worrying about Vivian on her trail leading nowhere.

"I love our life too, darling. And I love us being ordinary. It's the most extraordinary thing being ordinary with you. I still can't believe it."

We are lying in bed at eleven o'clock on a Saturday morning, after a sweet hour of love followed by Finn's early feed, followed by more sleep. And now, with coffee cups, bits of brioche and peach stones all around us, we are just talking.

I really didn't know what men were like before Mark. Except Fardie, of course, and he doesn't count as a normal man. I knew what they wanted, but not what they were like. I didn't have the remotest idea. I mean there was Char and Vivi and Mrs F and Elsie and me, then Westfield with its pashes and periods and Johnson's talcum powder sogging up girly smells. Then came the years sharing a London flat with Arabella and Tawda. When I think back, I remember hours in the bath under a line of drying nylons and knickers worrying about whether I might be pregnant or not. Most of the time it was physically impossible, but I wasn't sure how much fooling around one could get away with. If an agile little sperm could swim upstream like a salmon who was to say it couldn't dart through the air?

When I did finally go the whole way it involved an American summer drink called a mint julep, which looked like iced tea, and a cricketer called Dave something who didn't ring back. And that led to a lot more worrying in the bath under the knickers and visions of Fardie subjecting me to eternal fire. At the end of all this I still didn't know what men were like. I'd no idea that they were really domestic animals. And I certainly didn't know they could talk.

It's not that I think of Mark every moment. It's more a long, steady dose of sweetness, feeling safe and knowing he's around. He's as tall as Charlotte, has floppy light brown hair, shy eyes and a way of listening earnestly. He's good at the things men enjoy, like shooting pheasants and playing games - but not obsessed, not always rushing off to courts. He's a barrister, cleverer than I am by far, but he's diffident about cleverness. His father is a competitive maniac. He sent his sons to Winchester and tried to pit them against each other. In Mark's case you can see it was hopeless, like trying to teach a dove to snarl.

Sex with Mark is lovely. Not a flat out race to prove anything, but slow and luscious. I can't imagine why he's so good at being slow, it's not what you'd expect from a British public school boy who has been locked up for years playing with racquets. He licks the rim of my ear till I feel my nipples hard and aching to be kissed, like pebbles longing for the tide to come in and wash over them.

"Do you miss house-party weekends?" he asks me. "Don't you find this domestic bliss a little stultifying?"

I remember how deathly shy I used to feel walking into rooms in the country, Suffolk or Surrey or one of those, with the parents of the boy I was with sitting there looking me over. 'And where do you come from in Scotland, dear?' the mother would say sweetly, when really she was thinking, 'What a little tart!' and me saying, 'Argyllshire.' 'Mmm,' she would reply in a detached way, 'how nice.'

"I want to be stultified, Mark. I'm loving it!"

Sometimes I ask him what his London-before-me was like. It's hard for us to imagine the other in a separate existence.

"Studying for my bar exams, cricket, squash, skiing in the Alps, dancing with girls not nearly as beautiful as you, dreading going home for weekends ... "

"You mean your mother?"

"Yes, actually."

I shouldn't have asked. The one thing Mark isn't fond of talking about is his family. His mother is an alcoholic. She used to forget to pick him up from school when he was little. She was never there for the things that mattered. She's lovely to look at but impossibly remote. There are bottles of wine hidden in the strangest places all over their house. I came upon some Nuits-St. Georges in her long, suede winter boots. And there's usually a little stash of Chianti in the spare room bathroom under the basin with a plunger.

"Let's not go to Claybourne!" he says almost every weekend.

I agree. He's tense there and anxious about his mother. At meals it's like being on a high-powered quiz show with his father firing questions at the boys and giving snorts of disparaging laughter when one of them flounders.

"Let's not go up to Scotland!" I find myself saying more and more, when the longer holidays like Easter come round.

He agrees. Mark's fond of Fardie, but resentful too. When we do go he's especially tender to me, making me cups of cocoa and smuggling coal up to our bedroom.

"You're spoiling me." I say to him as he kneels down on the icy floor in his pyjamas, blowing life into the fire.

"About time!" he says. "It's about time somebody did."

Our wedding was pretty well taken out of my hands by Vivian. I thought it would be a nightmare with nothing but Scottish cousins and seed cake. In fact it was lovely. All sorts of treasures I'd never seen before were brought up from the cellar and there was plenty of Dom Perignon. The biggest surprise was Fardie, who was looking positively decorous in his medals. An old Highland trout called Jane Ansty, the kind that only comes out of the woodwork once a year weighted down with diamonds nobody knew she had, was there. And when the orchestra played *Tales of the Vienna Woods* they waltzed together with embarrassing nostalgic smiles on their faces. We couldn't believe our eyes!

Charlotte was completely supportive, not at all jealous. The only dramatic thing was when Fardie gave me Olivia's portrait as a wedding present. I feel dreadful about it, knowing how Char loves it. But there's something in me not quite prepared to give it up. Why should she have it after all? By rights it belongs to both of us. I'd consider coming to some sort of sharing plan, but I can see she's mortally insulted. When my sister gets like that you might as well give up.

***

I wasn't really for having a baby or against it but Mark loved the idea, so I agreed after two years. I felt more lethargic than usual when I was pregnant. Mark was determined we should do it the natural way. There were ten of us in the La Maze pre-natal class given by a Swedish teacher called Gunilla. She was like a model with short silver-blonde hair and wonderful skin. It was pleasant lying on mats with a background of Grieg and her voice like clean water, light and reassuring, flowing over us. The other fathers-to-be wore jeans. Mark looked out of place in his suit trousers, but he was frightfully good at it. If I opened my eyes - the music made me drift off - I'd see his eager face concentrating like mad on what she was saying. She had slides of the different stages of birth. They made it look easy, like an oyster slipping down a throat.

But it was all a lie. Once the birth got going it was like being in the grip of an earthmover that couldn't care less about breathing or relaxing, hands of hot pain tearing me apart. I yelled and swore and Mark was distraught when he saw how unlike the slides it was. All I wanted was dope and we'd signed something saying I wouldn't need any. In the end they gave me a spinal and the last part was a blur of contradictory instructions, more pain and the sound of Mark choking back tears.

Grunilla or Gunilla hadn't told us how wonderful it would be afterwards, either. I felt elated and full of slightly unhinged, swampy emotions when I saw Mark with the tiny Finnlet in his arms. At first my baby reminded me of Fardie, but then he began to look like himself - absolutely beautiful. I love the confident way he has taken to being a baby. He began appreciating everything straight away, fitted neatly into his white basket and loved the mobile Char made for him. Other babies I've seen are so agitated. Arabella, who lives only three streets from us, has two. I feel sorry for her, really. They are pathetic little creatures with faces like plums. Charlotte came to look Finn over immediately. She gazed at him for ages and then started lecturing me.

"You realize that he's ours? Ours forever! It's up to us - I mean he must have a perfect childhood with no punishments or psalms ..."

I started to laugh, but then I realized how serious she was. It was as if she'd had him too.

There really is this nesting thing. Every day I'm metaphorically lining ours with sheep's wool, flying back with something or nothing in my beak, but always flying back. When I go out I leave Finn with June. She's an unusual baby sitter, I'll admit. More of a hippie than a nanny but Finni absolutely adores her and lights up when he sees her bright hair with purple streaks. She sings: *Someone left the cake out in the rain* and *You've gotta friend* rather than lullabies and carries him around in her backpack with holes cut into it for his legs. It's far more fun for him than a pram.

Anyway, the other day, I was looking for trousers in Covent Garden when I banged into somebody I hadn't seen since school. 'Iona MacIntyre! Haven't seen you for yonks,' she exclaimed, taking in my blousy figure and comfortable flat shoes. 'Hello, Liz!' She looked very smart and *with it*. After a few preliminaries she asked me if I had time for a sandwich. I did, but I felt the magnetic pull that exists between Finn and me. Not just a heaviness in my breasts but an overwhelming need to be leaning over, picking him up, hearing his crying stop with a breathless jolt of relief. I love his serious, quick sucking and the way he presses one hand against my breast, fingers splayed. Gradually the tugging slows, the lashes flip up and his navy blue eyes lock onto mine, while his chin keeps on moving in little, pretending-to-suck movements. 'Sorry, Liz, I must rush. I'll give you a ring.' It's not that I don't like her, it's just that I'm caught up at the moment, nesting.

***

I feel guilty sometimes, feeling so happy in the midst of Char's turmoil. But I feel selfish too. Why should I always have to worry about her? It was agony for me when she took off with Daniel the Demonstrator. Alright for Charlotte, but agony for me sandwiched between her and Fardie. She forbade me to tell him where she was and he was furious, guessing I knew. I supported her, of course. But I was envious really, stuck in my London job while she was living on groats or oats or whatever the basic Irish food is - in love in a hut in the West of Ireland, growing her own food and smoking marijuana in the rain. I went to see her once but left after two days it was so uncomfortable. To be honest it wasn't the magical place she described in *No Earthly*

Trappings. It was damp. And the famous garden was mainly cabbages when I saw it. Also it was pretty obvious to me they were hopeless at catching fish. Daniel was sweet, but one of those pure, pure people, content to spend hours mending a fishing net. I could tell Char would get bored before long - and she did.

There was a lot of excitement when their book got taken on, but then it was never published. When the editor found out that Daniel and Charlotte had split up he was furious. He said the public would expect them to continue living with no earthly trappings, and that it would make his company look farcical if they found out Daniel had joined MRA and Charlotte was playing Amanda in Private Lives.

Fardie does realize when he's made a mistake. He was so distraught over Charlotte taking off that when she came back she could do no wrong for a while. The fatted calf was killed in the shape of a leg of one of our own lambs and the best redcurrant jelly was released from the larder. As if this weren't enough pleasure a mass of our for-export-only strawberries were served with real cream. I felt like the prodigal son's older brother who'd been faithfully tilling the land for months while the younger son was off wasting his substance with riotous living - not that Char had any substance to waste and Daniel was hardly the riotous type. Actually, I was thrilled to have her back and I've always had a weakness for strawberries.

It turned out to be an important week as Fardie revealed the fact that we had both inherited money from our mother. Having told us this exciting news he then dragged on about it not being money we could use. However, after a lot of lecturing from an insipid Mr. Craig, we discover that they really can't stop us getting at the interest. So Charlotte is able to study drama, after all. I'm still working on Craig, Creary and Calquhoun Ltd. I have high hopes as Calquhoun has a weak spot for me.

Fardie little realized that Gil Grey was round the corner. He can't stand the sight of him. I will say that when Char brought Gil up to Scotland he didn't try to make an impression. He never went out, even when it wasn't raining. He just lounged around in a caftan making jokes about the barbaric north and inventing a crazy fictional background for our clan.

'Give him a chance, Fardie!' Char said. "What's wrong with him?"

"Chap wears a frock, damn it!"

'Nonsense! It's a caftan - a Turkish man's dress. Heaps of men wear them in London.'

'Books. If he's interested in our history ... in the library.'

'He's not interested, obviously.' Charlotte said, tactlessly. 'Don't you understand, Fardie, he's an actor, on the lookout for material.'

It was an absolute disaster.

'Get me out of here, Charlie darling,' Gil said after three or four days. 'I've got gangrene, frostbite, hypothermia from your bathroom and a case of acute skeletal tedium.'

And that was that. They left on the next bus. The tragic thing is Charlotte and Fardie are still hardly talking. He wouldn't even go to their wedding. It was the most romantic one I've ever been to. They had it in a field in Wales and they both looked utterly beautiful. Charlotte wore an Isadora Duncan type of dress with daisies wound through her hair. The ceremony was mainly poems and American folk songs, followed by a long Felliniesque lunch at a wooden table with masses of wine. Later they changed into leather suits and went off on Gil's motor bike.

It makes me sad looking back on all that now because they haven't made it - at least I don't think they have. There's something terribly wrong with my darling Char. She's too thin. She draws her hair back and her face is white and strained. I went to their flat the other day and found her huddled up on her bed. She looked as if she'd been in the same T-shirt for days. She's closed off, even from me. I haven't a clue what's going on. Mark suggested we should take Finn up to Scotland to give her a break. Char didn't want to come, but her play was closing and he managed to get her to change her mind.

So we got on the night train to Glasgow, like millions of times before. When we woke up in the morning we hauled back the sleeper window and pushed our heads out. The blissful smell of heathery hill swept in and a smatter of rain hit our cheeks.

***

We hadn't expected Vivian to be at the station, but when we got to Craigmannoch there was still no sign of her.

"Where's Vivian?" Charlotte asked immediately.

"She's away at the moment," Fardie answered, as if that might work, as if he could possibly get away with such a vague reply.

"Where?" we asked. Vivian is never away at lambing time.

"America."

"America! Why on earth ... ?"

"Suddenly left," Fardie told us. "Said she'd always wanted to see 'the Big Sky Country,' her interest in cattle - all that."

"But Vivian isn't interested in cattle. She's interested in sheep!" Charlotte said in a baffled voice.

"She left you a note."

When we heard that I slotted Finn into the crook of Fardie's arm and we ran for it, pushing each other on the stairs like we used to as children ... and there it was, on our old homework table.

We learned what I've always half known, or quarter known, ever since I read her diary when I was fourteen. Vivian had a baby in France, a boy, years ago when she was only sixteen! The whole thing was hushed up and the child was adopted and now this son of hers, a man older than we are now, is looking for his real mother. And Vivian has just blasted off into the unknown - to America of all places - to find him.

The whole thing is fraught with danger. I mean he could be a travelling salesman with Brylcream in his hair - or a criminal. He could be resentful. And how is Vivian going to cope in the USA? She's only been abroad twice in her life, apart from France. Both times to fish in Norway, hardly the best preparation. Her clothes are peculiar. They'll laugh at her. And how is she going to be able to meet this person in front of other people if it does come off? She's so shy she shuts her eyes when someone takes a snapshot.

Worst of all, if it's the wrong person she won't have us there to bring her home. She hasn't even left an address.

***

Fardie had mended and cleaned one of our old prams himself. Each morning we wrapped Finn up and put him out under the oak tree for his rest. When he cried I ran to pick him up.

"I thought babies were meant to cry till lunch," Fardie said one day. Charlotte turned on him.

"No! No, Fardie, funnily enough that's not what's meant to happen." They are supposed to be picked up and kissed and," she went on, "children aren't meant to be punished when they are three, or controlled with a dog whistle or forced to learn psalms ..."

I can't bear it when she attacks him like that. He looks so lost. You can see he loves the baby in his way. When Finn laughs Fardie can't resist him. He says, 'Well, well!' and smiles and 'well, wells' again. When I put him on his knee he sits like a statue, hardly blinking. He's probably never held a baby ... after all he didn't know us until we were almost two.

We've hit heavenly weather. Everything's coming out in a rush. Baby birds plonk out of their nests outside the dining room window in the middle of lunch, just like they used to. Char's been walking for miles and helping with the sheep. She still won't tell me what's wrong. There's something flintish inside her, something that hurts. I stick around with Fardie and do most of the cooking now that Forrie's retired.

***

Does the space ever close over, I wonder? The space with no mother in it. As a child Mrs Forrester remembers me as easy and placid - but she doesn't know about the nights. I used to dread Char falling asleep.

Not knowing my mother's breast, voice, the feel and sound of her, I invented these things. I tried to wrap myself up in my own inventions, but it didn't always work. Once, when I was about seven, I awoke in motherless space, terrified.

I went to find Fardie. He wasn't in his room so I felt my way downstairs, flailing my arms in the dark, like being a child in a game of *blind man's buff*. Then I saw a light under the library door. I was about to push it open to run to him, when I heard sobbing. Dry sobs, so lonely, so full of their own emptiness that I couldn't go in. I felt my way back up to our room and climbed into Charlotte's bed. In the morning our father was eating his porridge at seven as usual.

I've never told anyone, not even Mark.

Chapter 5

CHARLOTTE

When exactly was it that I met Toby? I'd been in LA filming *A Diamond as Big as the Ritz*. It was after my first Christmas there I know, for I remember the Styrofoam reindeer galloping over Beverly Hills' lawns in eighty degrees. They had sweltering Father Christmas figures on sleighs behind them and lots of beautifully wrapped boxes. Americans are good at wrapping things up. They make the presents look too pretty to open.

Anyway, I was driving along looking at all this and thinking that the deer at home would be down below the snow line by now, stripping bark off the young trees, hurling themselves at the deer fences, when an announcement on the car radio cut into my thoughts. 'Whoever wins this contest,' the disc jockey was saying, 'will wake up to a white Christmas! Yes, real snow will be put in your yard with our Sno-Buddy machine and real icicles will hang from the tree of your choice.'

I remember these details because it was at a time when I was questioning sanity – theirs and mine. Wondering why anyone would want to wake up on Christmas day to a whirring snow machine and a lot of slush when they could be swimming and drinking margaritas. I know I hadn't met Toby at that point because after I met him I wasn't worried about sanity anymore - and I was so happy I took Styrofoam reindeer in my stride.

***

Billy and JJ - script writers on my film - invited me to join them at a lunch party in Toby Vane's house one weekend. Having read *Freeways Leading Nowhere* and loved it I thought it might be interesting and went along.

The house was high above Malibu beach with a thread of steps cut into the rock winding down to the sea. It was a cold/hot day, bright sun, but a strongish breeze. We could see a cluster of people far below us on the beach. Billy and JJ went to join them. I decided to wait for them up there.

The house was made of concrete and pale wood. It clung to the cliff in the most natural way, or rather seemed to grow out of it. There was a long deck with a kitchen behind it. A Mexican lady was preparing lunch. I asked her where the bathroom was. She pointed down some steps: 'Go through Señor Toby's office ... '

The walls of his office were white and the only furniture was a large table which served as a desk, and a plain wooden chair. Along one side of the room were bookshelves. The whole front wall was taken up with one vast window. There was no glass, only shutters. All one could see was sea and sky. It was like a large, rocking, abstract painting. I used to tell Toby later that I first fell in love with his desk and the surprising discovery that he used pencils.

I went back to the deck and helped the Mexican lady, Leticia, because she was behind with lunch. She gave me some quails' eggs to peel. I've always been good at that. The trick is to give the tip of the egg a sharp smack, making sure you pierce the transparent membrane. Then it's easy. You just lever the little egg out of its shell.

Toby says his first sight of me was sitting in front of a pile of slaughtered quails' eggs. According to him each one had the incision of my fingernail. He tells me he loved my winterwhite face amongst the bronzed Californian ones. He says that the minute he saw me he visualized my living there with him, which is odd because the moment I walked into his house I felt an overwhelming sense of recognition. I felt I had arrived at last, after a long journey.

"I'm Toby Vane ... you've got to be Billy's friend, Charlotte."

"Hello!"

"You're not good at peeling quails' eggs, are you?"

"It's one of the things I'm very good at, as it happens."

"What are a few of the others?" he asked, in an amused voice.

"Let's see, rowing on a rough sea, gutting mackerel, cribbage, memorizing poetry," I said, showing off.

I tried to close my lips on a silly smile, but it kept wanting to break away from me. He was smiling, too. I was running ... jumping into his arms in my mind.

"Acting?" he asked.

"Yes."

"Please don't tell me you're in some Hollywood film," he said.

"I am, actually."

"How tragic!"

"Mmm ..."

All the time I was looking at his bony face and his blown-about hair and noticing the fact that he didn't seem to care a hoot about clothes or image like most Californians - no dark glasses, no French shirt, rather bulky, non-designer jeans and what we used to call sand shoes in Scotland - plain and flat, good for rock-climbing.

The rest of the people had gathered. It was the usual Los Angeles scene - a few talented people and a lot of hangers-on. Two or three cokeheads and one old director everyone was listening to.

"Don't go away, Charlotte," he said quietly. "Be here when I get back." And he went to look after his guests.

***

Much later Iona asked me how I reconciled the fact that Toby was a married man with what she calls 'my religious mania'. All I know is that from the first moment I met him I felt cleansed. I instantly knew that this was what God had had waiting for me. I've often wavered, not in my knowledge that He exists, the listening face, the almond Giotto eyes ... but I'd begun to think that I didn't deserve happiness. I'm irascible like Fardie. I fly into passions; leave undone the things that I ought to have done - all that.

The day I met Tobias Vane I was thirty-five and he was fifty. I sat on the deck feeling pure and full of light. I remember the feel of the wooden planks under my bare feet. I felt confident for once, not minding my long legs, unashamed, knowing that it was a matter of time until we were alone.

That first conversation was not typical of Toby - normally there is not a hint of flirtatiousness about him. That he was having a party at all was unusual and the fact that I was living with him within three weeks is, in retrospect, the most unusual thing of all. Toby is cautious. He is a quiet man in a noisy business. He guards his peace like a Bengal tiger, pads softly round the perimeter of his cliff wary of anything that might disturb the tranquillity. He covets simplicity as others covet possessions. He literally winces if someone gives him a present. When he won an

Oscar for his work on *The Dollar Laundry* his main concern was where to put it, so that it wouldn't disturb the calm of a wall.

He doesn't like me acting but doesn't ask me to stop. I slip out of bed early and leave for the set feeling a sense of betrayal. But the person I betray is myself. When I get back he never asks me about my day and I don't tell him. We just start our time together. We don't do big things. We slice fruit, make bread, read aloud, walk for miles along the sand ... or nothing. Often we do nothing. The other evening we sat on the sand at dusk feeling the spray on our faces, not touching, not discussing it. It was enough feeling the light breath of seawater spinning a web over my face and hair and knowing that it was happening to him too.

But it isn't all spray. I've never known such passion. Toby has a habit of going down to the sea very early, just plunging in and out. I'm still in bed, only half aware that he's gone. He comes up from the sea sealwet and the first thing I taste is the salt on his tongue. His skin against my skin, these early mornings, is clean and cold. I feel his accelerated heartbeat, I feel the length of him hard and long. The rhythm of the sea is inside him. Its sweeping strokes stroke me, his coldness inside my hotness.

Afterwards, I can't help it; I become the worst sort of mewling sailor's girl. I long to say, 'Stay - don't ever leave me!' I want to say, 'I love you,' and to hear it said.

"I ..."

"Don't!" he says.

"But I lo ..."

"Charlotte! - No Hollywood lines, I beg of you."

"But Hollywood does pick up on real life lines occasionally ..."

"And ruins them ... we have to find something more for us."

"But how, when it's straining to be said?"

"Quench!" he says. "You quench me." His lips lie lightly on my eyelids.

"You are my poem," I say.

"You see, we can do it!" His voice touches, leaves, returns. It is only for me.

The truth is I'm planning to stop working for a bit when the film is over. Is it instinct or dread ...? Instinct screams inside me to be with my mate. But it's dread too. I'm not sure that earthly bliss is allowed - and I'm right in the very heart of it.

***

Most Californians are from somewhere else, usually somewhere interesting like Poland or the North of Ireland - at the very least they are from the East Coast. Toby says they're snow-bunnies from the Midwest who've seen the Rose Bowl game on TV on New Year's day and followed the sun. Toby was born in California. He's a serious writer who got into scriptwriting to make money. That struck me as curious since he doesn't care about money. In fact, he hates Hollywood. He sees it as a machine that pampers and engorges. He says it belittles talent.

"Why work for it then?" I asked him. "You don't seem to need much money."

"My cliff costs a lot. Peace is expensive in the USA, Charlotte. And there's Rain - Rain needs money. She may need more ... and more. I worry about her."

I don't like the sound of this. I know this woman is officially Toby's wife, I didn't know he was still so involved.

"Why do you worry about her?"

"Because she's fragile."

"Why ... ? What's wrong with her?"

"We did stupid things together, got into LSD years ago. I escaped. Rain never will."

"She still takes it?"

"No. She wouldn't take an aspirin now. She's afraid of her own heartbeat. But she can't work ... or make decisions."

"I see," I said, not seeing at all.

"I thought you would."

What a name - Rain Vane! He also has Missy, who is eight. I made a faulty decision. I decided they were nothing to do with me.

***

"Missy is coming for the weekend!"

Will she hate her father's woman? I wondered. Will she be one of these Barbie doll little girls I see in Beverly Hills carrying a miniature make-up kit?

They arrived via the beach. Missy likes climbing up the one

64

hundred and forty-six rock steps so Toby collects her, leaves the car at the fish restaurant, and they come home that way. The minute I saw her I realized there was nothing Barbie-ish about her. She had a shock of short brown hair with sun-bleached stripes, an intense little face with wide-apart green eyes and a thin, boyish body with very big feet for her size. She wore cut-off jeans and a faded T-shirt. There was a cat sticker on her forehead and Guatemalan woven bands round her bare ankles. The whole effect was rather charming, but I didn't have time to be charmed as she galloped right past me and began jumping about on the rocks behind the house. I recognized the gait and understood she was being a horse.

After that she swarmed up the lemon tree, calling out to Toby:

"How many lemons today, Dad?"

"Twelve. But you've got to get them into the basket."

The lemons flew out of the tree and they both shouted 'Right on!' when she got one in.

At lunch Toby attempted to introduce us properly. The child was not rude but she seemed to have tunnel vision that excluded everything but her father. I had made spaghetti as Toby had told me it was her favourite food. She gobbled it down, telling him a long story between mouthfuls of pasta:

"There's this great kid at school, Dad, called Mackenzie Donnelly and her Dad's a real stuntman and he gets to ride horses for actors that can't 'cos they're too dumb or too old or something and he does all the fun things like jumping off burning buildings and being with real tigers and Mackenzie gets to ride the horses after school ..."

After she'd finished eating she stood close to Toby while he was drinking his coffee. Close, closer, leaning into him, gradually sliding one hip onto his knee, until finally he leant back and she was on his lap and, in a few minutes, they were both asleep in the sun.

By the next day all I could think was 'clever!' It is clever to spend from twelve noon on a Saturday till after breakfast the following day without saying more than one syllable to someone in the same house. Clearly the spaghetti I'd made for her on Saturday and the pancakes we'd eaten the following morning had had a physical form, whereas the arm that ladled them onto her plate and the person at the end of that arm didn't.

When she left in triumph on her father's shoulders, her skinny brown legs drumming possessively against Toby's chest, one unlaced sneaker falling off and her hands fondly grabbing a clump of his hair, I had the curious impression that I'd been rendered invisible.

The second time she came it was the same. The third time, just as I'd settled for a mute relationship, a conversation took place. We were alone on the deck. I was reading and Missy was lying on her stomach glueing shells onto a collage she was making for school. Suddenly I felt uneasy. The hostile green eyes, like murky algae, were fastened on me.

"He's my Dad!" she said abruptly.

"I know."

"He's got my Mom and me!" Her tone was challenging.

"I know, Missy."

"So ... ?"

"So what?"

"So how come you're here?"

"I love him too ..."

"You're dating him?"

"You could call it that."

"What does that make you to me?"

"Nothing official ... whatever we want, really." There was a pause while she considered this.

"Is it true you've got a twin?" For the first time there was interest. She got up and stood, scowling, directly in front of me.

"Yes."

"Yeah?"

"Yeah."

Missy did a back flip and then came back - now she was intrigued. The algae cleared and I could see questions floating through her seagreen eyes in little golden darts.

"So?"

"So what, Missy?"

"What's it like having a twin?"

"Fun!"

"I thought it might be," she said a little wistfully. "I guess you share stuff and everything?"

"Yes."

"Charlotte!"

"Yes."

"Since you're my Dad's date and you don't have kids or anything you could tell me stories about twins. I mean about what you did and about the fun and ... and stuff like that."

"I'd love to, Missy."

"OK! You can if you like." A sudden transformation - her freckles scattered like dandelion fluff, a smile - wide, generous, cheeky, illuminated her face for a moment before the scowl relocated itself and she wheeled around and cantered back to her shells.

It was a breakthrough of a kind. I didn't know about Missy then. I didn't know that her war had hardly begun, or how she would tangle through my life like the Moss rose - which hurts when you try to pick it and never will live in a vase.

***

Vivian and her son, Morgan, live an hour from here by plane. We had a three day break from filming so I went to visit them. I wish I hadn't gone now. I wish I'd never listened to my cousin's muddled thinking and got into a flat out fight with Vivian.

When we first got the news about Morgan it was the most exciting thing that our family had ever experienced. It was February 1969 and we hadn't had a word from Vivi since she left for America. Then suddenly she sent us all elated letters and included a 8mm movie and a tape recording of the day she was united with her long lost son on Louise Leroy's radio programme. The voices and picture weren't in sync, but it didn't matter. We watched it in Iona's house. Even Fardie, who hates leaving Scotland, came down for the event.

Louise was a coloured lady, oozing with sympathy and emotion. Every so often she paused to say, 'Isn't that byu-ti-ful folks? Isn't it what we're all about?' We had to sit through the first half while two vast sisters from Mississippi were reunited with a father who'd walked out on them when they were babies. He was immense too. They did all the right things, cried and hugged and exchanged carnations. The father said he'd never meant for it to happen and he was real sorry. They exchanged more flowers and wobbled together in another hug. We couldn't imagine Vivian behaving like that, and we were quite right!

The camera switched onto a tall, thin, dark-haired man. It was obvious to us all from the first moment that he was Vivian's son. Despite his accent he had the same jerky way of talking and shy MacIntyre eyes. There was something of Fardie about him too, a gauntness, an odd-man-out impression.

"Our next guest is Morgan. He has been looking for his Mom for ... what is it, Morgan?"

"Eight years."

"Eight years! Well folks, several years ago Morgan came to us for help ... what had you found out yourself, Morg honey?"

"My birth certificate was French. I guess my mother must have been a young French girl, Catholic perhaps ..." he said in a hesitant voice. He looked as if he was hating the whole thing but was determined to go through with it.

"Now, Morgan, if she were to walk in here today could you forgive her?"

"Forgive her?"

"For having you adopted by what turned out to be a real harsh Mom and Dad?"

"I wouldn't be here if I couldn't," he said curtly. He kept cracking his knuckles like I used to and looking around anxiously.

"Well, Morgan, have I got news for you! What would you say if your mother was not a French girl at all but a Scottish lady - a real lady from a real old family in Scotland, England?"

Morgan didn't have time to answer for at that point Vivi was pushed out. She stood clutching her bag and blinking. There was silence while they looked at each other. You could see from the young man's shoulders that he was trembling. Then he took the initiative. He walked up to her and tentatively reached for her hand. Vivian just stared at him. Her eyes filled, emptied, filled again ... and gradually smoked over with love.

"I couldn't help it," she blurted out. "They took you away ... by force."

"I knew it." Morgan said, putting a long arm round her, fighting back tears.

Louise sighed. "Is this meaningful or what?" she said. There was the sound of canned clapping. At that point the film-maker seemed to have got distracted. The camera wandered over Louise's bust then concentrated on someone making faces at her from behind a glass window. Suddenly it swerved back onto Vivian. She was heaving herself out of her chair.

"Tell these people to go away!" she shouted. She seemed to think the mike they'd pinned on her blouse made it necessary to raise her voice. She must have pulled the wire out of its socket because for a while we just saw her mouth moving.

When it got going again Vivian was back in her glass box and Louise was saying:

"Now Mom, do you have something special to say to your son?"

"Tell me your name again?" Vivi said, looking at him the way she used to look at us when we were children, intrigued, her voice husky and amused.

"Morgan."

"Morgan's a surname! I called you Malcolm, but never mind ... it'll do," she said. Then, without lowering her voice, she boomed out: "Can we go home now, Morgan?"

Louise must have had enough of them for that was it, except for a glimpse of the united and reunited people at the end. The Mississippi lot were locked together sobbing with joy. Vivian and Morgan were giggling.

Since then we've seen quite a lot of Morgan. He lives in Arizona and teaches at the biology department of the University as well as working as a landscape gardener. Vivian spends most of the year with him. I look on Morgan as a brother now - we both do. That's the trouble, really. He's so delighted to have a family he's trying to understand all about us. How can he possibly, when we don't understand ourselves?

The first two days I was with them were great. I told them all about Toby and Missy. We played bezique and Scrabble and lazed about. The trouble started on my last evening. Vivi had gone to bed and Morgan and I were finishing off the wine. He always wants to hear stories about his mother.

"I guess you and Iona got a lot of her - when you were kids."

"Yes."

"I'm kind of envious of that, Charlotte."

"I can imagine ... but she was never ours, exactly. We always had Olivia - our real mother."

"But didn't she die before ...?"

"Yes, but we had our dream of her."

"Even, although ..."

"Even although what?"

"Well, my mother has told me a bit ..."

"Yes?"

"Of our family history, your poor father, the horror of his war ... and Olivia."

"What about Olivia?"

"It's just that what you went through and what I went through was sort of similar."

"I don't see why?"

"I mean we were both given up ... and both developed this dream."

"What do you mean we were given up?"

"Nothing!"

Morgan felt like a brother at that point – irritating.

"Go on - you can't start and stop like that."

"I just meant when she heard about what they went through ... the conditions ... and Ormonde's dreadful ..." he blundered on. "I didn't mean she gave you up ... I meant she gave up herself, as I understand it."

"Morgan! She was ill. She wasn't strong. Get your facts straight."

"Sorry!" He looked terribly worried.

"And what do you mean about Ormonde?"

"Look, you'd better ask my mother," he said abruptly and hurried off to bed.

I stayed awake most of the night thinking about what he'd said, and the more I thought about it the more incensed I became with Vivian. The next day she drove me to the airport.

"You might have had the decency to tell me about my own mother before you told a perfect stranger," I exploded, the minute we were alone in the car.

"Morgan is hardly a perfect stranger."

"That's not the point, Vivian. Olivia is our mother - not Morgan's. If you're going to start revealing our family's darkest secrets I think you might start with us."

"Stop shouting, Char!"

"I thought she was ill. And what the hell did Ormonde have to do with anything?"

"She became ill, when you were about one."

"And before that? Didn't she want us? *Didn't she want us?*"

"You've got to remember the war was on. You've got to remember how young Olivia was. There were so many deaths: her brother's, then Ormonde's ... what happened was terrible for all of us."

"What happened? *What?*"

"Get a grip on yourself, Charlotte! I can tell you a bit about Olivia. But I swore to Harry I'd never tell anyone what happened in Germany."

"Damn you, Vivi! Damn you! Just because everything's worked out for you, you think you have the right to keep our mother from us."

"Stop it! You can't know what it was like. None of us can. It was war. When I saw how little was left of your father, when I see that ... the very least I can do is respect what he wants."

"But Olivia?"

"She hadn't grown up herself, Charlotte. She was beautiful ... and self-centred. Most people are at that age."

"You're telling me she didn't want us."

"Did you want a baby when you were nineteen?"

"Not really."

"Does that make you a dreadful person?"

"So nobody wanted us! Fardie was away. You had lost Morgan, so you didn't care. Our own mother didn't want us ... I'm surprised you didn't exchange us for ration stamps."

Vivian cut across two lanes, bumped the car over a cement kerb and jerked to a stop on a grass strip. She cut the engine, turned round and grabbed me by the shoulders.

"Look, Char! I'm not much good at this sort of thing. But get this straight, when you two arrived the house changed. You kept us alive. In our own different, damaged, screwed-up ways Harry and

I loved you. We aren't good at showing it. We never had any of it ourselves. But, goddamit, we did our best. So shut up, kiddo. Shut up! And don't blame Olivia. She was numb. When everything dies around you, you daren't start loving something else. I held out at first. I tried not to care. But ..."

"Don't cry!"

I'd never seen Vivian cry. It was horrible. Her long MacIntyre face was contorted. Her mouth was in a sort of silent shudder.

"It's too complicated. I can't explain ..."

"You seem to have managed to explain to Morgan."

"I haven't. I was simply trying to give him a feeling of belonging. There's a lot I don't know myself ... my own dearest Ormonde. Just stop asking questions. Stop it!"

She started up the car and cut fearlessly back into the traffic. I made my plane by seconds. I was furious with Vivian. I still am. I must make Morgan promise not to discuss any of this with Iona. It would upset her dreadfully.

***

When I got back the house was empty and there was a letter for me on the kitchen table.

Dearest Charlotte,

We were so pleased to hear from you. How splendid that you've found the right man. Toby sounds great. I look forward to meeting him.

I'm afraid things are not so good this end. In fact they are very worrying. I am writing to ask for your help. I don't know where else to turn.

I have to tell you Iona hasn't been right since the baby was born. But, in the last two months, she has slid into a real depression. I don't know what set it off. Little Olivia had to have some tests as her responses were slow (I was terrified she might have MS, but she definitely doesn't) that could have made Iona's post-natal depression worse. But now that we know the baby has a common complaint, which will correct itself in time, nothing has changed.

I've managed to get people to take care of the children. But it's her

I'm worried about ... it's terrible, Char, seeing her like this.

She says she's tired all the time but it seems more serious than that. It's more like profound sorrow. Worst of all, I'm unable to help her. I've tried everything. But I've become enemy number 1. I don't know where I've gone wrong. I've encouraged her to see someone but she flatly refuses to accept professional help.

I am sorry to write to you at this point in your life when I'm sure you've no wish to come home. But I know you wouldn't want me to keep this from you. I wouldn't write unless I was desperate. You will understand the agony of watching her slipping away. We need you - all of us. I haven't told Iona that I'm writing to you.

Love,

Mark

My first reaction was 'not now.' But then I began to concentrate on Iona. I emptied my mind and waited. Usually her face - the sound and roundness and flippancy of her - rushes into my head. But this time the picture was faint. The harder I tried the more distant she became. The sea was disturbed that afternoon. Waves bullied the rocks and slapped up against the sand. The sky was boot grey. I wiped my mind clean and waited. I held the letter in my hand and spoke her name out loud. A black cloud was moving in towards the shore. Rain skidded over the wooden slats of our deck.

***

The following morning, when we were drinking our coffee, I was wondering how to tell Toby, when he looked across at me.

"You smell of the sea today - and salads - those delicious lettuces with a crumpled red frill."

"You smell of pencils and cotton."

"What does cotton smell like?"

"Flat, I think. Cottony!"

"On Saturday I thought I'd take you to see the sequoias."

"What are they like?"

"Immense. You'll love them. The bark is padded round them loosely like a quilt."

"Toby, I can't."

"Can't what?"

"I can't come to see the sequoias. I've got to go home."

I gave him Mark's letter. He read it carefully. Toby's hands look older than his face or the rest of his body. His fingers are long and graceful, but they are hesitant - the veins show and the skin is very thin.

"Has Iona been depressed before?" he asked me.

"Never! She's always happy. She's someone who sidesteps the gravelly side of things. I've never seen her sad."

"There's no doubt at all you must go."

"No, none."

"When, Charlotte?"

"This evening."

"I see."

We sat in silence, trying to get used to the idea.

"Don't move!" he said after a while. He looked at my profile, then he got up and leant against the railing and looked at me from a different angle. He walked round behind me. I could feel his breath on the back of my hair.

"What are you doing?"

"I need to draw you in my mind," he said. "Fix you here."

"I won't be long."

"You might be ... if she wants you to stay."

"It feels hazardous, Toby."

"Leaving?"

"Yes, leaving this deck and this house and you. I've never ..."

"Come here!"

"You were going to work."

"I'll work when you've gone.

Chapter 6

IONA

"What's this one?"

"This what?"

"Harvey Nichols - two hundred and seventy pounds."

"You said, 'Cheer yourself up!' You said you like Olivia to have pretty things."

"Of course I do, darling, and I'm glad if it did cheer you up, it's just ... "

"I hate all this tension about money - never being able to have fun with it."

"You see, the way a charge account works is ..."

"Isn't the whole point of things like charge accounts and banks that they're there to make life easier for people? I mean when families are growing and they need bigger houses and more holidays."

"No, it isn't, actually."

"Well, please don't tell me how they work now. I'm so tired."

"Never mind the money. Iona?"

"Yes, Mark."

"I thought next month might be a good time for Olivia to have those tests. I mean if it suited you."

"What tests?"

"The tests we discussed with Dr Ingles. Just to be sure. Just to check her condition."

"Olivia doesn't have a condition."

"I didn't mean she *had* a condition. I simply meant to be absolutely certain that she doesn't ..."

"Olivia is perfect!"

"I know, darling. We know she is perfect. It simply makes sense, don't you think? When you see something not developing as it should ... to have it checked?"

Mark's changed! He's become fanatical about money and education. But it's the horrible way he's going on about Olivia that upsets me most. Anyone can see she's the most adorable little girl. She's all I ever wanted. She's like us, thank God, not at all like Mark's side of the family. Finn and Hughie are delighted with their sister. We all are. But Mark seems to think she isn't developing at the normal rate. He wants to subject *my* daughter to tests. He bases this on the fact she isn't sitting up at ten months. Well, I've looked it up and all the books say that children develop at different rates. Olivia doesn't feel like sitting up yet. I make nests of cushions for her and she half lies, half sits. She prefers that position. If this goes on I'm going to start hating Mark soon.

Things haven't been going well with us since Olivia was born. To be honest I haven't felt like sleeping with him. It's such an effort having an extra bath when you've just finished having a first bath, when the baby is asleep and you're feeling downy and drowsy, just beginning to slide ...

Mark seems to think that having June three days a week should solve everything. But I'm tired. I'm so tired. I don't understand how other mothers with three children manage to look after them and go to gyms and take part in local politics and write novels. I meet these mothers at school. Several tidy children climb out of their Land Rovers and there's usually a sponged, contented baby in its seat in the back. Nobody's forgotten anything. The mothers are bright and positive and on their way to volunteer for something or other. It's their cheerfulness at eight A.M. which I find dispiriting.

I plan things carefully. For instance, I like Olivia to have fresh vegetables. What's the point in having moved to the country if one can't at least do that? I push her down to the vegetable garden. On the way we visit the ducks. If I go to the edge of the pond and point her at them she certainly does respond. She waves her hands in the air and laughs. Then I dig up carrots and a young leek or two and, by the time we get back, it's time for her rest.

When I get to the kitchen the breakfast dishes have hardened into a crust of egg and cereal. Then it's time to start cooking lunch. One of the things about being a mother is the way meals come at you like bullets: shepherd's pies, fish pies, salads, stews, sandwiches ... my whole life is paring and slicing and mashing and spooning food into wayward mouths. Then there are the children's clothes and cleaning up and driving them from one place to another.

I'd love to belong to an extended family with lots of extra mothers and aunts and great aunts. Female relations forever dropping in with homemade raspberry jam and sweaters they've knitted for the children. Women, whose whole concentration is on the young fertile wife, who gently remove dirty pans from her hands and take the older ones off for a while. Tribes, some of them, share responsibility for the children. Or is it elephants? I can't remember, but whichever it is, all the females pitch in. I could do with some of that ... Mark's mother won't miss even one of her AA meetings ... and Charlotte and Vivian are in America. I suppose I'd counted on having Vivi around for ever. How wrong I was!

***

Ever since Vivian found Morgan she's been different - transformed! Once she'd got over the shock of the programme she changed. She's like a bride, her son's bride. And he's sweet, a good sense of humour, knows how to deal with her, he even gets on with Fardie. She sent us a film of their reunion - the day she met her grown-up son. The whole thing was recorded, that was part of the agreement.

We all watched it together. I'll never forget it. Vivian looks startled and very uncomfortable when she first appears. Her hair is set in baby doll curls which don't go with her tweed suit and moth-eaten fur pelt. She's clutching her bag and blinking at the bright lights looking as if she's about to make a bolt for it. Then the coloured lady Louise introduces them - and when Vivi sees Morgan everything changes.

It's the most moving thing! Even though the film and their voices don't quite line up there's an instant connection between them. I felt an affinity with him too, as if I'd known him all my life. I can't imagine how I'd have borne it if I'd had one of my babies taken away.

They are inseparable now. Morgan is into gardening and teaches at the University of Arizona. Vivi's bossy and always interfering with his work, but he doesn't seem to mind. He seems to love it, in fact. She spends most of the year with him in his split-level ranch house. She does the most unlikely things now - takes Spanish cookery lessons and goes to some sort of transplanted Indian guru. You'd hardly recognize her. She looks almost like a normal American mother. In one snapshot she's wearing a track suit.

We only see her in the spring when she comes back for the lambing. I'm happy that it has worked out for her. But I miss her. I miss her dreadfully. Perhaps it's selfish of me, but I need her, badly.

***

"Mama! Hughie is getting out again."
"Make him sit still, Finn."
"I can't. I'm holding Olivia."
"Hughie, stop that!"
"My knee's blooding!"
"Oh dear, we'll wash it when we ..."
"I hate blooding!"
"Finn, hold the baby while I get Hughie in. Shh, shhh ..."
"Mama! That man's driving over our bread ..."
"I thought you'd put all the bags in the car, Finn."
"I thought I had ..." he swallowed anxiously, trying not to cry.
"It's alright, darling."

I reversed over the squashed supermarket bag. It didn't matter to me, but it worried my son so for that reason it mattered. Finn understands so much, about Hughie hating blood and Olivia not sitting up. Worst of all, he's worried about me being exhausted - and I'm the one who should be supporting him.

Actually, it's not just tiredness. It's more to do with an immense sadness. I feel it lapping over my feet, like water. It's breast-high now, pulling me down. Another thing, everything is so bright ... I need somewhere to get away to. A quiet room with shutters, like those sloping wooden ones in French houses that only let a muffed, half-light in.

Mark's at it again. He's obsessed. He's been going on about tests for Olivia. He puts Panda just out of her reach and watches her. When she doesn't react he starts lecturing me. He talks to me as if I were a patient being encouraged to have something off or out for my own good. I have difficulty hearing him. His voice has become so monotonous it keeps fading out.

"... for the best, darling."
"... just to reassure us."
"... on the right track."

I agree in the end, too tired to argue.

And the boys ... I find myself losing contact with them, too. I hear them chattering together, dancing chords, a tree full of birds, but one step removed - just beyond my reach.

***

The trouble is you trust people and then you can't. They change. Elsie, our Elsie who looked after us all those years ago at Craigmannoch, turned up when I was pregnant with Olivia. We'd been in touch off and on, then her husband Andy was sent down to Salisbury and she came to live near here with her girls. Anyway, she took a bus one Sunday to see me and meet the kids. She brought a wooden boat for Finn and a jar of tadpoles for Hughie. I thought it was lovely of her.

I'd made us a nice lunch. I shouldn't have given her any wine, I suppose. I see that now. It loosened her tongue and made her say those horrible things which stick like tar in my mind.

I can't remember how it started. I think we were chatting about how embittered Fardie was when she suddenly said:

"You canna blame him."

"Because of the war, you mean?"

"It wasna the war that fluttered its lashes at every mon in troos ... !"

"How can you imply ..."

"And one in particular as I've heard ..." she said with a little grin, "tho you'll not find me telling tales out the school."

"What? What are you saying? Elsie, it's my mother you're talking about."

"Some mother!"

I should have stopped her there; I shouldn't have given her a chance to get into all that breast-feeding nonsense.

"What do you mean? Our mother wasn't well. She wasn't strong enough to look after us."

"She was well right enough when you lassies were born. 'Elsie Buchanan,' my auntie telt me, 'it'll be your job to do for them two babies and the first thing'll be getting them to take the teat.' 'And how's that?' I asked. 'Do they no have a mother?' An' she was explaining that it wasna seemly for a lady to be nursing like we folks do. There was a right row going on, so there was, with me and auntie struggling to get yon wee Charlotte to take the bottle and she wouldna.

Then it was the third day an' I heard the doctor mysel fra the passage trying to persuade her. An' she was saying, 'Have a heart, Dr Cameron! You really can't expect me to let myself be hauled about any more.' An' he was saying, 'I'm worried for the little one, Mrs Harry. We'll have a tragedy on our hands if you won't feed the child ...' Then she changed her mind and I was telt to bring the wee soul in. She was sitting up looking a picture, so she was, with her lacy nighty on and one of they satin jackets ... 'Oh, you poor little mickle mouse!' she said when she saw her. 'Well, we'll have a go if we must!' But it didna work for she wasna a natural mother. And in the end Charlotte took a hold of the teat and growed into a fine wee gurl, just like yoursel."

"Lots of people can't breast-feed."

"There's them that canna and them that willna!"

"I'm sure she made up for it afterwards."

"Och, you'd no see herself in the nursery in a month of Tuesdays!"

She smirked and looked at me. At that point I think she realized she'd overstepped. I wanted to ask questions, but I wasn't going to give Elsie the satisfaction of gossiping any more about Olivia. She sat there squashed into her pale blue suit with her ugly, big red arms and her horrid, frizzy, permed hair and I couldn't wait to get rid of her. I couldn't wait to get her out of my sight.

***

"Come down in your dressing gown."

"I don't feel like it."

"Come on, darling, I've made some soup. We can watch television. We can eat off trays ..."

"Will the lights be on?"

"No, sweetling, just us on the sofa in the dark."

"Will you go on about doctors?"

"No doctors."

In the firelight I see Mark's face. His soft, straight hair is swept with white, brush strokes in snow. His eyes are wired with anxiety, which he tries to contain.

On television there's a documentary about POW hospitals in WWII. I read some books about great escapes when I was at school. They were about British officers and men digging tunnels and making maps and false passports. When someone escaped he usually managed to meet up with a beautiful resistance worker fairly quickly. She would mutter 'the birds are flying south' as she served him a beer, so he'd know it was going to be alright. It didn't seem bad at all, almost fun.

But this film we are watching is about a camp hospital. It's a black and white film that was taken during the war. The men are moaning - some are delirious. Uniformed orderlies march in and out. They take one young boy away. Another is brought back from the operating theatre without any legs. They tip him casually onto a grey sheet and plonk a wooden frame over his stubs.

Fardie's arm was amputated in a POW hospital. I'd forgotten that.

"Let's turn this off, Iona, it's too depressing."

"Please don't. I didn't know ..."

"Iona! I shouldn't have let you watch this."

"Fardie was there."

"Nonsense! What makes you think it was this hospital? I'm sure it wasn't."

"He lived through this ..."

"You're not being logical, darling, there's no reason to suppose ... "

"I know he was there."

"How can you ..."

"He used to sob in the library, Mark, after we'd gone to bed. This would account for it."

***

Charlotte's well. She's immensely happy. She's found the perfect man at our age, thirty-five! She describes a house hanging over the sea - a clear, clean view of sky and ocean, a wall that is all window, light spilling onto a wooden floor. I'm glad for her - but I couldn't bear so much light ... there would be nowhere to go.

I can imagine her in her high, light house in love with a man called Toby Vane. But I don't think she can imagine me.

Charlotte knows nothing about being a mother. She doesn't know what it's like sitting in a room with charts on the wall while a lady doctor puts toys in front of your baby and scribbles notes. She's got no idea about temperatures that soar in the night and curls sticking to hot foreheads like damp daisies. She hasn't learned that children need their own mug, the one with the cow on it - not their brother's mug, not the green one. And she's never had to remember everything: yoghurt, football boots, the composition about 'a bad penny', a note for somebody, a tick ... a tick you were supposed to put somewhere to show you'd agreed to something. Charlotte would never remember the tick.

Char doesn't know about Finn's friend Andrew, and how he changes things. The way he makes Finn spurt water out of his mouth and talk in a boastful voice. I hate Andrew and so does Hughie. But Finn loves him ... so he has to come.

Would she understand about being needed and needed and needed, I wonder? How it drinks up every drop of you and leaves you as parched as old skin?

I've been a mother all my life. Fardie made me into Charlotte's mother - I see that now. I remember one summer day when I was about six. I was a little girl eating porridge, spooning it into my mouth with a big Scottish spoon.

"Where's your sister?" Fardie asked me.

I was feeling happy about the tooth fairy, considering what to do with my sixpence.

"I don't know, Fardie."

"Boots, child? Did she have her boots on?"

"I didn't see."

"Teeth, Iona? Did she remember ..."

"It's kippers, Fardie," I said to distract him. "Your favourite!"

Even then I knew that she had to be protected. I should have reminded her to brush her teeth. It was up to me. I remember that day clearly. The sun was coming up behind the island. Her bare feet had scattered dew over the lawn ... drops of light, bending the blades of grass double.

***

"I've made an appointment, darling!"

"What for?"

"For us to go together to see Jamie's friend. He's a highly thought of psychologist. The sort of reasonable chap who can really help when you're feeling ... when you need a bit of a boost."

"Is there something wrong with you, Mark?"

"Iona! You know it's you I'm talking about. We must get you better. Feeling depressed is nothing to be ashamed of. Please come and see this man with me. Please! Just to talk things over ...."

"I can't leave this house."

"That's ridiculous! The appointment is on Thursday. June will be here all day."

"No, Mark. *No!* Can't you understand anything anymore?"

***

Char! I need to tell you things. Mark has changed. He's a spy after all. He watches me and reports to doctors. He watches Olivia too, and she's only a baby. If I could lie down for a while it might be alright. If only I wasn't so tired ...

There's a violent glare today. I drew the curtains, but it still wasn't quiet enough. Light jangled on my dressing table. I covered the mirror with a blanket. I try ... but there are things missing. Things we had before. I'm careful. I never leave the house. I avoid the bright things - sentences, taps, knives ... instruments of all kinds.

Chapter 7

CHARLOTTE

She wasn't expecting me. I arrived by taxi from the station and walked through their exuberant May garden, flowers bursting their buds, leaves fattening against the stone walls of the house. I could see Iona through the kitchen window. She was podding peas, or about to - moving around the room with uncertain steps, sitting down in front of the bowl, looking at it without seeing it, then staring at her hands.

"Hey!"

She didn't answer. She was frowning at the bowl in front of her.

"Iona!"

"Who is it?" she said slowly, without moving.

"It's me! Charlotte."

She turned. When she realized it really was me she didn't get up. She just sat there, hunched over, tears falling. I ran in and put my arms around her.

"Char, I'm not ... I haven't been able ... lately."

"It's alright, Puff. I'm here now."

"Char, I'm tired!"

"I know."

Her skin was paler than I'd seen it, all the sun and wind and the little flushes that normally come and go with her were drained out of it. She was wearing an old dressing gown and her hair was lank and unkempt.

"Why are you here?" she said, after a while.

"To be with you ... I can help you now. When you're better we can go to France, or up to see Fardie."

"I would be too tired."

"You might not ... after a bit."

She looked at me in despair. The lines around her mouth were wooden with fear, her skin as taut as a hospital sheet.

"I don't know what to make for lunch, Charlotte."

"I can cook. I'll make lunch."

"Hughie doesn't like beans."

"Then I won't make beans."

"The baby ..."

"I want to see her! I'm longing to ... you're so clever to have had an Olivia."

Iona collapsed at the table and started to cry again.

"I can't manage!"

"Shh, it's alright now."

"Mark's been a brute, Char, he ..."

"Hush! Tell me later."

"He's given my baby to June ..."

"I'm sure he hasn't. I'm sure he's just trying to help. "

I should have agreed with her that first moment, seen it through her eyes, for I lost her trust then and there. She looked at me doubtfully, then her eyes glazed over and avoided mine.

"I can't ..."

"It's alright, I know ..."

But I didn't know. It came as a shock. Most of my life force comes from Iona, her insouciant love of pleasure, her disregard for anything tedious ... her sweetness. Even as a small child she had an instinct for happiness. She could manage Fardie better than me. She would hum her way through our bible lessons in the library at Craigmannoch. While I was agonizing over Saint Peter and demanding explanations she was playing little games, and humming.

Then was Jesus led up of the spirit into the wilderness ...

Our father read slowly in a monotonous, cheerless tone. We had an hour of the bible after breakfast every day.

"Why?" I wanted to know.

"To be tempted of the devil."

"Why, Fardie? Why?"

"Be patient, Charlotte:"

And when he had fasted forty days and forty nights, he ...

"What's fasted?"

I needed to understand. Iona was tying her hair ribbon. She had beautiful hair the colour of wheat. Elsie used to buy her blue velvet ribbons in Oban.

"It means to eat nothing ... during that time."

"Why didn't he ... ?"

"Be patient, Charlotte!"

He afterwards hungered. And when the tempter came to him, he said, if thou be the son of God, command that these stones be made bread.

"That was a good idea, Fardie," Iona said, pleasantly.

"No, Iona. It was the wrong idea. It was the devil's idea:"

But he answered and said, it is written, Man shall not live by bread alone ...

"He could have made cakes if he'd wanted to," Iona offered. She was fond of cake.

"Bread, Iona, bread!" our father shouted, exasperated.

But the distinction was lost on Iona who had started to hum. I remember her pretty face with the bemused, slightly detached look that children have while daydreaming. She hummed her way through the roaring and rebuking at church too, and any troublesome lessons at school. She was the first to smoke a Gitane and the first girl in our school to go topless. We didn't know about going topless. It hadn't really been invented. Iona did it because she liked the feel of the sun on her breasts.

But it had gone from her, all of it. Something had happened. It was as if she'd been bled with a cup and scalpel by a medieval barber-surgeon.

***

I took over Iona's life. Hughie, the middle one, was an easy, affectionate little boy who lived in a fantasy world. 'Pretend to be wind!' he ordered me, or 'Charlotte, I'm the brave soldier and you're the other soldier'. He didn't like most food but if you pretended hard enough you could usually get him to eat.

Finn was altogether different. A grave child, preoccupied with his mother. Our first conversation was more in the nature of a lecture. He was checking me out.

"Mama is sad!" he told me. "She doesn't get up when she's sad."

"I see."

"Please play Monopoly with my father so he doesn't get sad too."

"Yes, Finn."

"And will you play with Hughie? He likes pretending games."

"I'll do my best."

"He hates beans."

"I won't cook beans."

"And tomatoes and soft stuff, like porridge ..."

"Alright."

"Our baby likes new noises - like this, Charlotte ... " he explained, blowing air through his teeth, then moving into a clicking sound and from there into an impressive whistle.

"I'm a fairly good whistler."

Later, he became more of a friend. "When my mother is better we're going on a private holiday," he confided, his face suddenly relaxed and boyish. "It'll be brilliant!"

"Private?"

"Yes! Nobody knows so far. Hughie is better off at home and Daddy will be busy."

"Where will you go?" I asked, intrigued.

"We haven't decided yet ... but it could be an island."

Olivia had a condition their doctor called delayed development syndrome. She took things slowly, but she was a delicious child, friendly and contented. When I held her I felt a tug, an almost cosmic pull, from our grandmother through our mother through us to this girl child.

In the evenings Mark and I drank a lot of Cava and discussed tactics. We debated taking Iona by surprise - getting a psychiatrist in without telling her, like calling in troops to storm a building to rescue hostages. It seemed that Iona was a hostage of a kind, although neither of us could make out who the enemy was. Mark had suddenly grown old. Under a thin layer of good manners and kindness to me I caught glimpses of the enormity of his desolation.

I was desperately missing Toby. I felt manacled in my single bed. I hated the walnut dressing table with its fresh white Irish linen scarf. I hated the subtle, faintly striped wallpaper, the Sheraton chest of drawers and the pretty Turkish rugs.

My mind strayed to Toby's bed, a white cotton island in a sea of space, and the way he needs nothing - just a few hooks on the wall. I could see Toby's jeans on one of the hooks; sea-faded, wrinkled, used to his body. I turned over in the narrow bed and thrashed with my foot to untuck the tucked-in blankets.

Iona was behaving like a whipped collie, slinking off to her room at every opportunity. I forced myself to be patient. I was patient ... day after day. But it's one thing to help someone grateful, someone who wants you to be there and sees you as her saviour. Iona didn't want me there. I could tell. One afternoon my patience broke. I blasted into her bedroom and drew the curtains.

"Iona! Snap out of it! What the hell is going on?"

Her face was turned to the wall. I hadn't realized how thin she'd become. Her shoulder blades overlapped like the blades of an old-fashioned lawnmower. I could tell she was awake, although she didn't answer.

"Listen, Puff! We know Olivia is alright, Mark's ready to talk over any problems. You live in this lovely farmhouse. What in God's name is wrong?"

"There isn't a point ..."

My sister's voice was small and distant, like sound that has travelled over many miles of dry land.

"Point?"

"When you lose sight of the point ..."

"What d'you mean?"

"A point, any point ..." Her voice trailed off.

"I'd have thought you had more point than most people, Iona. Specifically the children. What about them? Have you thought about what you are doing to them?"

She turned to face me. "I'm no use to the children. Don't you see? If you're young like they are, wanting to know things like Finn or full of glossy ideas like Hughie ..." Her mouth sank.

"Exactly! Like Finn! Finn loves you. He needs you."

"The worst thing for Finn is a mother who knows there isn't a point ..."

"Stop! Stop it, Iona! There is a point - you've just lost sight of it. How can you see it anyway if you sit inside all day with the curtains closed?"

"I'm tired."

"And what about the baby? Olivia needs a mother. Wasn't it bad enough for us?"

Iona put her hands over her ears. She crumpled, like tissue paper, like something thrown away and useless.

"You aren't trying to get well. You won't even agree to see a psychiatrist ..."

She scrunched up her knees and turned back to face the wall.

"You've always been selfish, selfish and self-indulgent!"

"Nobody cares."

"Stop it! Why d'you think I'm here?"

She was breathing oddly, crying again I supposed.

"We're going for a walk now - as far as the chestnut tree."

"No!"

"Yes!"

I dragged her out of bed and pulled her outside. I had one hand around her wrist and the other in the small of her back propelling her along. It wasn't difficult, she was so light. Her resistance was passive, like a child when she goes limp and trails her legs behind her. It was a windy afternoon, branches tossing, bright patches of ground, dark patches, clouds tumbling over each other, a square of glassy, sunlit raindrops hanging over a field of barley.

I was crying too. I was remembering the twin picture, the one at school in the medical dictionary, two unformed heads and a tangle of tadpole limbs united from the moment of conception, belonging together, the womb wall enclosing them in a world apart. If she lost the point what about me? When I'd just found one, at long last.

When we reached the chestnut tree we collapsed on the grass. Above our heads the leaves spread over us like lampshades, white tree candles licked and flickered upwards, rounded waxy lights in a green baize shade.

"You came," she said at last.

"Yes."

"But you'll leave, won't you?"

"Not until you're well."

"And if I don't get well ..."

"Then I'll stay ..."

"You'll have to go soon ..."

"I won't leave you, Puff. But you've got to try. There are people who know about losing the point better than Mark and me. You have to promise you'll see Mark's doctor. You have to try."

"I'll see the man."

"Good! Thank God!"

"Olivia knew, Char."

"Knew what?"

"That there wasn't a point."

I looked at my sister. Her eyes were closed again. I wondered what she had found out and if this was the reason for her depression. The skin of her eyelids was almost transparent, like the membrane that covers a bird's egg before the shell has formed. Her breathing was shallow.

"Put your arms around my neck, Puff. I'm going to take you back now."

I braced myself to lift her. She stretched up slowly and clasped her hands behind my neck. I carried her back to the house.

**

After that she began to get better and, by the middle of August, Iona was well enough to go to Craigmannoch. Mark was infinitely relieved. He managed to get June to help him with the children and encouraged us to go.

Our father fussed over Iona. He made her lie on the *chaise longue* in the garden, clumsily tucking rugs around her feet. Every morning he poached two eggs for her, making a nest in the water with a wooden spoon then, putting it down, he picked up the first egg which he cracked against the hen's bucket and swiftly dropped into the water. Next he tossed the eggshell away, picked up the spoon again, and ruffled water over the egg. A laborious business with one hand ... not the sort of thing he'd do for me!

Things had changed at home. The rest of us just had porridge for breakfast while Iona had two poached eggs on slices of buttered toast, as if they alone might assuage her sorrow.

We hadn't seen Fardie for ages and didn't know what to expect. Apart from his concern for Iona, we found him strangely elated. His old friend Murray was staying and we arrived, as it were, in the middle of a conversation which did not include us - a duologue which continued off and on through those late August evenings. They were re-living parts of the war and there were times they were so wrapped up in their talk that they hardly noticed our presence.

"Anzio." Murray said one evening as they sat companionably drinking their brandy. "I never thought we'd make it out of there alive!"

"It was the best time," Fardie said.

"Wouldn't have made it out - if you hadn't run a marathon through the whole bloody regiment to warn us of the trap!"

Harry smiled. "Running," he mused. "I can't remember what running feels like now."

"You ran like a bleedin' hare through those dunes. 'Go back to the beach! Back! Back to the beach!' You put yourself at risk, Harold."

"Managed to save the first lot ..."

"Indeed! And got your medal for it, if my memory serves me."

"Yes ... not that it made much difference."

"It made a difference to the first lot right enough. I was having my tea. Not the foreign stuff - the good old Red Cross tea ..."

"Came in a tin!"

"That's it! And suddenly I saw this bleedin' greyhound without its helmet on, black hair flying, diving in and out the lines like a lunatic."

"What was it, Murray? Another two weeks before they got us? Before they shipped us off to the camp at Bebra?"

"Three!"

"Three."

"That was the first time your brother ..."

Fardie started. He glanced across at us. "Bed, Murray! Time for bed," he said, interrupting him. "What in God's name are you two doing still up?"

"We aren't children, Fardie!"

"Bed!" he shouted. Then, in a softer voice, to his dog, "C'mon old girl. I'll take you out." And he hobbled stiffly into the warm night.

I'd thought Puff was getting better ... the protective early mists, the salty smell of seaweed and fish that comes up off the loch. It's what we know. It's what we are. She'd been eating more and listening, as I had, to the men. She'd actually stayed downstairs after dinner two nights in a row.

But that night she slipped back. I tried to get her to talk about what we'd overheard. I remarked on the odd way Fardie had shut up when Murray mentioned Ormonde.

"They are so fucked up," she said mournfully. "Have you noticed? Nobody loved their children."

"Who?"

"All of them. Our whole family. Our grandparents didn't love Fardie and Vivian and Ormonde. And Fardie didn't love us. Now I am failing with my own children. It's a pattern. It goes on and on."

"Nonsense! There's Olivia's side of us." I said it quickly and automatically because it was the sort of thing we used to say. But I could hear a false note in my own voice. "Anyway, Fardie did love us. He does still ... in his way."

"Mmm." she said. But her voice was distancing itself again.

"Don't be silly, Puff! You are getting better, miles better ... and you know you love your children."

She got into bed and turned away from me. Later, when I kissed her goodnight, her cheek was wet and cold.

Iona had to get well. I had to get back to Toby. Mostly it was his face that I thought about, although sometimes I couldn't visualize it and had to re-assemble each feature in my mind like constructing the portrait of a criminal.

But there were times when it was more of a yearning inside me for the feel of him - for what he does to me and my readiness for it ... and the precious, ever-astonishing fact that it's him, not somebody else.

That's the strange thing about *want* in the person you love. It's so much more ... Toby is a contained person so there's a sybaritic sensuality in his becoming uncontained with me. Once, on the beach, when it wasn't even quite dark, and there was a man throwing sticks for his dog not far away, he couldn't wait to climb up to the house. We couldn't. 'Charlotte!' His voice was thick with wanting. My body answered. I moved against him, felt him against me under his loose clothing. Rushing! We had to rush. Sand got into my mouth, sand stuck to our bodies. It was a race. We forgot about the man and the dog.

***

Murray's an odd fish. Who is he anyway? After all this time we don't know a thing about him: where he lives; if he has a family;

what exactly he has to do with our father. He doesn't notice us most of the time. When they aren't talking or eating - Murray is a great eater - he's always drawing. When I peer over his shoulder I see maps and complicated drawings that look like the foundations of a building. The same thing - over and over again.

This afternoon it rained. Iona stayed in bed and I didn't have the strength to rout her out. I went downstairs to read my book. The door into the library was open. New tobacco from their pipes mingled with the acrid thick smell of old tobacco that clings to the worn curtains and saturates the carpet in the library. I settled within hearing distance. Fardie was actually laughing. I was so close I could hear the grunts they made as they stuffed their pipes.

"Those buggers!" Fardie was saying.

"It was a good try."

"Mad to try, really. Nobody got out of Bebra."

"You know I went back there? A wee while ago."

"Christ, Murray!"

"Our tunnel's still there. They show kids round it. We paid for it alright! We'd a long whack in solitary, the longest ..."

"Yes."

"But it was worse for your brother. It broke him ... before they rounded us up for the march."

"I don't think of him."

"On the march, Harold, we'd the one Red Cross package to last us a week ... do you remember?"

"I do."

"And the cold?"

"It was March. It was hellish cold!"

"Weren't we all near the end of our courage? I was near the end of mine. Blaikie and Blair were near the end of theirs."

"Then they let us rest for a day or two at the farm."

"They had to, Harold, there were that many dropping out. We'd the dysentery and sores. We were two days into the march to Colditz."

"It was a sugar beet factory, Murray, remember? Those Russian workers said they'd help. It was the only chance for us ... and for poor wee Blaikie ... and Blair, who'd been with us all along."

"But your brother wasn't up to it. He wasn't lasting. We should have seen that ..."

"Damn you, Murray. I don't want to hear his name in this house!"

There was a long pause. Then I heard Murray's soft, even burble. "Well now, Harold, that'll get you nowhere. I was thinking it over when I was out there and it occurred to me we should never have pushed him into it. I was remembering that wee bit in the bible about being your brother's keeper and ..."

"He was in no way a brother," Fardie shouted. His voice was hoarse, but underneath was a tear of sorrow, like ripping cloth.

"Is that right, now? Ah, well, I must be mistaken for I'd an idea we were all supposed to be brothers ..."

There was silence. Then I heard a sound, an odd, rough sound, muffled, repetitive. It was a minute or two before I realized it was coming from my father. I jumped up to go to him. But when I looked into the room I saw that Murray had got there first. He was standing beside Fardie cradling his head in his arms. 'There now, there now ...' he was saying in the sing-song voice that country people use with their babies. They were rocking together - two pink old men ... Murray was patting Fardie's head. 'There now, Harold,' he repeated. And, like an exhausted baby, Fardie was quieting.

***

It took the whole summer and most of September for Iona to get well and for me to fulfil my promise to her. One hundred and thirty days out of Toby's life. One hundred and thirty days out of our life together.

There's good and bad in not knowing what is to come. The good is that you are unaware. Rolling in the sweet-smelling hay of your time together. The barometer doesn't work. You wouldn't look at it if it did.

The bad? I've thought about it a lot. The bad is that you aren't memorizing moments, the proximity of the other person working only a room away - so close you can hear the tiny wooden peck of his pencil as he starts to write. And reading, for example, when the other is reading too. Knowing that one of you will get up soon to turn on the lamp. There's a difference - turning on a lamp for yourself or turning it on when a room has both of you in it. When you are by yourself you strain your eyes. There is less point in getting up, hardly any point at all.

But thinking like that can be dangerous. My sister Iona lost sight of the point for six months. My father had it blasted out of him in the Second World War and never regained it.

I try to remember that.

Chapter 8

IONA

Last autumn everything mattered. Everything! The voluptuous scarlet berries, leaves loosening their greedy summer hold, drifting downwards, landing, drifting on again - bigger, emptier winter skies. And the bite in the air - a cold bite! Being able to feel it again, unbuttoning Livla's red jacket with cold fingers, touching the tip of her cold little nose.

I felt better every day.

One evening I came home in the dark and saw the children through the window having tea inside - tea and toast and raspberry jam. Finn's history book was lying on the table; the children were by the fire. I stood in the flower-bed watching them, knowing I could go in, could actually be with them again.

When I was ill I used to see my children at a distance, as though they belonged to somebody else. I had the illusion ... I used to have the frightening illusion that they'd been bussed in for the day and would leave me again cold and empty, like an abbey when the tourists have left.

Not that it was easy at first. June gave me a tough time. It was as if she were punishing me for having been ill. Depression doesn't exist in her book. June is a full-time traveller these days. She takes off alone, travels till the money runs out, then comes back to work and save up for her next journey. She adores the kids but makes it her business not to get too attached. It's one of the things I've always respected about her. However, when I came back from Scotland this time the lines weren't so clearly defined.

'Who loves her Junie bug?' she'd chant in an irritating voice to Olivia. 'Who's coming to Zambia in Junie's backpack?' Livla would laugh and snuggle up against her Sid Vicious tattoo. Hughie preferred June's Aborigine stories to our favourite books and he'd only eat her food: 'This is an ostrich egg,' she'd tell him. 'Whoever eats it will be the fastest runner in his class!' I could see they had a brilliant relationship going and I was very grateful for all she'd done. But I wanted my babies back.

Finn was the only one who hadn't been brainwashed into June's cult, but my depression had made him over anxious and insecure. I tried to explain what I still don't understand myself, that sadness can be an illness, like measles.

"Will I catch it, Mama?" he asked.

"Of course not, darling."

Still, despite June, I was adoring each day. Twice a week I put on a track suit and went to my yoga class. With each deep, controlled breath I sucked life back into my lungs. It moved in a wave down my body, into every finger and toe.

I went up to London, just for a day, and allowed myself a quick dart into Harvey Nichols. Such pretty things! I bought myself a coffee-coloured silk bra and knickers and a smart pair of trousers. I mean I absolutely had to. I was putting on weight again and nothing fitted. Mark was a little sulky. It's not the shopping he objects to, it's that particular shop. He's got a thing about it. When he saw the bill I heard him say under his breath that he hoped Harvey Nichols would be the IRA's next target.

Looking back on it, I was perhaps too conscious of my body, too happy to have one again. But why not, after all? I think that God, if there is one, must have wanted us to eat strawberries and wear coffee-coloured French silk knickers. If He hadn't why would they exist?

In October we went to a party. I was wearing glittery trousers and my black shirt. Just walking into the room was a buzz, having a glass of wine in my hand, talking to men again. A man called David flirted with me. I felt a scatter of feelings blow through me - that strange thrum that can happen between strangers.

"Time to go home!" Mark said, coming up to me and putting my shawl round my shoulders, then turning to say goodbye to our hostess.

"You didn't tell me you had a keeper." the David said.

With one hand he straightened my slipping shawl while, at the same time, a stray finger paused on the back of my neck. It was exciting, I don't mind admitting.

"You make me sound like a zoo animal!"

"Not at all," he said. "I would classify you as definitely wild."

Of course it meant nothing. Men often want me, well they used to... it was just another step towards wellness. How could I hurt Mark, after all I'd put him through?

***

Mark and I ... we were in the process of getting together again. We hadn't quite slipped back into the simple, easy way it was before. We used to stay in bed on Sundays, for instance, letting the boys watch cartoons on television and help themselves to the wrong kinds of cereal. But it didn't work like that anymore. We were too tightly wired. Mark always had an agenda, like making scrambled eggs for the children or bringing me tea in bed - when what I wanted was him. Or, to be strictly honest, what I wanted was to want him.

We were getting there, slowly, when the Caroline Rawlstone-Pares thing came up.

June had gone to buy boots for her trek across Zambia. I was happy to be alone with Olivia. I was looking a wreck, with the baby on one hip and the washing under my other arm when a thin, blonde woman in riding breeches and boots came into the kitchen carrying a large box of vegetables.

"Hello-o!"

"Hello," I said.

"Oh, Hello! I've just bwought a little pwessi for Maak ..."

"Thanks! I'll tell him."

"I'm Cawoline - Cawoline Walstone-payas."

"Yes?"

"They're aw-ganic!"

"Mmmm!"

"You must be new." she said, sizing me up. "Jolly good!"

I should have told her who I was, but I admit I was enjoying the situation.

"Just tell him they're from Cawoline."

"Certainly, Mrs Rawlstone-Pares."

"Bye-ee!"

I was looking forward to teasing Mark about her but June turned up first. I thought we'd have a good laugh and told her what had happened. Her reaction was unexpected.

"Well, you know what they say, Iona!"

"What do they say?"

"Use it or lose it!"

"June! You're not telling me Mark had an affair with this Caroline woman?"

"Probably just comfort, you know, a few glasses of sherry sort of thing. But you want to wake up and smell the coffee, kid."

It enrages me when June says kid to me. She always has - and she's younger than I am.

"What are you saying?"

"Mark's a handsome bloke!"

"Of course he is, but ..."

"Don't think I haven't noticed, myself."

"Really?"

I felt suddenly uneasy, as if I was about to be told about a traffic accident. I didn't really think he'd fall for the riding lady who couldn't say her r's, but June was another matter. Intrepid, funny, tough, she travels light with nothing but two T-shirts, an extra pair of knickers and a waterproof that rolls up into a pocket. She has a long, pencil-thin torch. Once, when threatened by a large man in Sierra Leone, she shoved the end of the torch into his eye, kneed him in the balls, stole his motor bike and got away. There's a lot to admire about June.

"Just kidding!" she said after keeping me in suspense for a second or two. "But you want to keep the home fires burning, know what I mean?"

"June! What the hell ..."

But it made me think ... I decided not to mention it to Mark. I determined to try harder to show him how much I love him.

***

In Scotland I began to notice how Charlotte has changed. Since meeting Toby some hard thing inside her has melted. She can have an unnerving, dictatorial look. Her eyes are shaded now, softer. And her body is different too. She used to keep her tallness reined in, like a horse on a tight martingale. She's become pliant, as though shaken loose from her own restrictions.

That November I got a letter from her, in reply to mine thanking her for everything she'd done.

Darling Puff,

You don't have to thank me. Just thank God you're back! You say you don't want to saddle Finn and Hughie with religion but bear in mind there are at least two of them (Gods). Fardie's one, spewing out guilt and grim warnings in a swirl of foggy Glasgow sputum and the real one - loving and forgiving - who got you out of that slough of sorrow and allows me to go camping in Baja California with Toby Vane!

Can you imagine it? We had an old L.L.Bean sleeping bag (double) and no tent and slept only yards from the sea (salty from our last swim). Toby's idea of camping is to take poetry books, water, a big frying pan, matches, onions and a few other essentials and to let the rest happen - which it did. A fisherman dropped shrimps from his net right into our sizzling oil. And a lovely Catarina, who lived at the other end of the beach, baked fresh bread every morning and brought it to us in a basket with a clump of bananas.

Every night we slept under a sky full of stars, mapped out for us in silver ink against the black. Easy to believe all they say about universes without end. You could believe anything!

We didn't want to come back, needn't have, really. If it weren't for Rain we could live anywhere. I admit that if I heard that Rain had choked on a piece of chocolate cake or fallen into her swimming pool ... I'm joking, of course, well almost.

Missy could come with us - I mean if we chose to live somewhere else. Remember how Jimmy used to call me 'a right wee bugger'? Well, Missy can be one too. She gives me a hard time. Told me to 'fuck off' the other day when I was trying to get her organized for school. Admittedly, It must be hell for her living in a semi-nursing home with Rain. Her conversation is bizarre. 'Mr Edward's goiter's better, Dad!' 'Hey, guess what? They're taking Janice off the catheter!' It's not exactly what Elsie would have called a healthy environment.

I will say she's a brave little creature. Always dreaming of things she can't have - a stunt horse, a stunt dog, training to be a trapeze artist, stuff like that. She makes me laugh. I could be accused of starting to love her.

Anyway, that camping, that sky ... it was concrete evidence of heaven, Puff. You ought to at least let Finn know that it exists.

Love,

    Char

I felt so happy for her, but fractionally envious too. I've always thought there was something deeply attractive about a certain kind of American man - the way they wear belts with largish buckles and use your name all the time. Not that I'd ever had one myself so to speak ... I must have been basing it on Bogart in Casablanca or the young Paul Newman. What I didn't know then was that just that sort of American man was about to play a role in my own life - in the shape of Morgan, Vivian's lost and found again son.

They came to stay that winter.

The glamour of California life seemed to have worn off with Vivian. She was in her element in the country, taking off early in her Wellington boots, crunching holes in iced-over puddles, offering our local farmer unasked for advice. She's as bossy as ever, but the minute she strides into the house we all love her. I can't explain it.

Morgan was affectionate from the start, and helpful. The kids thought he was cool and in some ways he was, but under the surface I was aware of dark spaces which he tried to cover up. We all mean so much to him. He's always trying to get it right, which is touching and quite abnormal in a family like ours.

"I-o-nna! Let me carry that bag for you!"

"I-o-nna! Now you just go take a nap and I'll get the kids."

"I-o-nna, sweetheart ... how about I cook dinner tonight?"

He's so physical! Having him at home all the time was like having a stag around constantly pawing the earth. And he's a nuzzler - lays his hand on your arm as if there's nowhere else to put it and hugs you at breakfast with the same sort of hug people give other people at airports.

One day I had a headache and the next thing I knew he was giving me one of those in-depth neck and head massages. It felt good - but it took place at tea. June looked disapproving and the boys started flicking cake at each other.

I have to admit I enjoyed all the attention. We had a lot of fun together. June was about to leave but, once again, she had to get involved.

"So what's with the cock teasing?" she said when we were cleaning the kitchen together.

"What?"

"That poor dope Morgan."

"Don't be ridiculous, June. He's like a brother. He's suffered a lot. You know nothing about it."

"Like hell he's like a brother!"

"How can you suggest ... ?"

"Because you're capable of fucking up your life, Iona."

I walked out of the kitchen, infuriated. What gave her the right to set herself up as my moral guardian? I wanted to throttle her but it was a difficult situation. The children adore her and I did realize - and always will - how wonderful she'd been when I was ill. I was a little nervous of coping on my own again. I knew that I'd miss her after she'd gone.

***

Mark is an accepting person. Nobody has a kinder heart. So I was genuinely surprised when he took against Morgan. It was upsetting, just as we were really getting to know each other.

"Why don't you like him?" I asked.

"In simple terms, Iona darling, he's a bit of a creep."

"What on earth do you mean?"

"Always loping around after you and cooking that wheat germ stuff. I hate that sort of food ... and having him in an apron in the kitchen when I come home from work."

"I can't believe you're saying this! Haven't you thought about the fact that this is the first time in his life he's really had a family?"

"He must have had some sort of life in the years before he found Vivian."

"He says the family that adopted him were screwed up themselves."

"What about later on - when he was grown up?"

"I tried to ask him about it. He said something about behaviour repeating itself, says he made the mistakes that were made with him. I think he was married at one point. But don't you see, Mark, he's trying to work it all out. He's finding out who he is. It's amazingly brave of him."

"I can't stand the way he's always fingering his own entrails - and ours!"

"Americans love that sort of thing. Roots are really important to them."

"I know," Mark said sceptically. "They're always dashing back to Ireland and routing out perfectly contented farmers with the same surname."

So far we'd been calm, talking in the restrained, slightly amused voice you put on when there's something bigger behind the words you're using. We've never fought. We're basically not fighters. But suddenly, I lost my temper.

"You're narrow-minded, Mark. Prejudiced! A whatever-it-is-phobe that doesn't like people from other countries, stuck in a mire of corduroy trousers, commuting, cricket, suburban stinginess and speechlessly dull people like Cawoline Rawlstone-Pares. Morgan's sort of a brother, for Christ's sake."

"Very touchy-feely for a brother, I'd say!"

"What the hell are you saying?"

We looked at each other, appalled. I saw Mark's older face, marked with a graffiti of anxious lines that I'd put there.

"Sorry!" We spoke together.

"What have I done, darling?" Mark whispered, putting his arms around me. "I just want to be with you. I've been selfish about Morgan. I'll try to be more understanding."

"I didn't mean it about ... any of the things I said."

"I know you didn't. As for Caroline ... she's one of those lonely people, you know? I was pretty down myself at the time. It was a consolation thing, just a few awkward hugs by the fire. She's really better with animals than people. I think she felt sorry for me - as though I were a horse that was off its feed."

"A horse that needed fresh vegetables ... ?"

"Well, yes."

Mark blushed and we both laughed. I felt closer to him than I had for a long time.

***

We squeezed in five days' holiday in the south of France by ourselves before June left and Vivian and Morgan went up to Scotland. Mark jokes that we are better off travelling than we are on a day-to-day basis. It's true! He's heaven to be with full time. We were in our element wandering down sunny avenues of pollard trees, talking our hopeless French and eating *moules marinières* in little ports. We drank the local wines and Mark had fun describing them: 'Jaunty! With playful undertones wouldn't you say, Iona?' or, 'This one is definitely cocky with a touch of pithy aggression that jostles for attention under its suave exterior.' 'Silly!' I said laughing, loving him for being silly again.

One special memory from that holiday sticks in my mind. We went to see the chapel decorated by Jean Cocteau in memory of the drowned fishermen of *Villefranche*. We arrived at the village late one afternoon. A jumble of tiled roofs tumbled down to where the sea blinked bright with painted boats. Working men drank *Pernod* at shaky tables. Old women, hurrying home with their evening baguettes, whispered '*Bon soir, messieuretdame,*' as we passed.

The chapel is built on a rock that juts out into the sea - inside it's more like a cave than a building. There are fluid charcoal lines drawn over the walls and ceiling, drawn as a child might draw, filling the whole page. At the level of the small wooden pews Cocteau has depicted sinking fishing boats in a violent storm. Angels swoop down from the ceiling, lifting drowned fishermen out of the heaving water up into a whitewashed heaven. I stood there dazed by the hazard of the waves, thinking of my sister Charlotte.

I'm slow to understand things. I don't think I'd understood fully until that moment how she saved me when I was drowning. All last summer she kept picking me up. I wanted to die, but she wouldn't let me. Once, like a soldier angel, she lifted me up physically from the long grass under the chestnut tree and carried me back to bed.

***

Morgan came back in April. He wanted to see some of the famous English gardens. Part of his job is planning gardens for people with no imagination and he was longing to see an English spring. Morgan loves seasons; I don't think they have proper ones in Arizona - just dramatic conditions like dust bowls and raging fires.

I met him at our local station. When he emerged from the train with two large skateboards for the boys and a lot of awkward luggage I seemed to see him properly for the first time. A rather gaunt figure wearing the most unlikely clothes: cotton trousers with sneakers and a thick lumberjack shirt, which he wore open over a tie-dyed vest. It didn't hang together. It didn't look right for a cloudy day. His dark hair was too short so I couldn't help noticing what a lumpy head he has. It sits at an angle on his unusually long neck. No one could possibly call Morgan good-looking!

But two things struck me as I watched him get off the train. The first was his irresistibly sweet expression. His dark eyebrows were contorted in their irregular way, one higher than the other, and he was laughing with an old lady who was getting off too. The second was odder. Somewhere around the temples and in the shape of the eyes themselves he looks like us. I did a double take. It made me feel as if I was meeting a male Charlotte, or a broken-off part of myself.

Yet why shouldn't he look like us, after all? Morgan is our first cousin. It must be the different culture thing that makes him feel more like a man than a cousin.

That April he double-dug my vegetable garden for me and we planted it out. I usually sprinkle a packet of one kind of lettuce and then have far, far too many when they come up. Morgan was strict about staggering, putting a tiny quantity of seeds into my cupped hand and showing me how to rub them between finger and thumb, slowly releasing them into the trench.

When it came to flowers I was able to show him the butter and eggs snapdragons that sow themselves in my old brick wall and the *anemones blanda* that crop up all over the orchard. He loved the *crocus angustifolius* which we call cloth of gold around here - and the wild bluebells which lie in the woods like amorphous pools of fallen sky. He met an old gardener at our local pub and was forever slipping down there for a few pints and flower talk.

Once, when we were potting out, he asked me if I had a favourite garden. I said that I had.

"Save it," he said, "for last!"

"Shall I tell you which one it is?"

"No, I-o-nna, don't. I'll know when we get there."

I realize now that I shouldn't have taken Morgan to see the white wisteria at Barrington Court ... but sometimes you walk right into things. Years ago I saw a fox's paw in a gin trap - just one furry paw, all by itself. The fox must have gnawed through its own leg to get free. They used to camouflage gin-traps with leaves and moss - the fox couldn't have spotted it until it was too late. The wisteria garden was a trap of a different kind.

***

But, thinking back on that month, it wasn't just the gardening - not at all! Morgan involved himself with every part of our lives. He was with us at the time Hughie was being bullied. My little son had been behaving strangely, clinging to me, eating even less than usual.

"I don't want to go to school!" he said one morning, for what I suddenly realized was the third day running.

"William's being mean to him," Finn offered up, looking troubled.

Mark and I tried to find out what was going on, but in the end it was Morgan who got to the bottom of it.

"So how big is this William?" he asked him.

Hughie flushed and looked away. "He's got big feet and a big face ..."

"Mmm, that is scary, but how smart is he? Does he know about badgers?"

"I don't think so."

"Does he know about Aborigines and ostrich eggs?"

"He wouldn't care ..."

"No wait! This is important, Hughie. It's beginning to add up." Morgan was stroking his chin like a detective. "Did he get nine plus for the witches composition?"

"Five, he got a five."

"You know what, Hughie?" Morgan said, seriously. "I think you and me can outsmart this guy."

My son looked interested in spite of himself, but still unsure.

"Wanna hear the plan?" Morgan pulled back his arm in readiness for the macho handshake, which both my boys find irresistible.

"Well, maybe I ..."

"Are you on for it or what?"

"Yesss!" Hughie said, in a somewhat shaky voice, allowing the yes to end in a reassuring hug.

I still don't know what happened, but somehow they worked it out and the threatening William disappeared from our lives.

***

In the evenings we were companionable. Mark was making a real effort with Morgan. We listened to Brahms and played games. When we were on our own, however, Morgan tried to get me to talk about myself. I fought against it, but at the same time it was something of a relief.

"Why do you think you got sick, I-o-nna? With all you've got going for you?"

I didn't want to discuss it. My depression was still only a thin wall away.

"The scary things ... you've got to stare them out. Take them head on, you know."

"I'm not in the mood, Morgan. Let's play backgammon."

But he went on, regardless. "Your mother, I-o-nna ... don't you see it must have been building up all these years, sweetie? From what I hear you were one brave kid. But just because of that, it's got to catch up on you."

"What's got to catch up?"

"Not having a mother. It hits you later on."

"It's more to do with not knowing what she was like, I think ..."

"Tell me about it!" Morgan said ruefully. "I've been there."

But when I tried to get him to talk about his adopted family he was even more evasive than me.

"Go on!" I urged him one evening. "They can't have been so dreadful?"

"It was her," he said, looking down at his feet.

"Your adoptive mother?"

"No mother to me, I-o-nna."

"Was she cruel to you, Morgan?"

"Fixated, more like - kinky."

He got up, strode out onto the grass leaving the door wide open, letting a cold draught into the room. I could see him standing on the lawn, gulping the dark, starry air. After a while he came back and, shouting at me "I'm for the hay!" went up to bed.

Another favourite topic of Morgan's was Vivian. He wanted to know how we'd found out about him, about his existence ...

"Did she tell you herself?"

"No."

"Then how did you kids find out?"

"We didn't know about you for a long time. Although we knew about your father ... and the fact that Vivian had had a love affair with him and been sent to France as a punishment."

"How did you find that out?"

"I read Vivian's diary when I was fourteen, Morgan."

"No kidding!"

"It was a wild night in winter - she was ill, asleep upstairs - and I was alone downstairs in the firelight. It was as if I were under a spell. I mean, I saw the diary - like the apple that tempted Eve - and I just couldn't take my eyes off it. You know the way books look when the cover is very, very soft and much touched? You could say I was seduced into opening it."

"This is an A movie, I-o-nna! Did it tell about my birth? And how she felt?"

"Oh, I just read a bit, where the diary fell open - with a little help from me, I admit. And I saw the cover, which said Normandie 1938."

"The year I was born!"

"After that we cornered Vivian and asked her if she'd ever been to France and she admitted she'd been sent there as a punishment. We plagued her to tell us why and she told us about falling in love with Oran and how our grandfather had been apoplectic with rage when he found out. It's the class thing, you see. His sixteen year old daughter and a local boy. Scottish people are weird about things like that. We must have been pretty thick 'though, for we didn't jump to the fact that she'd had a baby in France. We learned that later - after she'd been contacted by Louise Leroy. She left a note, telling us why she'd gone – and about you."

"I know about my father. I tried to track him down, too. But he died in a truck crash, shortly after he was exiled, shipped off steerage class to Australia on a P&O steamship by our mutual grandfather."

"I never knew that."

"I don't let myself think about it."

"So it must have been all the more wonderful when they contacted you about Vivi."

"I'd been looking for her for years. It was the greatest, like suddenly someone up there was listening after all. I hated the Louise bit, but look what happened! I got my whole family ... and you."

***

Barrington Court! You see I'd been there before, twice. For me the place is what a religious experience might be to Char, I love it so much. Two days before Morgan was supposed to leave I took him to see round it. There are several gardens there. I led him into my special courtyard quite casually.

It's an old stable yard. There are tears of white wisteria on four stone sides. White, weeping ... they make me think of the sheep on the hill at Craigmannoch bleating for their lambs - only this crying is soundless.

"You see," I said, "it's the *wisteria floribunda* ..."

There was silence between us.

"It's your church, I-o-nna."

"Yes."

We were close. His arm was slung loosely about my shoulders like it often was, casually. But I felt it tighten. Morgan moved my hair away from my neck and touched my cheek with the back of his hand.

"You're so, so ..."

"Morgan ..."

I don't know which one of us initiated it. It could have been me. It might have been him. All I know is that one of us kissed the other and for a minute, just a minute or two, it spilled over and we stood there lost in that kiss, with the white flowers dripping their sweetness around us.

We said nothing. We drove home in silence. That evening we spoke very little. At dinner Morgan told Mark that he needed time in London before flying back to America. Then he left - the next day.

People often say, 'it just happened'. I'd love to think that. It would make sense, like buying something you didn't mean to buy, or finishing off a whole box of chocolate truffles on the spur of the moment. But that kiss didn't just happen. It had been on the edge of happening since the day I met Morgan off the train. Through those evenings listening to Brahms and Hughie's dilemma, through the hoeing and planting ... it had been in the April air.

Chapter 9

CHARLOTTE

A stray bullet. Bullet is the sort of word you can get your teeth into. It was a .38 calibre round, shot from a stolen police pistol at a 30 yard range. One of these bullets travels at a rate of 2000 feet per second. The bullet that hit Toby on his way to deliver an idea to his agent was a .38 calibre round. A witness said he fell to the ground without a sound.

The word I can't get hold of is *stray*. The fact that the bullet just happened to be there, like a stray dog that has no specific home or a stray lock of hair which is simply out of place. As if bullets were a natural hazard. As if bullets can be excused or understood because they are stray, blasting through the air into people's brains for no reason.

There's lots for me to do. There's Rain. Her nonexistent, leftover life to organize. The lady who takes care of her told me she didn't feel grief. She hasn't taken in the fact that Toby was hit by a stray bullet.

Which makes two of us.

And there's Missy. Missy is with me in a sense. She has locked herself into Toby's office. She won't unlock the door and she won't talk to me. She's got her sleeping bag in there. I know she's alive because there are periodic thuds and because the spaghetti I left outside the door has vanished.

Last night I talked through the door to Missy. I described the island at Craigmannoch and explained how we pull the dinghy over the stones into the sea. I told her where we keep the round logs and how we space them in front of the boat and heave. 'One - two - three, heave; one - two - three, heave; one - two . . .' then suddenly the sea catches the boat, reaches out and lifts her in bouncing arms. I explained that there were two kinds of seals - the Grey and the spotted Atlantic, although they all look black and shiny in the water. I told her how they swim behind the boat if you sing, lifting their whiskery faces out of the sea to listen. When I got to this part the thudding almost stopped. But then it started up again. I explained how we weren't allowed to row out to the island until we could swim twelve lengths and that there always had to be two of us. I said that I thought she and Finn would qualify, although he wasn't as strong a swimmer as she was.

I concentrated on the future. Because, as Missy's whole past had been eclipsed by a stray bullet, it seemed the best thing to do.

At eleven o'clock I told Missy that Toby would want her to get into her sleeping bag and to go to sleep. I heard nothing for a while then I thought I heard the sneakers coming off. A few minutes passed, then a little voice said, "OK, Dad. Okey-dokey ... Dad."

***

I met Rain for the first time today. I begged Missy through the door to come with me but she wouldn't so I decided to risk leaving her for a few hours.

Rain came out to meet me with a weird hostEsse smile which she kept on her face all the time I was there. It didn't go with her empty eyes. They were green, like Missy's, only bigger, surrounded by a lot of light blue eye shadow. You could tell she'd been petite once, although now she has the puffed up look people get from pills, her wrists and ankles have little purses of white flesh attached to them. She was smartly dressed in a '50s light blue silk dress with a matching handbag.

"Why hello, Charlotte!"

I hadn't expected the southern accent. Toby never told me that. Somehow, hearing my own name set me off. I started to cry for the first time. Stood there on the doorstep of the condominium where she lives beside a kidney-shaped turquoise pool and wept.

"Come on in, honey, you don't want to do that now, do you?"

I began to howl.

"You'll start me off in a minute! And I've been looking forward to visiting with you."

It was unreal. The fixed garden party smile, the vacant eyes. But I couldn't stop and my crying began to upset her.

"Nurse Polly!" she called out. A woman appeared. "Y'all know Tobias? Well he's had a little accident and this poor lady ... she's all tore up and ..."

"That's OK, Mrs.Vane."

"We were going to have tea," she complained.

It ended badly, that first meeting. Rain was led away and I found myself being given pills in an empty bedroom.

"Missy's at home!" I gasped out between sobs, before I fell into a chemically-induced sleep. Three hours later I woke up and rushed back to the house to release Bob, one of the staff from Rain's condominium. He reported that she still hadn't come out, although a hand had reached round the door for a jelly doughnut.

***

Toby's parents came this morning. His mother, Alice, has been most kind to me. She says I may stay here as long as I want. She's organizing everything. She's organizing Toby's death. She's organizing Missy. She says I don't have to worry about a thing.

Mr. Vane sat in Toby's chair and wept.

They are not at all Californian, the Vanes, although they've never been out of the state. The drug culture, love-ins, starlets and the aftermath of the Vietnam war seem to have passed them by. They live in a mock Tudor cottage with a cocker spaniel called Cinders. They have teacups with rose buds on them and an embroidered *Home is where the heart is* sampler on the wall. There are photographs of Mr Vane fishing and a stuffed marlin with a glaring glass eye above his desk.

Toby doesn't like fishing. I mean Toby didn't ... he liked sitting by the sea on the sand when it was getting dark or diving into it when it was getting light. He likes ... he liked hermit crabs, their fragile sideways scutter ... all sorts of things. Toby liked all sorts of things about the sea.

"Melissa!" Mrs Vane said firmly, standing outside the office door. "This is your Grandmother Alice. I want you to open the door and come out now!"

Almost immediately the door opened. Missy looked smaller and very dirty. I wanted to hug her.

"You know your father is dead?" Mrs Vane talked kindly, but in the same firm tone.

Missy nodded.

"We are all very sad, aren't we?" she soldiered on, without waiting for an answer. "But we must be brave and ... Melissa, are you listening to me?"

Missy nodded again. Her little face was as pale as Toby's typing paper.

"It's time for you to come home with us now. Grandma will give you a bath and you can help her to choose some lovely flowers for Daddy's funeral."

Missy's lip wavered.

"Cinders can sleep in your room, just for tonight."

"Can Charlotte ... ?"

"You will see Charlotte on Thursday at Daddy's funeral. Now give me your hand."

"Will Mom ... ?"

"Your mother is being looked after nicely. Come along, now! Patrick, take the child's other hand."

To my surprise Missy put her hand meekly into Mrs Vane's and walked out of the house by the door, without insisting on leaving by the rock steps. Mr Vane shuffled out behind them.

**

I could go and see him tonight. Toby's mother has told me where the funeral parlour is. I've read about these places. I know what to expect. I'm prepared for the fact I'd find Toby made up, at least I think I am. I've seen the fridges they use for bodies in films. I could take that ... I think. I'll wash my face and brush my hair and go ... just to kiss him one more time.

**

I've been driving around for hours. The sky is black with only a frill of moonstruck cloud. I don't make mistakes anymore. After Topanga Canyon I hit the 101 and drove east. I found the Encino exit, passed two traffic lights and saw the building on the left. I drove around the block. I drove around it five times.

I hit all the wrong freeways on the way home, Toby. I missed the Topanga Canyon Blvd. exit you showed me our first week together. I overshot Malibu Beach. I was crying so much I couldn't see the road. So many lights coming at me, so tired ... I didn't go in, darling. In the end I didn't. I couldn't bear to see you dead.

***

I've made our bed. It's all white - big white cotton sheets, big white pillows, white extra cushions. I've made it up, but I'm not sleeping in it. I tried sleeping in the rattan chair on the deck, but it got too cold. I tried going to sleep in the kitchen. Now I'm in Missy's sleeping bag in Toby's office. She got it right. It's the only place to be. In the morning I'll ring Iona.

***

"Rain! It's Charlotte. I'm so sorry about the other day."

"That's all right. Nurse Polly told me you were going through a real hard time ..."

"Would you like to come with me to Toby's funeral tomorrow, Rain?"

"In your automobile, Charlotte?"

"Yes, of course ..."

"I'd like that very much, dear. You know Tobias Vane was my husband."

"I know."

"Our little girl, Melissa Eliot Vane, is on a visit with her grandparents, isn't that nice?"

"I know Missy, Rain."

"Of course you do!"

"I'll be there at noon."

"Charlotte?"

"Yes?"

"After the ceremony can we have tea? Tobias always takes me to tea."

"I promise."

***

They make you drive through a sort of shop. One sign actually said: Choose your own angel. The angels were made of plaster, most of them had painted, golden curls. There were plastic flowers and an odd assortment of stone rabbits and squirrels. Rain bought a big vase of imitation freesias. There were multiple-choice question forms in the reception area. One of the questions was:

Would you like?
a) A specific religious service
b) Our ecumenical ceremony
c) A non-religious event with our Positive Peace Chorus

There were about thirty people. I recognized three of Toby's friends. Otherwise there were some Hollywood contacts and quite a lot of strangers. Missy was standing across from me beside her grandfather. Somehow they'd got her into a red skirt and a blouse. An incongruous beret was crammed onto her hair. I noticed that nobody had managed to sever her from the sneakers, a fact that was considered helpful later on. Toby's coffin, an elaborate shiny box with an American flag over it, was placed on one side of an open grave.

The Vanes must have ticked c) for, instead of a priest, there was an odd little group of cemetery staff. The event began with *You've got a friend* sung by a failed starlet in black cowboy boots. After that there was a 'good guy' talk about Toby by someone who didn't seem to have any idea what he was like. It was during an appalling attempt at a poem —

Just passin' on
not really gone
You're still our
Hon-eee-bee

that I lost it. How dare his parents exclude God? I accept that some people don't believe, but God has everything to do with Toby, his quietness, his searching. He once told me how he found the phrase *Lord, help thou mine unbelief* particularly reassuring. 'After all, Charlotte,' he'd said to me, 'to whom else could one address such a major plea?'

"I would like to speak!"

I don't know what anyone thought. I didn't care. I spoke for Toby and Missy, and for Rain, who was holding onto my hand with trembling, gloved fingers.

'*Let not your heart be troubled: ye believe in God, believe also in me,*' I began.

Then after the gospel of St. John 14, verses 1-6, I launched into George Herbert's beautiful poem *Jesu*. My voice was driven, like loose snow, from somewhere beyond myself. I felt Fardie at my side giving me courage, helping me to remember the words. I started in on the Gaelic Blessing that Toby sometimes read to Missy when she couldn't sleep,

Deep peace of the running wave to you,
Deep peace of the flowing air to you
Deep peace of the quiet earth to you ...

And lifted my eyes to see if the child was remembering it too. I looked across at the place where she'd been standing by her grandfather, with her missing front teeth and her mossed-over eyes, as lifeless as dry stones. But the space was empty. Missy had gone.

***

The police were called in. The Vanes made an appeal on television. Posters of Missy's bright little face were circulated. I tried to think like Toby. I scoured the beach and visited and revisited Sam's Spaghetti Spot, her favourite. I drove the school run - both ways - and rushed back to touch base with Rain and the house on Malibu beach. The second night after her disappearance she was still missing.

The third day I sat on the rock behind the house and concentrated with every fibre of my being. Where might a child like her go? A child that dreamed of doves flying out of top hats, ponies with pink manes and trapeze artists clasping hands mid-air? Suddenly it came to me. I remembered her telling Toby, only ten days ago, that a circus was coming to Santa Monica.

I arrived just as an audience was queuing up to the strains of calliope music. The smells of elephant dung, candy floss, sawdust and perfume hit me. I felt certain I must be right, although I couldn't imagine how she could have found it or managed to get there without any money. I went to the ticket vendors first. They didn't recognize the poster but organized an interview with the manager. He was a little man with rouged cheeks and a middle parting. The picture of Missy and the story of her disappearance made him nervous. 'If there was a kid around here I'd be the first to know,' he assured me. 'Anything of that nature is reported immediately.' I got permission to look at the stables and cages where the animals were kept, but found no trace of the child.

On my way out I passed a clown juggling half-heartedly outside a trailer. I decided to have one last try and showed him the photograph.

"Inside" he said. "Eatin' ..."

I ran up the steps. Missy was filthy. The red skirt was torn, the beret gone and the blouse had green stains on it. She was sitting on an Indian bedspread being fed soup by a fat fortune teller - beaming from ear to ear.

"Hi Charlotte!"

"Missy!"

"Guess what, Char? Zepo figures they might have a slot with the monkeys."

Her mouth was full of food and her eyes were alight again, glinting green with excitement.

Luckily for me the fortune teller didn't want trouble either. She told Missy that she was on the young side for the monkey job and explained that circus kids had to go to school just like everyone else. Missy listened without putting up a fight, then slowly, a little hesitantly, made her way over to me and leant up against me, just as she used to with Toby. Close, closer ... until she was on my knee and her head flopped heavily against my breast.

Something happened in that instant. We counted on each other now. Yet it was more than that. I'd been searching for Toby's child. The anxiety I'd felt, the spaghetti I'd cooked, the stories I'd told ... had all been, I thought, for Toby's sake. But with Missy's weight splayed out across me and her muddy legs dangling against mine a mechanism started up inside me, small golden wheels like the inside of a clock began to turn. It hurt. It was an epiphany! I realized that I loved her.

"When are we going home, Charlotte?" she murmured, half asleep, apparently having forgotten about her grandparents, apparently unaware that half the L.A. police squad was out looking for her.

***

I gave us one day together. I let myself pretend that it could be like this, me and Missy in the Malibu house forever. I knew her disappearance was on the news. I realized that the police might be watching the house on the road side. I unplugged the telephone and the television set, cognizant of the fact that I could be had up for kidnapping.

For just one day we had each other. When Toby's absence became too painful we went swimming ... as far out as we dared, as far out as she wanted. When we felt like crying we curled up on his bed with a little nest of sweets between us. In the afternoon I taught her how to play gin rummy, but suddenly she got tired again. Then I was ready, with my knees available ... and my arms.

"I don't want Dad dead, Charlotte! I want him to put me to bed," she cried.

"I know, Missy. It isn't fair."

"He'll hate being dead without me there."

"I don't think so. I think he'll be happy you're living and well."

"Sure?"

"It's what I believe. I think God's taking care of him. I don't think he'd want you dead too. There are exciting things for you to do - and perhaps he can see you doing them."

"Well I'm going to show him stuff." she said bravely. Then her body re-aligned itself against mine.

"I guess I'll hang out with you here ... OK, Charlotte?"

***

But I had to tell them where she was ... I had to. It's the worst thing I've ever done.

The Vanes have taken her over. I tried to fight it but Alice Vane rustled up a lawyer who produced a will Toby had made two years before we met. In it he left everything he possessed to Rain and Missy. The will also stated that, if his daughter were underage at the time of his decease, Alice Vane was to be her guardian.

Mrs Vane has said I should feel free to communicate with Melissa whenever I want. I've rung the house in the San Fernando Valley twice, but she won't talk to me. Hardly surprising when you think how I sold her out to the police and condemned her to middle-class mediocrity. I could have left her with the fortune teller, I suppose. A circus career might have been preferable to suburban life with a narrow-minded grandmother for an adventurous child like Missy. She would have been happy learning the double somersault and dressing monkeys in little skirts.

Which has left me suddenly ... leaves me ... alone with Toby. Alone with Toby gone. And nothing of Missy but a few toys and a pair of grown out of sneakers. I haven't told Iona yet, or Fardie. I think it has to do with not wanting anyone else to come here. Even with Toby gone this is still our house. On his desk there's a sharpened pencil and notes on his last idea. The one that he was taking to his agent in downtown L.A. the day he was hit by a stray bullet.

Chapter 10

IONA

'NO BOYES' is written on her door. It's Olivia's room, her first. Up until now she's slept in an annex off ours. We spent the morning together painting stars on the midnight blue ceiling and walls. I wasn't sure about bringing the Milky Way down to floor level, but it's her room, her choice. The full-size single bed is installed with her own duvet cover - also celestial in its way with flying pink pigs against a background of fluffy cloud.

And I might have missed this. I might, so easily, not be here.

She sticks stickers everywhere. A horse one over the shelf that has her jeans, a shoe over her dancing slippers, a smile over her paints. Frown, lick ... stick. It's important. It's exciting! Every now and then the decorating is delayed while she bounces on the bed. Her fair hair flies round her face and her cheeks flush as pink as raspberries.

"Other girls' Mummys don't let them bounce," she says, generously.

I let her. I let her do almost anything.

This June our garden is a haven. Over the years we've added steps and paths, two live willow arches and a stone fan for my herbs - sage, tarragon, thyme, coriander and parsley flare out like a pianist's fingers. I wake up and want to be outside as early as possible. We are opening the garden to the public at Finn's insistence. He wants the money to go towards the families of the hunger strikers in Northern Ireland.

You wouldn't think a boy of thirteen would be worried about the hunger strikers, the conditions in the Maze prison and the world in general - but Finn is. Mark and I can't quite believe we've created a child so unlike either of us, so right about things, yet so fragile.

When I got back from California last year I noticed changes in him. He wasn't behaving like a normal twelve year old. He was withdrawn from us, busy writing letters to the newspapers and Amnesty International. Last summer he was involved in a school project helping in a camp for disturbed children. Since then he's lived sparingly, as if he only had a small backpack to rely on in day-to-day life, washing one

T-shirt over and over, never buying anything for himself.

"He's never going to be run-of-the-mill like I was," Mark said thoughtfully the other day. "We have to prepare ourselves ..."

"What do you mean? He's the dearest, kindest ..."

"That's just it, darling, haven't you noticed?"

"Noticed what?"

"The spiritual side of his nature ... I wonder if he can bear so much of other people's pain."

I do notice. I notice every little detail about my children now. I'm aware of how easily you can lose people, or almost lose them. It started last year when we received a letter from California. It wasn't from Charlotte it was about her and, although it's not supposed to be physically possible, my heart stopped. Literally closed down for a minute or two, while I absorbed the peculiar information.

***

The letter was from a Mr Jake Cohen who started off by saying that he assumed we knew. Knew what? We'd no idea what he was talking about. Cohen went on to explain that he was Mr Vane's attorney and he felt it right to let us know that he'd gone to the house at Malibu beach two times and found it deserted. He said that Charlotte hadn't been there for weeks. He didn't mention Toby. I couldn't imagine why he didn't say *they* hadn't been there for weeks. Char and I had been out of touch for some time. It's not unusual. Normally, it doesn't mean a thing. Mark suggested they might have broken up, but something told me it wasn't that.

In the days that followed we found out that Vivian and Morgan didn't know anything either and Fardie hadn't heard from her for ages. Mark kept trying to get in touch with the lawyer and being told he was out of town.

It got more and more ominous.

I couldn't see Charlotte clearly. Usually she's with me all the time. I hear her laugh when Hughie does something outrageous. I tell her things in my mind and know exactly how she'll react. She always butts in before I've finished a sentence. She pushes me into thinking about things and, when I don't bother, I sense her giving me a nudge. But that immediacy had evaporated. I couldn't see her face.

I tried to pray, which isn't easy when you're fairly sure there's no one there. Because I was out of the habit I fell back on the prayer Fardie taught us when we were children, but it came out all wrong, with threatening overtones, not humble enough.

Jesus, tender shepherd, I started off, *I repent for everything - for extravagance - for being selfish - for finding my cousin Morgan tremendously attractive. Now it's over to you. Just keep Charlotte safe. Surely, surely you can see ... nothing else matters.*

After five days I couldn't stand it any more. I had to find her. While I was packing, I kept passing Olivia's portrait on my way to get summer clothes that were hung in a downstairs cupboard. Every time I passed it I felt conscious of her eyes upon me - reproachful - demanding my attention. Gradually it came to me that it was time for Char to have the painting. I lifted it off the wall and lowered it gently, lingering, dusting the radiant young face, the exquisite neck, the pale, voluptuous bosom. Mark made a crate. We wrapped her up together.

***

I flew straight to California. It was instinctive, but physical too - as though I were a star being sucked into a black hole. I'd never travelled alone before, never really been alone and I wasn't sure how black the hole I'd find might be.

Los Angeles gave me the illusion that I was part of a child's game. It was unreal - white toy buildings, green toy grass, unsteady plastic palm trees all set up under a big fake sun that never wavered. Enormous cars slid slowly about. Boutiques, fast food places, funeral parlours, vets, beauticians all looked strangely similar. I saw one woman drive in one side of a building then reappear on the other with a shampooed be-ribboned dog on her knee. I wondered if everyone who drove in there got a shampooed dog, or if they'd had hers ready and passed him through a window like a carton of chips.

My first afternoon there I tracked down Mr Cohen and learned about Toby Vane's death. For the first time I felt really frightened. I couldn't imagine what Charlotte would do, where she'd go, why she hadn't told us. I begged him for answers but he didn't have any. He'd never even met her. He gave me a key to their house and made an appointment for me to talk to Leticia, a Mexican lady who was clearing up. She was the first real human being I met. She took one look at me and burst into tears.

"*Señora Ilona,*" she said, "this is a tragic house! They killed *señor Toby*, then they took away the child *Missicita*, and now your poor sister ... how she suffers!"

"But where is she, Leticia? Do you know where she is?"

"I made her some tacos. I brought bread and eggs and milk from the farmer's market, but she wouldn't eat a thing. She said God had abandoned her."

That was a bad sign, a terrible sign in Charlotte's case. I felt faint, dazed with emotional exhaustion.

"Sit down, *señora*," she said kindly. "I have a sandwich for you in my bag."

"But do you know where she went?" I pleaded. "Please tell me what she said."

"She said, 'Didn't I know that California had its own God?' She told me she was going to a place which made you forget bullets. She said, 'Didn't I know you could buy peace for sixty dollars a day and get a new skin at the same time?' She was *loca, señora Ilona*, crazy, *pobrecita!*"

It sounded like Char at her most hurt, her most sarcastic. When I pressed Leticia for details she thought she remembered that the place was somewhere north of Los Angeles. Then we found a pad by the telephone with the words: *Normandy DS Sanct. approx. 90 miles* scribbled on it in Charlotte's handwriting.

***

The receptionist at my hotel helped me to work out where it was. I rented a car, got an early start and arrived just as it was getting light. A large sign reassured me that I'd come to the right place.

THE NORMANDY DEWFALL-SCHWARTZ SANCTUARY
Grief Therapy / Yoga / Inner Cleansing / Moving On

It was a divine place - long and low with wild sage growing all around it. There were little cabins scattered about between blue oaks and eucalyptus trees. A white-coated receptionist sang out 'Greetings!'

and handed me a glass of sparkling water as I went into the hall. I asked her if she knew Charlotte MacIntyre. She directed me down a sandy path to some dunes where she told me that Normandy was officiating at her morning sun ritual.

'Greet the day!' I heard a voice shout out. I rounded a corner and saw about thirty women rising slowly from recumbent positions on the sand, turning their gleaming, moisturized faces towards the sun. 'Day! Day! Day!' they repeated. 'Greet your new life!' a small shining figure in a two-toned leotard urged the ladies. 'Life! Life! Life!' the women sang out in response, waving their arms in the air. I scanned the faces for Charlotte's and couldn't find it. At that moment Normandy noticed that one towelled hump had failed to rise to the greeting call. She switched on a Debussy tape which the women continued to sway to, and made her way towards the hump. It remained dormant with two long red legs sticking out at an unattractive angle.

"Is something wrong?"

A half-snort, half-sob came from under the towel.

"Now, dear, It's all OK. I just want you to breathe with me. In and out, in and ..."

"Fuck off!" said the hump, in a familiar voice.

I kicked off my shoes and ran to her. "Char! Char! It's me, Iona ..."

She sat up slowly. Her face was thinner and older. Oyster white bands shot through her black hair.

"Thank God I've found you!"

"Toby's dead, Puff," she said.

"I know."

"Excuse me; are you a paid-up member of my Grief Therapy Class?" Normandy Dewfall-Schwartz asked me, quite reasonably. "See, this dune is reserved ..."

I held Charlotte's hands. "I'm her twin."

"Well, what d'you know?"

"Toby's dead." Charlotte repeated, looking only at me.

"I'll leave you two to visit," Normandy said, observing that one large lady had dispensed with her robe and was making for the waves, still chanting 'Life, Life, Life ...'

***

To my eyes Charlotte's cabin really was a sanctuary. It had a pretty wooden terrace, its own little kitchen, large white wicker chairs with bright appliquéd cushions, a rag rug and a big table with a bowl of fresh fruit on it. I couldn't think of a better place for us to be.

"Let's just stay here," I suggested.

"I can't take it," Charlotte said. "It's so ... intrusive."

"What do you mean?"

"They want us to massage each other's feet and meditate ... and share."

"Share?"

"Feelings. I don't even know them, Puff. They don't know Toby. Didn't ..."

"But they're only trying to ..."

"They want to swill our problems together in one big soup. They think they can make pain go away in a bubbling sauna. Nobody even *knew* him. Nobody knows Missy ..."

I felt my chest tighten with her pain.

"Where do you want to be, darling Char?"

"Nowhere!"

Normandy Dewfall-Schwartz was very understanding when I explained the situation. I think the twin thing got to her.

"Iona, honey, this is a sanctuary!" she said. "You don't have to participate if you don't want to. We are here to heal. You guys take all the time you need. You coming here all the way from Scotland is like a spiritual thing ... kind of otherworldly."

That night I cut up bits of peach and fed Charlotte like a baby. I ran the shower for her and dried her on the rug, just as Elsie used to dry us in front of the nursery fire. We slept together in Char's single bed. Dry shudders went through her like a cough that wouldn't loosen. They'd given us a camp bed for me, but my sister needed to be held.

We stayed there for a week. I tried to comfort her, but couldn't reach her desolation. One evening I was telling her about the children and, for the first time, her eyes filled with tears.

"I'll never have one now," she said.

"But Charlotte, you might one day. It's not impossible. You could fall in love again ..."

126

"You don't understand, Iona. I had a child and I lost her."

"What? Charlotte, I'd no idea ..."

"Missy," she explained.

"I thought you meant ..."

"Toby's mother took her."

"Does she want to be with you?"

"She hasn't said so, exactly. But I think she does. It's what Toby would want, it's what he does want, I'm sure ... and I love her. I love her as much as you love Finn - only more. I love her with all my heart."

"Any chance at all of getting her ... ?" I asked tentatively, ignoring the 'only more'.

"None whatsoever," she said.

Shortly after that Charlotte told me she was going to New York where she thought she could get an acting job. I tried to stop her leaving, but she wouldn't listen.

"Thank you for coming, Puff," she said. "It's the best thing for me, I think ... to go somewhere different, somewhere that isn't home, or here ... or where we were."

***

Only then, only after she'd gone, did I allow myself to think about Morgan. Tucson, Arizona was about four hundred and fifty miles from where I was - no further than from Somerset to Argyllshire - and the roads were so straight, so easy.

I stayed on at the Normandy Dewfall-Schwartz Sanctuary for another three days doing all the things Char hadn't wanted to do, greeting the sun, basking in the Jacuzzi, drifting around in a white towelling dressing gown, having my hair conditioned with sesame oil and my body massaged with something that smelt like a forest on a hot day. But, all the time, I was thinking 'shall I go or shan't I?' I rang Mark. 'Go!' he said. 'You'll never have another chance to see the desert. Vivian and Morgan would love to see you.' It wasn't fair of me to have asked him. I blame the massages for my decision. They make you vibrant, salty, years younger ... your body smells as sweet as butter.

***

I arrived on a blinding hot day about five in the afternoon to find Vivian alone, sitting on the terrace steps of their L-shaped ranch house mending a chair. Her sixty-year-old scrawny legs and weather-beaten bare feet protruded from a pair of army shorts, a lit cigarette dangled from the corner of her mouth. She was thrilled to see me and anxious to hear about Char.

"Poor dear!" she said. "Well, she'll get over it. Sheep do. It just takes us longer."

She proudly showed me round. Morgan's area was plain with simple wooden furniture and lots of books on gardening, biology and ecology. The window ledges were cluttered with seedlings in various stages of being brought on. It was Vivian's part, the foot of the L, that touched me. Clearly Morgan had done it up with the things he thought a mother would like. There was a heavenly bathroom with a shaggy, fitted rug and an art nouveau dressing mirror in an alcove. I couldn't imagine Vivi using it as she never gives herself a second glance. On the wall of her bedroom were framed copies of Henry Moore sheep. He must have chosen the sheep too, to make her feel at home.

After that are gaps in my memory. I mean when exactly did Morgan arrive? What did I feel when I saw him again? Later that evening we were on the terrace. Dry grasses, long and red, come right up to Morgan's fence, beyond are dusty hills with splurges of flowering cacti and prehistoric mottled iguanas. The day-hot air hung on. I must have looked cool in my Marrimekko black and white cotton dress. Morgan looked cool too. He was wearing a crumpled linen jacket, I remember, and a sea-green shirt. He made us all gin fizzes. We clinked the icy glasses together and laughed. Vivian was full of chat, glad to have her beloved son and her niece together, innocent of the sense of foreboding between us - a greater, hotter heat less than a millimetre beneath our clothing.

The following day all three of us spent together. We're going to get away with it, I thought to myself. It will be alright.

But that night Vivian had to go to a meeting and we found ourselves alone. We tried to behave normally. I made Morgan laugh telling him about the Normandy Dewfall-Schwartz Sanctuary. We cooked sea-bay scallops and made an endive and goat cheese salad. But when we carried it outside onto the terrace into the warm waiting dusk we paused and looked at each other, paralyzed.

"I-o-nna," Morgan said desperately. "It would be incest. It would cancel out everything."

"I know."

"My mother ..." he said plaintively. "I couldn't bear for her to ..."

"I know, I know. I don't want it either ..."

"Darling I-o-nna!"

"It's alright Morgan, I'll leave. I want to leave."

Crickets let out a trilling wail. My breasts stuck to my cotton top.

"Don't leave!"

"I love Mark," I said. "It's all wrong."

"I love Mark too, and the kids, especially Hughie ..."

"I'll leave," I repeated. "Tomorrow!"

Two fingers, rough from planting, touched the palm of my hand. His eyes grew into mine, like thirsty flowers and, without meaning to, I felt mine alter, widen, and gradually answer his.

"Stay with me now," he said, opening his arms.

***

We lived through the two days that followed as if a stopwatch were ticking in our heads. We didn't know how long we had ... it could have been a matter of hours until she found out. The first of those days Morgan told Vivian he was taking me to the university for the day. I don't believe it even hurt him to lie at that point - we were in so deep already, cut off from reality like divers locked below the surface of the water in soundless space. We had hardly driven ten miles before we found a motel.

I remember nothing about the place except that it had Japanese wallpaper with blue bridges in the pattern. If I opened my eyes, when I opened my eyes, there was a surreal background to Morgan's hunger, our hunger for each other - glimpses of humped blue bridges and fluffy flowers. Between the heat of our bodies, the wet, the sweat, the licking, long aches of pleasure ... bridges. Luckily there was a fan. It whirred so loudly I don't think anyone heard us cry out.

Then we were tired, so tired we could only lie on one elbow and look, touching the other's eyes, chin, lips with one finger, whispering, touching.

I can't remember what excuse Morgan gave Vivian the second day. We walked for an hour and found a river bed. We'd brought sandwiches because the previous day we'd forgotten to eat. Vivian had given us soup and salad for supper, believing us to have had a large lunch. We had wanted to laugh, noticing the other devour every crumb of bread. But we didn't. We did nothing to give ourselves away. We were like Bonnie and Clyde in the last stretch, ruthless ...

Lying naked on Morgan's jacket amongst bright turquoise insects and golden butterflies, we were both happier and sadder than on the previous day. It seemed nothing could assuage the longing we felt, nothing was enough. But we guessed the shoot-out was round the corner. We realized we hadn't a chance.

And then she knew.

It was the next morning at breakfast. Vivian looked at us both slowly, took a cigarette, lit it, then fixed her gaze on Morgan. He was the one she looked at because he was the one that mattered.

"Morgan?"

Morgan was silent.

"You couldn't have been such a bloody fool ... surely?"

Morgan slashed his fingers against the wooden table. He held her gaze. It was as if I didn't exist for either of them.

"For Christ's sake," she said. "She's almost a sister."

Morgan leant over the table and held his head in his hands. From the way his back humped I thought I'd never seen such grief.

"You're my son ..."

A harsh sound came from his chest.

"Vivi ..."

She turned on me like a viper. "Shut up, Iona! You spoiled, idiotic, greedy, faithless little ass ..."

*　*　*

Within an hour Morgan had gone. Vivian wouldn't talk to me. I heard her rattling about in the tool shed for a while, then I saw her cross the grass with her trowel and fork, shoulders hunched, a frayed denim cap on her head. She lowered herself shakily and began to hack away at a stubborn root. It was far too hot to work but she kept on hacking.

I got into my rented car and left without a word.

Flying home I felt a rash of shame spreading between my fingers, under my nails, along my gums ... my heart palpitated, my stomach turned to water. All I could think of was my family, each child in turn, and Mark - especially Mark. I was filled with sheer terror. What if he wouldn't forgive me? I longed for home, to be listening to Radio Four in my kitchen, brushing Olivia's hair, picking up Hughie's tapes - all I wanted was to be doing the little things, but doing them innocently, in a state of innocence.

Miles above the clouds, cutting sleekly through the dark, the actuality of Mark, the knowledge that I love him beyond anything or anyone was clear to me. I had been, as Vivian put it, 'a spoiled, idiotic, greedy, faithless little ass.' For two days and one night of passion with Morgan, who only wanted a family, who wasn't looking for passion anyway, I'd risked everything.

I ran out of the 'Nothing to Declare' channel into Mark's arms and burst into tears.

"Mark! Listen! Please, please forgive me ..."

"Steady on, Iona! For what? Let's sit down."

"No, here! Now ... please." We were standing in an enclave of telephones, hedged in by my trolley.

I told him everything. I went back to the kiss in the wisteria garden ... and how I'd tried to cut Morgan out of my thoughts after he left, banished him, pretty well entirely. I wept on Mark's shoulder. We slipped down and sat on my coat in a sea of dirty cigarette butts. I admitted to him how the massages, Jacuzzis and the Californian sun had started it all up again. I told Mark about the drive to Tucson, how I'd pressed my foot down on the accelerator of the rented Mustang, belting through the desert listening to Aretha Franklin on the radio, knowing - knowing in my heart - what would happen.

"Shh, shh," he said, holding me.

"Then at Vivi's ..."

"Don't tell me that part, ever."

"But ..."

"Do you hear me?" Mark said slowly and severely, "This is

important. Don't tell me what happened between you and Morgan. I don't want to know."

I couldn't bear the hurt in his eyes. They looked as if they'd had all illusion drained out of them. I had let him down, just like his mother.

"On the way home in the airplane, Mark ..."

"Yes?" He was looking away. He'd turned up the collar of his coat so all I could see was the back of his head and his red ears.

"I realized - I understood the only thing I couldn't bear on earth would be to lose you."

"Give me time," he said, gathering up the cases. "You're going to have to give me time."

"I'm so, so terribly ..."

"Don't cry any more, Iona. We are very married, you know. We have a safety net - it's caught us before. And ..." his voice was husky, he avoided my eyes, "and I wouldn't know how to love anyone else."

***

I should have known that Mark would be generous enough to forgive me. I should also have known that that sort of mistake isn't over because you are forgiven, but drifts between you like a film of oil in what was once clean flowing water. I have every privilege. We walk into rooms together. I'm Mrs Mark Eyers. I'm well tied up in a safe harbour. But when he says, 'Did you have a good time, darling?' and I quickly, truthfully, say that I did and add exactly what I bought and whom I saw, there's an undertow. Mark is thinking, 'Does she believe that I believe her now?' and I wonder, 'Is he thinking that I'm thinking that he might not be believing me ... ?'

Chapter 11

CHARLOTTE

On hot New York evenings after I got back from the theatre I used to camp out on the grey fire-escape outside my apartment I spent a lot of time there because inside was even hotter - and lonelier. At least that's what I found. The only possession I had that meant anything at all was Olivia's portrait. In an act of utter generosity Iona gave it to me in California, no strings attached. Having my mother on my wall was a reason for going home at night, my one and only reason.

In summer the fire-escape was my refuge. You've got people to watch outside and sometimes you call down or they call up. My apartment was right above a fire hydrant and when it was unbearably hot a policeman would open it up. It spewed out water in a misty, drenching arc. Children would appear from nowhere and dash through it, tipping their heads back, opening their mouths and screaming with pleasure.

When I saw the children tossing the drops out of their hair and spurting water at each other in littler arcs, I used to think of Missy. I thought about her at other times too. Alice Vane was my only tenuous link. In her 1982 Christmas letter I learned that Rain had died the previous September.

It was for the best, she wrote. *The poor creature always was unstable. I warned Tobias but he wouldn't listen and ended up pouring good money down the drain to support her. In my opinion, they never should have had a child.*

Rain fell down a flight of stairs in her nursing home, carrying a tea tray. She broke several ribs and ruptured her spleen. The matron wanted to know if we wished her to be sent to City Hospital or a private one as she needed an operation. Mr Vane agreed with me City Hospital would be best as naturally we wish to save Tobias's money for Melissa's college tuition.

I thought it wiser not to tell the child. It would have been unsettling for her to visit her mother in hospital.

As it happened, Rain contracted an infection during surgery and died three days later. I told Melissa and suggested she come with us to her mother's funeral. She flew into the most terrible rage because we hadn't let her know before. She said she had better ways of remembering her mother than 'that place where you put poor Dad'. She is ungrateful and thoughtless. Really no girl could have a lovelier home to grow up in and we have her in the most expensive school in the Valley.

We had a nice little ceremony for Rain with some of the ladies from her condominium in attendance but, while we were there, Melissa disappeared again and we had to call in the police. It was extremely embarrassing. Our neighbours saw everything. We have always taken pride in our quiet street which, as you will remember, is mostly tudor with only two ranch-style houses. I need hardly tell you Melissa is now under close supervision ...

So Alice Vane thought it would have been better if her granddaughter had never been born. I imagined Missy alone in that bright, white, anonymous city and tried to remember myself at her age. I made up a parcel for her of the War Poems, two P.G. Wodehouse novels, striped knee socks, my bible and a box of fudge and sent it off with a letter. I hardly dared to hope for an answer, which was just as well as none came.

During the years I lived in New York I tried to absorb Toby's death but it was immiscible, oil that wouldn't sink into the water of my brain. Phrases from the bible would come into my head:

I stand at the door and knock ... harden not your heart ... come unto me all ye that are heavy laden and I will refresh you ...

They were words I used to love. But something had gone from them. They repeated themselves in my brain in a lifeless mantra. What I yearned for, what I felt I deserved, was a sign - an indication that Toby was safe and that God had not abandoned me.

I took classes in meditation. I opened my mind, creating a space for His voice, but it never came. My efforts were met with bigger and bigger blocks of silence, solid glass blocks like the ones that formed the graceful buildings surrounding me. I would have settled for a dream, a glimpse of Toby and me as we once were, the replay of a single breakfast ... but sleep when it came was as sterile and empty as my waking hours.

Not long after I'd started living in New York I received a letter from Fardie:

Dear Charlotte,

I hope you are recovering from the tragic death of your husband. At times like this one's faith is put to the test. But I have confidence in you. I am sure you will not falter.

I write to you today with a specific purpose in mind. Our good Logan is retiring after fifty-two years with the sheep. I had hoped he would carry on until his seventy-fifth birthday, but his hip is giving him trouble and he can't manage the hill walking. Neither of his boys is interested in taking over. Malcolm is working in the motor bicycle industry and the younger boy is a bad lot.

This distressing news coincides with our longstanding tenants moving out of Loch Cottage.

It occurs to me that you must be tiring of your artificial profession and living so far from home. Although shepherding is a man's job I have always felt that you, like your aunt Vivian, have a way with the sheep and I would like you to consider coming back and taking over the flock. You could live in Loch Cottage and I would pay you a fair monthly stipend. A local lad could come in to help with the dipping and shearing.

Have been having a bit of trouble with the old wounds. These damn stairs need work. Had a fall the other day but the doctor put me to rights.

I wonder what has happened to the Vane child of whom you spoke so fondly?

Yr. affectionate father

Funny how just a few words of his could enrage me at a distance of three thousand miles. My *artificial* profession! *A man's job!* And why did Toby have to be a *husband?* I replied immediately telling him it was out of the question. It did not strike me as particularly odd that he should have slipped on the stairs. They were always losing their runners. I failed to heed the frailty of my father's handwriting which, never strong, had faded into a faint spider web - the kind which flits across your face like gauze and disintegrates before your hand reaches your cheek.

It was completely out of the question yet, as I walked to work through the whine of ambulances and honking taxis, I couldn't help thinking of Loch Cottage alone on its rocky promontory with the waves sighing below and the wet backs of gulls lifting and sinking as they skimmed the sea for fish.

Not that my life was all bad. There are things I love about New York, glimpses of bowling-along cloud framed between the sharp edges of skyscrapers, Soho warehouses which turn overnight into galleries, coffee houses and dark, pounding jazz clubs, boutiques with kinky hats and baggy trousers - all that, and the sandwiches! I love the way boys hurl bacon onto hot grills, crinkle it, dry it, and slap it between slices of toast with tomato, mayo and lettuce before you've had time to unzip your bag. I ate a lot of BLTs when I lived in New York; it was pretty well my staple diet.

During that time I had two off-Broadway leads I really cared about - both O'Neill. Anna Christie was probably the most interesting character I've ever played. But more often the shows were shallow - leading nowhere. I used to roller-skate to the theatre when the weather was fine like everyone else. But at night, roller-skating back to no Toby, the phrases came back unbidden: *harden not your heart ... I stand at the door and knock ... if any man hear my voice ...*

When this happened I did my best to block them out. I got good at going into bars and ordering a Stolichnaya vodka on the rocks, or several. In fact, as 1982 slid surreptitiously into 1983, several Stolis became the norm. The first swallow jolted me into an easier world. With the second the phrases retreated and, after that, a lazy warmth spread through me. I loved the smoky closeness of the bar. I forgot the pointless monotony of my life. In bars I heard my name again. Nobody actually spoke it, but it floated back by itself, round and real and whole.

Then at Christmas - last Christmas - something happened. I was in Punch's bar, drinking Stolis. A young man was staring at me. I didn't feel like talking so I looked straight ahead, past the bartender at the rows of bottles. I looked beyond the bottles and suddenly caught sight of myself in the glass. For a moment I thought I'd seen my own ghost - my skin was like ashes, my hair was drawn back tightly in a scarf and my eyes were hollowed-out shadows. No wonder the man was staring at me, he obviously thought I was a ghost. I got up and walked unsteadily to the lavatory. I took off my scarf and shook out my hair. It wasn't bad hair, still shiny black despite the grey strokes. I found some eye-liner in my bag and slowly, carefully, painted my eyes. I put on a strong vermilion lipstick and outlined my lips with a thin black line. Then I went back to the bar and sat down.

"Let me buy you another of those."

He was young, years younger than me. The sort of young that is laid-back - all legs and arms with a smooth, tanned, been-skiing-recently face. He had the kind of smile that is too damn easy, not suitable for approaching a wintercold widow like myself. I nodded.

"You drank that one fast enough!" he said, moving to the stool next to me and making short work of his own.

He was wearing a business suit. His striped shirt was open at the neck and his tie was half stuffed into a jacket pocket. His socks didn't match, I noticed, and the laces of his shoes were undone.

"Is this a competition?" I asked.

"If you want it to be."

"What are you?" I asked, vaguely aware that I wasn't actually dead, that something in the nature of blood was chugging slowly through my veins.

"Name's Rob. I'm a useless adman who wishes he was a writer," he said. "Bored at work, in the process of separating from a Junior League, charitable, well-loved-by-everyone-except-me, caring-to-everyone-except-me, joyous-to-everyone-except ..."

"I get the picture!" I said.

"... pretentious female!" he went on, "Who just happens to be pregnant with my child," he added, knocking back another drink.

"Oh, dear."

"How about you?"

"Charlotte. An actress of sorts," I told him, hearing myself slurring my words. "Lots of baggage, Rob, miserable baggage, fucked up, childless, miserable baggage ... and a few minutes ago I got the distinct impression that I was dead!"

"I see signs of life." he said, leaning over, putting a strong, young arm round my shoulders.

"That's a relief."

We had another drink. Our stools were so close that I could feel him against me from my hip to the top of my boot.

"Feels good," he said.

"What?"

"You feel good, baby ... Hey! It's Christmas time! Haven't you noticed?"

"Jingle Bells! Who cares?"

"What about it, Charlotte? My one room, no-furniture-yet apartment is only two blocks away."

"What about AIDS, thrush, gonorrhoea, viral beriberi ... that sort of thing?" I asked, not really caring. He laughed.

"Junior League partners don't have these diseases! Actually they don't fuck, except once in a while to get pregnant."

"A one-off?" I asked.

"A one-off!" he agreed.

***

I don't know what changed my luck. It might have been that young man, or maybe God had seen my face in the bar mirror too and thought to Himself, 'this servant of mine is at the very end of her tether'. I don't know, but soon after that He sent me a sign. It didn't come in a dramatic form, no angels bursting into song above my apartment, no visitation from my darling Toby. No, it came in the form of a telex - from Mr Vane.

Things had gone from bad to worse, he confessed. Melissa had been smoking marijuana and had stayed out all night twice. They'd had to ground her. His wife was very distressed. There was to be a private hearing to discuss their granddaughter's future and the school psychologist had suggested it would be a good idea if I were there. He gave the date and wanted to know if I could possibly come despite the short notice. He knew it was a lot to ask ...

I went straight to Shaun, the director of the second-rate play I was rehearsing for in Greenwich Village, and told him I had a family emergency. He threw a fit:

"Nobody does this to me, Charlie. We got two weeks till opening! What sort of an emergency, anyway?"

I couldn't think what to say that would make it sound urgent enough.

"A child ... my child is in trouble," I told him. He looked at me suspiciously.

"What child? You haven't got a child!"

"Just a child I had once," I said weakly. I didn't care how unconvincing it sounded. I had to go.

"I'll sue, you English bitch!" he screamed after me as I left.

***

I got onto the first available plane to Los Angeles and arrived late at the address I'd been given.

"Stealing what?" The woman judge was saying as I slipped into the back of the family courtroom.

"Mainly food and silver." Toby's mother pursed her lips. She looked put upon and very angry.

"Silver?"

"A picture of my son's graduation ceremony in an expensive silver frame."

"Is it not possible that the frame was incidental?" the judge suggested.

"She's an untrustworthy child, Your Honour. We took her into our home, pay for her education, and this is all the thanks we get ..."

"And when your granddaughter came back from spending a night out for the second time what explanation did she give?"

"She was extremely insolent and ..."

"In the child's own words, please."

"She said it was her life."

"And when you confronted her over the marijuana issue, how did she react?"

"She said it was her life again. The girl talks like an uneducated ..."

"Thank you, Mrs Vane," the judge said firmly. "I'd like to ask Melissa to give us her view of the situation."

A tall girl got up, wearing jeans and Doc Martens. A tanned child, growing out of childhood, yet still a long way from becoming a woman - awkward, yet not without grace. She had thin dreadlocks with clumps of beads and shells at the ends. I had expected her to look browbeaten and depressed, but she was animated and launched into a breathless monologue.

"It's like they don't get it, Your Honour ... I mean *she* doesn't! Grandpa's kind, but old. It's my grandmother - she didn't even tell me till afterwards when my Mom died - she always thought me going to see her was just an excuse to hang out with my friends - and I could have been around when they took her to hospital. I could have stayed with her and done the things she liked, like singing along to the *BeeGees* and making ginseng tea. And I wasn't there ... and know what, Your Honour, she's got me in this dead school that doesn't teach you anything that matters, like about the Greeks and Icarus and those great stories. It doesn't teach you about native Americans or animal husbandry ... so I skip. And my grandma thinks stuff, having stuff, is all that matters. And it isn't! There's lots going on that's real. Like last month the police shot a blind kid and all he'd done was try to run away. See this boy was with his friends and they'd been looting, though he hadn't. I mean how could you loot if you couldn't see? He was just hanging out with them so when they ran away he ran too but being blind he couldn't run so fast ... and they shot him. And like I relate to this because my Dad was shot with a police pistol, even although it wasn't a policeman who shot him, it was a police pistol so I'm into ..."

"Gun control?" the judge asked.

"Right ..."

"It's an important issue, Melissa," the judge said gently.

Later I had a long talk with Toby's parents. Alice Vane was defeated and wanted to put Missy into foster care. The old boy was anxious to avoid any kind of institution. He felt guilty, but impotent. Gradually, gradually it dawned on me why I was there ... that if Missy wanted to, and if the authorities involved agreed, I was in there with a chance. Apparently she had talked about me to the school psychologist who had been seeing her since Rain's death. The fact that I had been with her father, in what appeared to them to be a permanent relationship, was another plus.

A feeling of utter amazement came over me. I tried to concentrate on what they were saying, but the possibility of having Missy in my life was flickering in my head, exploding into Catherine wheels in the sky of my mind.

***

At that point we had seen each other, but hadn't spoken. It was arranged that we should meet the following day. The venue chosen by Missy was a playground near the Vane's house.

When I got there she was sitting on a swing, her long legs stretched out, her sneakers scuffing channels in the sandy earth. Her body language was not encouraging. My only choice was to sit on the grass, just out of reach of her large feet.

"Hi!" I began nervously.

But my 'Hi' was ignored.

"So things don't look good?" I started again, stating the obvious.

"Huh!"

"You aren't happy living with your grandparents?" I continued, helplessly, feeling foolish.

Half the sun-striped dreadlocks were covering her face. She went on swinging and scuffing in silence. At last she looked up. Her green eyes looked directly into mine.

"How come you left, Charlotte?"

"Missy, your grandmother had custody of you - your own mother was alive. You didn't want to see me ... don't you remember?"

"So ... ? How come you left California?"

I should have remembered she's no pushover, I thought, a stubborn little pain in the arse! Yet my mind was racing. I was thinking about the letter from Fardie. I wondered if Loch Cottage was still empty.

"So?" she said again.

"Because I couldn't be with you, Missy."

"You don't know a thing about kids do you, Charlotte?"

"Not a great deal," I admitted.

"See they want you to wait for them, hang in there, because they've been hoping to be with you all along ... like they seem to be mad about something, but they aren't really."

She began twisting herself round and round on the swing, knotting the chains into a spiral coil then releasing it. As it unwound I got flashes of young child and flashes of hurting teenage girl - child, girl, child, girl, child. The shells and beads whirled round her head like a dervish.

"I should have hung in there," I said.

"Yeah."

"But I'm here now, Missy. Do you want to try it ... coming to live with me in Scotland?"

There was a long silence. She stopped and steadied herself with her heels making a deeper rut in the red dust.

"And you'd be like my mother?" came out after a while, in a voice with a hole in it. "And we'd be where that island is and the boat with the five logs that start it off ... ?"

"More or less - there's a good school there now."

"Forget it! I hate school."

"How are you going to fight materialism or take on the L.A. police department if you haven't been to school?" I said. She thought this over.

"But do you want a kid?" Her voice was caught on barbed wire, raspy and brittle ... yet soft as sheep's wool underneath.

"Not any kid - I don't like most of them. It's you ... I want you Missy. More than ..."

I hardly ever cry, hadn't for ages. I didn't want to. I particularly didn't want to put emotional pressure on Toby's child, but tears collected in my eyes, like rain in a pregnant cloud. The girl was still now, staring at me with rapt attention. I blinked - trying not to let it happen.

"Gee!" she said, as the first drops fell. "Awesome!"

"Sorry!"

"It's OK, Charlotte. It's OK."

She got down from the swing and knelt beside me on the grass, stroking my cheek, putting her arms around me. I remembered how affectionate she'd been with Toby, grabbing handfuls of his hair, falling asleep on his knee in the sun.

"And I'll go to school,' she added, "so long as it's not private."

We sat on the ground for some time. Two boys were whirling down a slide. Mothers with toddlers gathered in the shade. My cheeks must have been smudged with tears and dirt.

"Dad'll still be around, right? I mean even in Scotland," she said after a bit.

"I think so," I said. "In fact I had a si ..."

"A what?"

"Nothing."

"See it's totally weird, Charlotte. I mean since Dad and my Mom died my life's been totally gross. Sort of like the poem you sent me about the blinds. Remember that bit ... *and each slow dusk a drawing-down of blinds?*"

"Yes."

"And now it's going to change ..."

"Hold on a minute. We've got a lot of work to do. We've got to convince your psychologist and your teacher and the judge ..."

"Don't worry about it," she said. "The psychologist's a pushover and Miss Kuhns is real sorry for me and the Your Honour lady can't bear Grandma but ..." she suddenly bit her lip and looked uncertain, "but Charlotte, don't go and get scared on me about being a mother, OK? I mean I'm going to try to be good."

"I'm not scared!"

She'd sensed it immediately - a fleeting moment of apprehension as the immensity of it struck me. Would she like Scotland? What sort of a mother would I make at forty-one, never having been one before?

"And I never thought of you as bad, Missy," I added quickly.

"I was aiming to be very bad, very soon," she said ominously.

"How?" I asked, although it didn't surprise me.

"Like getting into a gang, and having sex to annoy Grandma and ripping off stores and stuff."

"You haven't done any of these things yet?" I asked anxiously, bracing myself to take whatever was coming.

"No, but don't tell her! Just smoking pot with the animal trainers at Universal, and that's a normal, you know, a part of growing up - like braces."

"Mmmm!" I said, thinking I might need some advice from Iona.

"You said you had a si ... like a sign?" she asked. "About me? About Dad? Who sent it, Charlotte?"

I thought back on the years since Toby's death, empty years of longing for some sort of reassurance from God. When Jesus cured the leper he had said: *Say nothing to any man but the leper went away and began to publish it much, and to blaze abroad the matter.* I looked at my very visible answered prayer, with her red sneakers and her torn jeans showing glimpses of knee and thigh. Behind her head a whitish rose light filtered through the Los Angeles smog. She was standing up now, having momentarily forgotten her question.

"I'm hungry!" my sign from heaven said. "There's a guy over there with ice-cream: Blueberry Bonus, Butterscotch Crunch ... Raspberry Ripple?"

I felt like the leper. I wanted to blaze it abroad, to tell Iona and Fardie and the whole world how God had heard my cry in the wilderness of Manhattan. I wanted to tell Missy, too. But I made up my mind to say nothing for as long as I could.

"Blueberry Bonus." I said. She held out a hand to pull me up and we ran across the park to the ice-cream van.

Chapter 12

IONA

When an affair is over you lose the lover, that goes without saying. But in my case I lost Vivian too and in a way that made it worse. Not that she was ever what you'd call a mother figure, not at all ... yet it rankled. I couldn't forget how she'd turned on me that dreadful morning in Tucson with the heat simmering like a slow sauce at nine in the morning, blistering the butter on the table and wilting the scrambled eggs that lay uneaten between us. 'Shut up, Iona, you faithless, idiotic, greedy ...' She'd said it as if I didn't exist, as if I'd never been hers and she'd never been mine and my whole childhood counted for nothing.

A few months after I got back from California I took a garden design course. It was Mark's idea. At first I didn't want to. I thought I'd be far too stupid to understand about perspective and soil chemistry. I left Westfield able to play the piano quite well, sing in harmony, speak French and smock - but otherwise dim. I've always thought of myself as dim. Mark has often told me that I'm not, only idle. But I never used to believe him. Anyway, he was right. The course was fascinating and I was one of the best. After it finished I got a job as part of a team bringing a sunken garden in Devon back to life. I discovered that I love working, especially with flowers. For two years I concentrated on the garden and the children and managed not to let myself think about Morgan - or Vivian.

But when my fortieth birthday came - our fortieth - I began to feel a heaviness hovering above my head, like claws about to drop on their victim. Things I'd put off dealing with pushed back into my mind. Charlotte for a start. She was still in New York and wrote occasionally, but when we talked on the telephone I was aware of distance between us, space that had nothing to do with the Atlantic ocean. And Fardie, I had a suspicion he wasn't well. Yet I didn't have time to go up to Scotland, or rather I wasn't prepared to make time, or perhaps I just didn't feel strong enough to go there alone. But worst of all was Vivian. I'd written to her three times but she hadn't even answered my letters. How can a mother - well, a stand-in mother of a sort - give up on a daughter? I mean how can she just stop caring?

At Craigmannoch, when a sheep had a dead lamb they often gave her another. We used to watch the shepherd bringing the ewe off the hill. He walked ahead dragging her lamb on a long string and the sheep followed, snuffling lovingly. At the farm they'd pen the sheep and skin the dead lamb - its coat would slip off like peeling a jersey off a child. Then the coat was tied onto an orphan lamb and it was shut up for the night with its proxy mother. It almost always worked. We saw this procedure so often that it must have sunk into my consciousness. It sounds pathetic now but I used to think we were like that, orphaned lambs, and Vivian had taken us on.

"Why do you mind so much?" Mark asked me. "Vivian didn't mean it, I'm sure. And you know she's an oddball ... she's not that important to you surely, or is she?"

"She's abandoned me."

"It's Morgan, Iona, isn't it? You can tell me."

"No Mark, it's Vivian."

He took me back to Gareth, the psychiatrist who'd helped me before. I really hate the whole process, rootling around in one's subconscious, waiting for something you'd rather not think about to float up to the surface, like a drowned body or a bit of one. But I needed to go. I didn't want it to lose it again, like the last time.

Then finally I got a letter from Vivian. She suggested we should join up at Craigmannoch to organize care for Fardie. 'Poor old Harry,' she wrote, 'he can't cope at all. It's pretty gruesome. The house is in a state of chaos. And, while we're at it,' she added casually, 'we've got some sorting out to do ourselves.' It made me furious! As if I hadn't been trying to make amends for years, as if I hadn't apologized.

I got there first and saw what she meant. The house looked like a boat that's smashed about on the rocks with so many leaks in it you can't quite imagine why it's still afloat. Slates had blown off the roof and the garden had grown into a wilderness with rhododendrons taking over the lawn and pushing their way up to the house. Inside there was pipe ash everywhere and piles of pans with old porridge stuck to the bottom. The curtains were threadbare, some had disintegrated and lay like shed snakeskin in silvery pools on the floor. Fardie looked as if he'd gone adrift himself. He was very thin; his wispy hair was long and uncut. I came upon him wandering around, mumbling to himself.

When he first saw me I was standing in front of the library window with the sun behind me.

"Fardie, dear!"

He stood still blinking against the light for a few seconds, staring at me.

"Livla?" he said at last, in a voice I'd never heard before, tender, astonished, elegiac.

"Fardie, it's me, Iona."

"Of course it is, dear," he agreed, recovering slowly. "The light, you know." he said apologetically. "Damned light! Thought it was someone else for a moment."

***

Driving Vivian back from the airport we were awkward together for the first time in our lives. I was damned if I was going to grovel any more so I hardly spoke. She kept looking at me sideways then surveying the countryside, making critical remarks about the farms we passed. Just as we reached the village she lurched into a clumsy apology.

"By the way, Iona, sorry ... ! Sorry for flying at you in Tucson. I've been meaning to tell you face to face. Not sure how to write it in a letter."

"It's been upsetting me a lot," I said. "I did write three times."

"It wasn't fair of me, I know. But you see, at my age you dry up like a pod. You forget what it feels like ... no sap. You've lost those urges, thank God! The ones that made you two take off like copulating rabbits. Morgan said ..."

"What did Morgan say?"

"That it wasn't fair blaming you."

"Well, it wasn't. I know what we did was wrong, but you pretty well brought me up. I was almost your child, for God's sake!"

"If you must know it was because of that I was so angry."

"What do you mean?"

"I think of you and Charlotte as my girls, that's what I mean."

"Really?"

"Always have since your mother died. That was what made it rabbitish ... and downright peculiar."

"We are cousins - not brother and sister, Vivi!"

We reached the gate. Someone always has to get out and open it. Fardie has never sprung to grids. 'Right, bletherers, whose turn is it?' she used to say - I could hear her, as if it were yesterday.

"I suppose it's my turn!" she said with a laugh.

She got out and heaved the gate open with some difficulty. I noticed that her arthritis was worse; her fingers were like the grotesque lumps of a ginger root. Her skin was crinkled from lack of cream and her marvellous eyes were beginning to droop a little - too much whisky, I imagined. Yet, as she stood there with the rain falling on her grey hair, sniffing the sea air and shaking herself like a dog, I felt an unbidden wave of fondness.

"Well, that's that!" she said cheerfully, as she got back into the car. "I hope Harry's got some decent booze. I could do with a dram, couldn't you?"

"Certainly could ..."

I realized we were back on track again, although she hadn't told me anything about Morgan and I suspected she wasn't going to.

***

We managed to get the district nurse to come in to bath Fardie every evening at six o'clock. It wasn't hard convincing him it was a good idea, however at five he began to fuss, making and remaking his bed, polishing his bedside table and cleaning his shoes - then he lay down rigidly on top of the sheet, staring up at the ceiling until she arrived.

"What on earth ... ?" I asked Vivian.

"Look at the card beside his bed," she said. I looked and saw he had printed: Major Harold MacIntyre – 44479310 – Date of birth: 21/10/1910.

"Poor sweet old sod," she said. "He thinks he's back in the POW hospital where they amputated his arm. Murray once told me a bit about it. Apparently he arrived in the back of a cattle truck half dead from blood poisoning. Then, as you know, there was the delay before the operation which almost cost him his life."

"What delay? What cattle truck? I don't know, Vivian. I don't know anything. I'm not psychic."

"It's a grim story - in character, but grim."

"Tell me, for God's sake!"

"Murray had friends in the Bebra camp who reported that when Harry arrived at the hospital, with his left arm almost hanging off, the head surgeon - a Kraut with some crazy personal vendetta - demanded that Harry salute him."

"Christ! I suppose he couldn't."

"Couldn't or wouldn't. The man was showing off in front of the other doctors, sneering and laughing. Apparently he said if a fucking Major thought he was too good to salute the Chief Surgeon then he didn't deserve to be operated on."

"Fardie should have given in."

"When has he ever given in to something wrong? He wouldn't make the slightest gesture to appease the doctor. So he was put at the end of a long list of prisoners. He had to wait for sixteen hours in unspeakable agony ..."

"And he'd been brought all the way from Anzio?"

"No, I don't think so. He just had a minor wound in Anzio which they soon patched up. When this happened he'd already been a POW in Bebra. I understand they were bringing him back there. I think the real crisis came when they were on a nightmarish march to a high-security camp. I never discovered quite what happened.

"But what about Ormonde? He was killed at Anzio, wasn't he?"

"I know my brother Mondy was dead by the time Harry got to the POW hospital. Don't ask me for details, I wasn't there, for Christ's sake!"

Vivian's neck reddened. I had the impression she knew more than she was telling me. She began her version of dusting, whacking the paintings with an old towel, then spitting on a corner of it and running it along the ridges of the frame. "You do the floor!" she said to me, as cobwebs, dead bees and bits of a bird's nest settled around us.

I felt sick. I longed to comfort Fardie. I wanted desperately to slice through the years of silence. I wanted him to know that I knew what he'd been through. That evening, after the nurse had left, I took in his supper tray and sat down beside him. But I hardly knew where to begin. We weren't in the habit of talking.

"Fardie! Finn wants you to take him fly-fishing again. Remember when you took him before?"

"He smiled. "Finn watches the water ..." he said quietly. "He understands."

"Fardie, Charlotte and I - we love coming back to Craigmannoch. We want to be closer to you ... again."

"Side's hurting. It's the old wound ..."

"Listen to me! Please listen, Fardie dear. We understand a bit now, I mean about what you went through ... We've left you alone too much. We want to come back - often."

"It's all in order, all the papers ... Crichton will help you when I'm gone."

"But that's not what I mean! There's nothing really wrong with you Fardie. Please ... don't just give up."

"I'm tired, Iona. Put the light out, my dear."

"The doctor said there's no reason why you can't get well again ... you know, keep going. And now we've got Bessie Wilson from the village. She'll cook you a good lunch every day and leave soup on the Esse for your supper."

"Can manage it m'self."

"I know, but it will give you more time - for other things. Then we'll be back in the summer."

"Put out the light ... that's a good girl."

***

We cleaned the house from top to bottom. The pantry was the worst. It smelled. Something had torn into a sack of flour and the damp remains were mixed with feathers from an ancient grouse which must have been hanging so long it had disintegrated. Our three-legged cat, Snooky, rescued from a gin trap as a kitten, was long since dead, but a family of semi-wild ones had moved in and skirted round our feet, mewing frantically.

"Charlotte ought to be here, too," Vivian said.

"We're all guilty, Vivian. How could we have left him so long?"

***

A few nights after my unsuccessful talk with Fardie I came upon the unlikely sight of Vivian sitting in our old nursery knitting an uneven blue square.

"Goodness!" I said. "What's that?"

"Sit down, Puff."

"I am ..."

"It's for Morgan's baby," she said, smiling an annoying old-woman-of-the-pack smile.

"What?"

"There's Susie," she explained. "She's a scuba-diving teacher and she's pregnant."

"Goodness!" I repeated feebly.

"It's the best thing for him, kiddo," she said. "I know you'll understand. He has to have his own family. Can't really rely on yours, can he?"

"Are they married?" I asked stiffly.

"Oh, I expect they'll get hitched somewhere along the line. It doesn't seem to matter much any more. Want to see a photograph?"

Vivian has adopted certain all-American habits like carrying photographs around in a handbag which she calls her purse.

"Alright," I said nervously.

And there he was, standing beside a youngish woman with an oval face and wet, wavy pre-Raphaelite hair, the kind I love which just shakes out and doesn't need brushing. She'd been swimming, although Morgan hadn't. He was wearing cotton trousers and a denim shirt. His hand was on her shoulder and he was looking at her the way he once looked at me under the wisteria at Barrington Court.

"Right!" I said.

I've been saying 'right' a lot lately. It happens when I need time to think something out, like the other day when Finn told me he wanted to be a Buddhist or the time Hughie asked if he could be the queen in his school play. On this occasion I said 'right' because I felt as if I were short of oxygen. If I cut myself I suspected a fluorescent green liquid might seep out in place of blood. I stood there, blinking back tears, trying to take it in.

"Right."

"It's for the best, dear," Vivian said, suddenly taking pity on me, standing up and putting an awkward arm around my shoulders.

"I know." I said. "It makes sense. It makes sense for you - and him ..."

"Course it does, and for you, too."

"I love Mark. I adore the children - so why is it such a shock, Vivi? What's wrong with me?"

"Sap!" she offered up obscurely. "Sap in the blood, it's the very devil. But it passes in the end."

***

The house was in order at last and Fardie almost docile and accepting of the new regime. Our last night, after he had gone to bed, Vivian poured herself a large glass of whisky and took out the knitting. I didn't like to ask what it was meant to be.

"You know," she said out of the blue, "it's odd but I still feel her presence."

"Olivia's?"

"Yes. Harry brought her up here when he was called up. It was only a year after my baby's birth and abduction - I was in a terrible state. I never addressed a word to Father and he was still fuming with me. Mother was always complaining. She'd hoped for a daughter who would go to the balls in a white dress with a MacIntyre tartan sash draped over her bosom, and landed up with me - a fallen woman at eighteen. It was a pretty grim household to come into, but when your mother arrived we fell like ninepins. She had that effect on people!"

"What was it about her?"

"Oh, I don't know. She made us laugh and she was ... exotic. I can see her now sitting at breakfast in a silk dressing gown pushing her narrow feet in and out of ostrich bedroom slippers, eating un-breakfast food - here, in this house! Normally, Father punished anyone who didn't appear fully dressed for morning prayers at six-thirty. But I don't remember her ever appearing at prayers and she got away with it. She got away with everything. I once walked in to the drawing room and she was teaching Ormonde the foxtrot. I was about to leave, but they wouldn't let me. She wouldn't. We three danced all afternoon! We weren't used to having fun ..."

"What did you mean when you said she was eating un-breakfast food?" I asked, fascinated, filling Vivian's glass when she gave the slightest sign of tailing off.

"Oh, I suppose she'd convinced Father she was allergic to porridge or something and Mrs Forrester was always sneaking her things. She worshipped her. When Olivia came back the second time, pregnant with you and Charlotte, the war was in full swing. I was doing the work of two men, surviving on the most God-awful rations, and I'd see old Forrie labouring up the stairs in her elastic stockings with titbits none of the rest of us ever saw - a dish full of blaeberries, six quail's eggs, sauteed chicken livers ... God knows where she got them!"

"You must have felt resentful."

"Not really, not about that, I adored Olivia. She had the sort of voice that holds you lightly at first, then weaves you down into it. She made me feel as if I were the only person on earth she cared about. I was knotted up with pain, as you can imagine. But she got my story out of me and I felt that I had a sister ... of course she did the same to everyone. She was a con man, by today's standards.

"You say 'when she came back?' You mean she didn't stay long the first time."

"No, once the boys had gone she got bored and went back to London. But Harry insisted she should come back here for your birth."

"Was she afraid ... at the thought of having twins?"

"To tell you the truth, yes. Once we were waiting for her before dinner and I suddenly heard a long melodramatic wail. Mother looked disapproving. By this time Father had died and she and Olivia were at loggerheads. Forrie and I went running to the call. She was standing in her room surrounded by a mound of dresses. 'I'm a sow, they'll never come ... never! I'll be like this forever,' she moaned. It was really very funny."

"But she must have known when we were due."

"Your mother was vague about dates."

" 'Dinna fret, Mrs Harry,' Forrie reassured her, starting to gather up the dresses. 'The full moon'll bring them on.' "

" 'Is that true, Forrie darling? How does it happen?' "

"She was so vulnerable then. I don't think she knew the first thing about her body, none of us did."

" 'It's the pull in it,' Mrs Forrester explained. 'It pulls seeds right out of the earth. It minds the farmers when to sow and when it's time for an ingathering of fruit.' "

" 'I wish it would ingather me,' your mother said mournfully. 'Will it hurt terribly?' "

" 'Well now, I'll not say terribly. Its nature, isn't it? It'll pain you, but you'll rise to it.' "

"It was a frightening time, Iona. You see we'd had no news for months from Harry or Ormonde. It was a dreadful winter, freezing cold. Every day we looked at the deaths in the newspapers."

"And did the full moon bring us on?"

"No! It came at last, lumpy and pale, but nothing happened. It was well into waning, into its third phase before she went into labour and Elsie was sent running for Dr Cameron."

Vivian was unusually relaxed, lifting her hand off the needle with each stitch and winding it around the point like a small child. A pattern showing a complicated matinée jacket, which seemed to bear no relation to the blue square, lay on the table but clearly the whole exercise was giving her satisfaction. Every so often she put the garment aside and had a swig of her drink. It was a unique chance to find out more, I thought. She was in a talking mood.

"Tell me about how Olivia was with us after we were born? You don't have to hush it up. I know a bit about it ... Elsie told me once. I know she wasn't a natural mother."

"Well, Puff, that's true up to a point. For the first year ... no longer, I'm afraid, she almost never saw you. I don't think you realized she was your mother. But then something strange happened and she grew very fond of you."

"Don't invent things, Vivi. It only makes it harder."

"The tragedy is it was too late, or almost too late. She was terribly ill by then - and I'm not inventing things. I'm the one she summoned, after all."

"She summoned you? Why?"

"It's not a story I come out of very well, Iona. In fact I feel guilty as hell. At that time I'd got a thing about them - babies - having had my own literally torn out of my arms. I'd been avoiding you two, never went near you. I didn't want to be reminded ..."

"Reminded?"

"... of my eight hours with my son."

Vivian topped up her glass and lit a cigarette. She had a glazed look, as if she were watching a film and the subject was so gripping that she couldn't look away.

"Of course, of course - but what did Olivia want? Why did she ask you to come to her room?"

"Blame me if you want, but I'm telling you it was still raw. Only five years had passed ... an easy birth, then this small creature was left with me - for eight hours. Eight trusting hours! I half knew what went on in that house. I'd half guessed. But alone with my baby, finding I knew what to do like a good ewe, steadying his little dark head, feeling his mouth against my breast, noticing eyes like Oran's ... those hours almost fooled me."

She was getting off the track. I didn't want to hear about Morgan. I wanted to know about my mother. But Vivian had the bit between her teeth and she was drunk.

"You can blame me all you like, Puff, but it was still raw ..."

"I'm not blaming you!" I said. "It's awful, awful! I just wonder why Olivia summoned you to her room. You said she grew fond of us? You said 'later she grew very fond of us?' "

But it was too late. I don't expect Vivian had ever told her story before. She told it with pauses, banging down her glass, sloshing drink over Fardie's embossed leather library table.

"I had eight hours with him, kiddo! Then the French bitch came in with a basket and I knew. I jus' knew ... it all fell into place."

"What did you do?"

"I curled over my baby like a lioness. I bit her wrists when she reached down to grab him. I tasted her blood and spat it back in her face ..."

"Jesus!"

"You should try having your baby taken away from you before you start blaming me."

"I'm not! I'm not blaming you, for Christ's sake!"

Vivian gulped and turned her face to the wall. Her hair was tough and springy like heather when the flowers are over. Her arms were flabby. You can't switch overnight from sheep and heavy gardening to knitting.

"That woman had done it before, Iona. It was her job, her ... trade. She'd been employed by my own father. She called the pseudo doctor in. He was small, neat and lethal. She grabbed my head and held it while he put a rag soaked in chloroform over my nose ... "

"And ... and when you woke up they'd taken him away?"

"I was on my knees, Puff, holding my baby against my stomach like a marsupial."

"It's so sad, so terribly, terribly ..."

"Blame me allya want, kiddo ..." The glass slipped out of her hand and smashed into bits.

"Vivian!"

She slid to the floor. I tried to rouse her but she was out for the count. I picked her up and half-carried her up to bed. It wasn't easy. Although she was scraggy her Scottish bones were long and solid and wouldn't line up. Morgan would have made a better job of it.

***

The next morning a wind from the west brought clouds tumbling in from the sea. Bouts of rain like temper tantrums crashed into the garden, glistening the leaves of the rhododendrons and turning the petals into flimsy chiffon rags. Neither of us had left time for breakfast. When it came to saying goodbye Fardie looked quite cheerful. I could tell he was relieved that the cleaning had come to an end and not unhappy to see us go. He had set out the electronic chess set which Morgan sent him from California. It's the only present I can ever remember him being pleased with.

"Goodbye, Fardie darling!" I said, giving him a hug, able to do that now, then I climbed into the driver's seat. With Vivian it was harder. She wasn't sure when she'd see him again. She knew more about his health than I did. They are fond of each other, but flounder about with words, like seals on dry land.

"Bye, old boy," she said. "Don't forget to pay Bessie ..."

"Yes, yes! Told me two times already."

"Don't forget the gooseberry jam ..." Vivian shouted into his good ear.

"Won't. Tell Morgan I'm on level two."

"I will. Remember to take ..."

"You'd better be off." he interrupted. "Timetables ... all that."

"You're an old fuss-pot, Harry - loads of time!"

At this point they made an affectionate swipe at each other, you could describe it as a pat I suppose, and Vivian got into the car with tears in her eyes. I couldn't see Fardie for the wind which virtually blew him back into the house and his chess game. We had planned that I would drop Vivian off at Edinburgh airport on my way home.

She didn't mention the night before or remark on the fact that she'd woken up in her own bed, in her own flannel nightie, with the knitting beside her. Picking up the dropped stitches had been a laborious business, almost as difficult as picking up my aunt. But I decided to let it go ... I couldn't bear to end our time together on a sad note.

"At least you got Morgan back, Vivi dearest. I mean that was a huge miracle, wasn't it?"

"Was it a miracle not having him for thirty years?" she asked. "Losses take the stuffing out of you, Puff."

"Losses?"

"Oran, Ormonde, Harry to a certain extent - thirty years of Morgan's life."

"God! I'm selfish. I can't imagine how you bore it. How did you ever get through it?"

"Sheep, mainly," she said. "There's nothing like hard work. Try spending a day dosing your hoggs against worms and liverfluke or branding each sheep with her age and hirsel. And remember what the lambing season is like? Up at four, climbing the hill paths, retrieving trapped lambs, helping the ewes when one is stuck ... it gets you through a day alright!"

I didn't remember most of it, but had a sudden memory of Vivian nudging a newborn lamb towards its mother with her boot. 'He'll do.' she'd say, leaving the sheep to lick her lamb in private, striding back to the farm with a lighter step.

"And children," she went on. "I mean you two became part of my life, after a bit, after the talk with Olivia. Told you about that, didn't I?"

"No, actually you didn't, Vivi. You started to, but ..."

We were arriving the airport. I should have driven slower.

"Loved you." she said gruffly. "Now don't go asking any more questions ... and don't come in with me. Can't stand all this goodbye nonsense and I'm perfectly capable of carrying my own case."

Chapter 13

CHARLOTTE

If I'd thought for a moment it was in the bag I was wrong! It's worse than a standard adoption. I'm like a prisoner here, a criminal in a halfway house, only permitted to see her every second weekend. Yet I have to be on hand for the questions: What school will she attend? Am I attached to a new partner? What male role models will be available? Finances? Nationality issues ... I take every job that comes along as my earning capacity is being assessed. When I feel desperate I remember Missy's reprimand the day we met in the park.

You don't know a thing about kids, do you Charlotte? See, they want you to wait for them, hang in there, because they've been hoping to be with you all along.

I've got the top storey of a clapboard house in Santa Monica. You can't see the sea from any of the windows. You can't even hear it. There's no point in trying to recreate things - we're both agreed on that. But however hard you try you can't ignore the ocean, just as you can't cut out stars or the way the moon bleeds into cloud, or clouds themselves when they are low over the sea, sweeping it, drinking the spray. So sometimes we do walk on the beach at dusk, each of us remembering him in her way.

And I have another problem - getting off vodka. It's become a habit, a comforting one, and on the days between Missy's visits I need comfort. It wouldn't matter if I were just one person but, under the circumstances, it could blow the whole thing apart. I've made a promise to God that if this works out, and while He's working on it, I won't touch a drop. Yet it's always there; the thought of a frosty opaque bottle, the way ice-cold vodka thickly, silently pours into a glass. My hand shakes. It curves round space. I drink Diet Cokes instead. If you drink them straight out of the can they taste alright. They have their own ritual, pulling back the metal horseshoe, a slight rip, a cold, circular feel. I was explaining this to Libby, an alcoholic actress friend of mine, the other day. 'Not nearly as classy as Stolis,' was her riposte. And of course she's right ... but then she isn't trying for a child.

I've established a rhythm for the days Missy isn't with me - fruit for breakfast, work, Diet Coke, BLT, Diet Coke, more work, a movie, Diet Coke, read, Diet Coke, supper, sleep. On Wednesday of week two I start planning for the weekend. I book horses for us to ride, stuff the fridge with her favourite food, get out the Scrabble, make up her bed. I feel tender doing this and slightly dizzy with excitement. Missy is thirteen now. She's cut off most of her hair, leaving behind a fringe for security and flicking. What's left stands up and sticks out like the petals of a chrysanthemum. She looks like Toby in ways - his open gaze and sweet, slightly protruding, upper lip. But her eyes are a wild card, lapis lazuli, embedded with chips of emerald green. Joy, doubt, compassion and curiosity flood in and out of them like shoals of fish in a clear sea.

Usually she bounds up my stairs talking non-stop as she flings her arms around me. But I can't count on it. The waiting is getting to her too and every so often she freaks out. Hardly surprising! It's even more of a nightmare for her living with Alice Vane now that the proceedings are under way. The more I come into contact with that woman the more I realize how manipulative she is. I'll never understand how Toby came from her tight-arsed, ungenerous loins. Last week there must have been a row because the child arrived in a fury. She pushed past me, threw herself onto the sofa and kicked off her sneakers.

"You're all the same!" she shouted.

"Who are all the same?"

"Adults! Social workers, teachers, grandmothers, judges ... they think they own you."

"What's happened?"

"Don't even ask ..."

So I didn't. Instead I told her about the poets in the Russian gulags and how they managed to keep their ideals intact despite terrible physical suffering.

"Think of 2244 Hyacinth Avenue as a Siberian prison camp and your grandmother as the KGB," I found myself saying, "and consider you get better food and your own room."

"Huh!" she said, shifting her long legs under her, calming down a little.

"We've got to hold out."

"Yeah, but don't think I'm staying here if it doesn't work out."

If it doesn't work out, if it doesn't work out ... that's the bitch of it. That's what we're both thinking most of the time.

"It will work out!" I said, pushing my voice up an octave, hearing it come out as steely and bright as a metal saw. She looked at me doubtfully.

"If it doesn't, I'm out of here!" she said. "I'm hitching a ride to Wyoming."

"Why Wyoming?" I asked, in spite of myself.

"They've got a ranch where you earn your own horse." she confided, cheering up and reaching for a banana. "You work for them for nothing, taking care of other horses, then you get to pick one out yourself. After that you start earning for real."

It was impressive. I didn't point out that she's underage and her plan is against the law. At least she has an alternative plan, which is more than I do.

Just as everything was moving along and I was beginning to think I might have Missy in Scotland for Christmas, Alice Vane put a spanner in the works. She suddenly became the hurt grandmother, making out I was conspiring to steal her grandchild, complaining that Missy was all that she had left of her dear son, insisting the authorities question why I wanted to take her from her native land and her blood relatives. It's insane! Everyone knows how desperate she's been to get rid of her. I don't understand - after all this work. Now Missy is the one who is keeping her cool.

"It's like this, Charlotte," she explained. "She's a cheat. Like a D student who wants everyone to think she's an A student. She'll write the answer on the palm of her hand if she has to. See, she wants the neighbours to think she's like the great grandma. Grandma of the year!"

And it turns out she's a good actress when she needs to be. She's picked up the psychological jargon and plays it right back at them.

"Charlotte's my mother now," she said in a pitiful voice to the social worker. "I need her to take care of me. It's what my birth Mom wanted for me because Charlotte's young and real loving and she's got the same values as my Dad had. And she wouldn't have the structure it takes to adopt a kid if she wasn't in her own country near her own sister and her kids, who'll be like brothers and sisters to me and, see, I've never had a wholesome family environment ..."

"Is it true about your mother wanting me to look after you?" I asked her, surprised.

"Could be." she said, with a shrug. "I can't remember. But we've got to fight for what we believe in, right, Charlotte? Like the Russian poets."

***

Finally, Alice Vane was defeated in June and, at the age of forty-two, I was granted custody of Melissa Eliot Vane. Yet still it wasn't over. At the last moment Missy had a bout of terrible insecurity.

"How do you know it will work? Your life wasn't so great ..."

"I just do! You'll love the animals and the smell of things and the space. Iona's children will become part of your life."

"So? They may not like me. Some kids don't."

"I think these ones will," I said, praying they would. "Finn is shy, but very kind."

"And Hughie?"

"He's fun - a bit mad like you. He'll love having someone his age ..."

"And the kid sister? I mean will she think I'm like invading her space?"

We'd been over it before.

"I don't think so. She'll be glad to have another girl around."

Then she asked me to take her to Malibu beach. The house had been sold, but she wanted to go to the bottom of the rock steps. I was reluctant. She begged. I told her you can never go back. She said if I didn't take her she'd go anyway. So, in the end, I drove to the fish restaurant and we walked along the beach as we had both done so often with Toby. And there they were, those steps leading up to what once was, leading back into my time with him, a lemon tree, a deck, white cotton pillows on a white bed. We were only writing the first pages of our life together ... we'd hardly begun.

Missy sat on the bottom step. It was windy and she hadn't brought a sweater. She pushed her bare feet into the sand as if by feel alone she could conjure him up. At least that's what I think was happening. She sat with her chin in her hands, staring unseeing out to sea. I walked on.

On my way back half an hour later it started to rain. I was suddenly afraid that she might not be there. I began to run. Panic that I could still lose her outstripped my own grief. Then, through a veil of grey drizzle, I caught sight of the iridescent colours of her tie-died T-shirt and a glimmer of white knuckles supporting a pale, childish face.

I held out my hand. After a minute or two she took it. We walked back to the car in silence.

One thing was clear to me. It wasn't the right time to tell her about Iona's telephone call. The important thing was to get her onto the plane.

***

Iona's family were there to meet us. Puff dived through the barrier and hugged me over and over. After that we stood around together - the children staring at each other solemnly. Then suddenly eight year old Olivia made a flying leap into Missy's surprised arms.

"You can sleep in my room if you like!" she said. "And I'm going to show you ..."

"Shut up!" Hughie interrupted. "She can be in the TV room and share my parrot."

"Welcome to England," Finn said gravely. I hardly recognized him. He was over six feet tall with two rings in his left ear. He was dressed in the sort of worn out jeans Missy normally lives in herself. I saw her noting this with approval, although she didn't relax her fierce expression until Mark produced a basket with Crunchie bars, chocolates, tapes, bracelets, Body Shop bottles and a pile of English comics.

"From us." he said, sweetly.

"Thanks!" She said, with a flicker of a held-back smile, allowing Olivia to take her hand and haul her along towards the car park.

It happened to be one of those late June evenings when English gardens are infatuated with their own warmth. Splurges of large white roses with heavy petals hovered in the air, pink ones were staggered against the walls of Iona's house like piles of giddy tea cups. During dinner Missy didn't speak much except for her usual *cools* and *so whats* but, under an assumed nonchalance and a lot of fringe flicking, I could tell that she was intrigued. And when they took her out to meet Jesse, the mare that the children ride, she caught her breath and looked happier than I'd seen her since Toby died. That night I told her about Fardie.

"Your father?" she asked, surprised.

"Yes."

"Was it an accident, Charlotte? Did he get shot or something?"

"He did get shot, as it happens, a long time ago in the war. But right now he's ..."

"D'you want me to come with you?"

"Missy, this is something I have to do with Iona. I think it would be too sad for you. I hate leaving you but ..."

"No problem!" she said. "I'll hang out here with the kids."

We were leaving for Craigmannoch at six the following morning. I'd known my father wasn't well for a long time, but pushed it aside. I was pregnant during those nerve-racking months in California. I'd even fantasized that I should be eating more green vegetables and getting nine hours' sleep a night. Forty-two is old to be having a first child. Anxiety wasn't good for me. I was anxious enough as it was. Then Iona had rung two nights before we left.

"Thank God you're coming, Char," she'd said down the phone in a frightened voice. "Fardie is dying."

And still I didn't let myself think about it. Not until we were driving up the M5, when hedges and walls fell away and the wild sweep of border hills engulfed us, did it begin to enter my consciousness.

Chapter 14

IONA

For the first part of the journey I just revelled in being together again. Having a sister! It's like lowering yourself into warm water when your body is tired. It's beyond parent, husband, even children - it spans time and place. I never have to point things out to Char. When we reached the Borders I knew she was remembering train journeys home from school. All night we were rocked and swayed as the heavy steam train pushed and hissed its way north. We woke to the euphoric shout 'Carlisle' in a Glasgow accent and the clink of thick tea cups against a brass tray. We squashed onto the top bunk, sliding back the heavy sleeper window, letting a swoosh of wet, glittering Scottish air into our cabin. There's no need to go over it. Charlotte knows what it was like. She remembers the elation ... and the dread.

She's more like a greyhound than ever; more linear, more self-contained, more beautiful. Well, I find her beautiful. Not that she tries to be. In fact it wouldn't hurt her to try a little. Her eyebrows are getting like Vivian's - a bit too savage, casting shadows over her eyes like an Edwardian tennis shade. When she arrived I thought I'd never seen her happier. I know it's partly to do with me but mainly, I'm afraid, it's the girl. I've got a hunch Missy is going to be trouble. I can see she's one of those children who has immense power over other children. Hughie and Olivia are in her thrall already, vying for her attention. Charlotte doesn't interrupt her or interject any of the '*Isn't it lovely?*' or '*Thank so and so for the chocolates*' that I'm guilty of. But she's obsessed. Her eyes trace the child's movements. She watches every reaction with loving attention. It's not natural.

After we'd crossed the border Fardie's presence began to invade the car. We automatically stopped talking. It became more and more intense. I felt a tight, almost bronchial thickening in my chest.

"Let's hope it's peaceful," I said.

"Has anything with Fardie ever been peaceful?"

"No, but people do change at the last minute, don't they? Aren't they supposed to reach out and explain ... ?"

"I've got a bit of explaining to do myself," Char said. "I've been keeping away, deliberately."

***

The one thing I hadn't expected was that he wouldn't know me; or rather that when he did he'd think I was Olivia. It's macabre! It's frightening sitting in Fardie's gloomy bedroom in heavenly July weather listening to him raving on about the war. He talks to Murray and Ormonde and to me, born-again in his imagination as my own mother ...

He talks to Charlotte as herself.

And it isn't peaceful at all, it's terribly sad. His one-sided conversations are broken up with stark terror. Every so often he rears up in bed and cries out:

"Get them off! Off, for Christ's sake!"

"Shhh, shh, Fardie dearest," we say, laying him back against the pillows and patting his face with a damp towel. Usually we can't hear him clearly. But last night, when we were both there, he was talking to Ormonde and we heard every word.

"They were going to shoot you anyway, Ormonde," he said. "Blaikie and Blair ... they might have got away. Could have! Both dead now. Blair went first. We attacked the ferret together, but the Hun shot him in the stomach. Saw it. Saw what they did to you too, boy ... had to run for it then."

"Where were you, Fardie? Were you escaping?" Charlotte asked.

He looked in her direction, but didn't seem to see her. Then he started to blink, and shrank back, as though the room were full of noise.

"Don't shoot me!" you cried. "But, Mondy, they'd have shot you anyway. Should have told you. Should have explained."

"Did Ormonde ... ? Was it his fault?" Charlotte insisted, trying to reach him. But he paid no attention. He was panting, as if he were running.

"We were nearly up with Murray - then I heard Blaikie fall. Tried, tried to pick the boy up. No strength left. I couldn't run with him. Thought he was dead ... almost certain. Laid him down."

He continued to breathe heavily. His legs twitched under the sheet.

"Told his mother I was almost certain."

His voice trailed off into a distance we couldn't see. I was in tears, but Char kept on questioning him.

"Was that when they shot you, Fardie? Was that what happened?"

"Ran! But they set the dogs on me. Kraut dogs. The dogs got me, for Christ's sake! But Christ abandoned me," he said, with a sob.

It was then that he talked to Charlotte, recognizing her, knowing she was his daughter. It was as if a spiritual rope was binding them together.

"He didn't abandon you, Fardie. He's close now. She held him in her arms. "Don't you remember? You taught me ..."

"Yes, Charlotte. Close now," he said.

"There are things I've been meaning to tell you. To thank you for."

"Thank me for? Nothing to thank me for, that's the pity of it ..."

"You made me see it all," she continued intently. "Jesus at the lakeside, the fishermen with their nets. And Simon Peter, above all Peter. It's made a difference - a great difference in my life."

"Charlotte?" he said, weakly.

"Yes, Fardie, yes?"

"The child?" he said, unexpectedly.

"Oran, you mean?"

Morgan's baby is called Oran after his father. We have photographs of a jowly baby who looks like Orson Welles, nestled in the crook of Morgan's arm.

"No, the child that is to live at Loch Cottage? Has she ..."

"Yes, Fardie. She's here! She's with Iona's children."

"A good thing," he whispered, his voice fading. "Pass it on, Charlotte. Andrew and Simon Peter, the Canaanite's daughter, the ten lepers ... all that."

His eyes closed and he slept peacefully, for once.

Later that night we were in the kitchen having a sandwich and a glass of wine when we heard a noise. We rushed upstairs. He was sitting bolt upright.

" 'Ferdammt feigling', they called you – Ahh, Ah ... shot you there, on the straw. Saw it ... Had to run for it, had to. In a row ... later, they laid us in a row: Blaikie and Blair - and you, on my torn side. You were close to my agony, Ormonde. They thought I was dead, too. But one of us had to live, for Livla."

"Shhh, shhh, rest now." We laid him back down.

But he was still agitated and went on mumbling in a voice so low that we only caught occasional words.

"Murray said ... said ... told me once ... should have been my brother's keeper ... brother's keeper ... sorry Mondy ... should ... sorry, old boy ... brother's keeper."

His hand continued to move spasmodically, pleating the sheet and letting it go, pleating it and letting it go.

***

This is the week they separate the ewes from their lambs. The bewildered lambs have been herded into a pen half a mile down the valley. The sheep are up here, huddled together in appalled solidarity. They let up a universal, anguished cry. The lambs bleat back in disjointed desperation. The bleating outsounds the river. It goes on all day. It continues into the night.

There are seven bedrooms at Craigmannoch in various stages of disrepair. Some have a view over the loch to where it flows into the open sea. We could sleep in any of them now, but we always go back to the room we shared as children. It looks out across the old vegetable garden and what used to be Minnie's field. It is twelve extra stairs from the upstairs landing and a long way from the only bathroom. The lumpy beds have mahogany head and footboards that are too short for Char. But we couldn't sleep anywhere else, we wouldn't think of it.

Last night I was lying in bed when a stain on the wall reminded me of the shadow creatures. Normally Fardie only came to our room to hear our prayers, but when we had measles he slept on his army camp bed outside our door like a sentry. After dark, by the light of a torch, he made animal shapes on the wall. With his one hand and his coat sleeve he could make a swan swim across the ceiling and a crocodile that snapped its jaws. We watched, feverish but entranced. I want to tell him that I remember the shadow dance. I want to forgive him for not letting us have a light in the passage. But, more than anything else, I want him to recognize me.

Yesterday he didn't talk all day. The district nurse bathed him in the afternoon and got him to take a little food. After dinner I went upstairs to check on him. It was a beautiful evening - there had been a downfall earlier and a light hairnet of raindrops covered the roses that clambered up to the sill. From Fardie's window I could see the farm children jumping from rock to rock and searching for winkles in pools which glinted like silver coins in the evening light. I moved back to his bed and stooped to kiss him. He looked at me strangely - then gradually a softness, a look of infinite relief crossed his face.

"Sweet Livla," he said, "you've come."

"Fardie, it's me. Me, your daughter Iona. Our mother's dead." But he didn't hear a word.

"Did you touch my face, my darling?" he whispered.

I couldn't bear it ... I decided to play along, to be my mother for his sake.

"Yes, Harry," I said.

"The two little girls, Livla, they're doing well. I've got it in hand. Charlotte's brave y'know. And Iona – she's just like you."

"Good, you can sleep now. All's well."

"No! Not yet, unfinished business. I've got to go back for Ormonde, Livla. I left him behind."

He reached out and grasped my hand.

"Help me! Help me up. I think I can find the place."

"I will," I lied, laying him back down on the pillows. "I'll help you - tomorrow."

"Dearest ..." he said after a while. "Are you still there?"

"Yes, Harry."

"Don't let go of my hand, Olivia. Please ... forgive me."

"Forgive you?"

"Should have been my brother's keeper," he mumbled, "Should have taken care of him. Sorry, Livla! Sorry, dearest one ... got to go back for the boy."

"It's alright, we'll go tomorrow. Sleep now, Harry. You did your best."

"It's not clear! It's still not clear. What do you think Ormonde did?" I exploded. "And, Char, he thought I was *her* ... again! And where were those dreadful dogs?"

It was our sixth day at Craigmannoch and we were both at the end of our tether.

"I have to go to Edinburgh tomorrow", Charlotte said, tentatively. "I've been thinking - I could try to find Murray. He lives in Edinburgh, doesn't he?"

"I believe he does."

"Could you manage by yourself, Puff?"

It was a good idea. It might clarify things. I told her I'd be fine and urged her to go. Besides, Vivian was arriving the next day.

We had a difficult time tracking him down. Most of the people in Fardie's address book were crossed out. Murray himself had been crossed out several times, but the last three addresses were legible.

Sgt. Grant M. M.	Murray Grant	Murray
22, N. Bevan Road	c/o Miss Elspeth Grant	Beeches Retirement
Edinburgh	(sister)	Home
	6 Bellevue Ave	Dunarvan
	Edinburgh,	*by* Edinburgh

After Char left the next morning I went to check on Fardie. There was something different about his face. The hectic red that usually clumps around his cheeks and nose had drained away. His skin was starched and bleached like a stiff napkin.

"Fardie?"

"Wake up, Fardie dear."

"Wake up! Wake up! Wake up!"

I've never seen a dead person, except in films. I couldn't bear him to die when I was all alone. I ran the cold tap and sogged up water with his sponge. I went over to the bed and squeezed it as hard as I could, letting the water drip over his face. I put my ear up against his mouth. His faint breath came and went in a drifting, uneven vapour.

Chapter 15

1985

CHARLOTTE

I found the place with difficulty. Any beeches or view of beeches had been eclipsed by blocks of flats. It was a Victorian house adapted for the elderly with linoleum floors and ramps for wheelchairs. A strong odour of antiseptic thinly disguised the smell of wet knickers, old skin and milky tea. They showed me to the day room, and there he was in a corner by himself, drawing away contentedly with a pile of papers in front of him. He was completely bald and stooped, but otherwise easily recognizable. They'd told him I was coming and when he saw me he got up smiling broadly and holding out his hand.

We sat together for a while talking of little things. Murray told me he was well taken care of, very well indeed. He explained that the Beech View Retirement Home was known for its afternoon tea which would be along in a wee while. It would be his pleasure, he said gallantly, if I'd be his guest. I assured him that I'd be delighted.

"You'll have news of your father for me?" he asked. "I hope he is keeping well."

"He's not well at all, I'm afraid, Murray ... I don't think he's got much longer."

He nodded his head sadly. "Ah well, he'll be ready for it. Harold'll be good and ready to go to the Lord."

"But that's just it, Murray, he isn't ready at all. There seems to be so much that's unresolved. He's been mumbling about Ormonde, and we can't make out what happened. Please, can you tell me about it - the escape?"

"Your daddy was a brave man, Charlotte. He'd not a thought for hisself - saved dozens of lives in Anzio and has the DSO to show for it! But then our company was captured and we were taken by train all the way to Bebra POW camp in Germany. It was there that we made our first attempt to escape."

Murray started to cough. His chest heaved like a frail boat in a storm; he anchored himself by holding onto the arms of his chair and let it run its course. I got him some water and asked if I was tiring him.

"No indeed, it does me a world of good to talk about it. There's not many has the least interest in the war any more. Is it the escape from Bebra you're wanting to know about, Miss Charlotte?" He pointed at his pile of drawings. "I've been rectifying the plans the past forty years. If I'd had the knowledge I have today we'd have managed it."

"No, I don't think so. I mean the last escape - the one when Fardie lost his arm and Ormonde ... ? What did Ormonde do, Murray?"

"I understand. You'll be needing to know."

"Yes!"

"After we were caught trying to escape at Bebra we were in the solitary a long while - the five of us. There was me and Harold and Blair, a brave chap, affable - we'd been together since Anzio. Then there was Blaikie from Dumfries, a great wee joker, never complained. And Ormonde, who'd have followed his brother anywhere. I'd an affection for Ormonde. He was never a strong lad, but when he got out the solitary he wasn't a well man. Soon after that we learned that a lot of us - three hundred men - were to be marched to a more secure camp."

"You must have been weak before you started out, Murray?"

"Indeed, indeed. They'd had the five of us shackled in six-foot-square infested cells for fifteen days without our clothes, if you'll pardon my telling you that, just two prison blankets was all." He started coughing again. "The damp got to my lungs," he said when it calmed down. "We all lost our strength. But we were better off than young Ormonde ... they'd broken him down, you see. He'd dysentery and a temperature. He was in no fit state ..."

"So how did he manage ... on the march?"

"We'd your uncle between the two of us, Harold and me. When he faltered we gave him a wee lift along."

"Then you stopped somewhere?"

"There were that many men failing they let us rest two days in a sugar beet farm. Some Russian workers there told us about a river a mile off. They were ready to help us with a boat."

Murray stopped and mopped his forehead.

"We decided to try for it, Charlotte," he went on after a bit. "The second night we managed to hide in some straw in a nearby byre. At six in the morning we heard the guards lining the men up and setting off. But there were two rearguard soldiers - ferrets we called them - left behind. They made a thorough search, kicking the piles of beet apart and pulling up floorboards. Then one of them went outside. The other stayed behind to relieve himself and on his way out he noticed the pile of straw. He must've been prodding it with his bayonet when he struck Ormonde."

"Oh, God!"

"Young Ormonde jumped up and cried out: 'Don't shoot me! Don't shoot me!' He was sobbing, out of his mind with fear."

"*Wo sind die anderen?* the ferret shouted - Where are the others? He'd a gun against his head."

"You mean Ormonde gave you away? You mean he betrayed you?"

"It was a sorrowful thing, Charlotte. There's not a man of us knows what he'd do at a time like that."

"How did the rest of you get away then?"

"Harold and Blair sprung up and wrestled the ferret, but Blair got shot in the stomach and died on the spot. The other German came running back and grabbed Ormonde. I made a bolt for it but Harry would not move, till he saw his brother shot ... in the back of the head. It would have been a terrible sight for a gentle man like your daddy, a sore puzzlement for a man wi' a strong feeling for the right and wrong of things. "

"Oh, Murray!" I said. I could imagine it. I could see him standing there watching his brother die.

"Then he and Blaikie came after me, like we'd agreed," he went on. "But your father was slowed when they hit Blaikie. He was slowed because he picked him up. I was the only one that made it to the river."

Murray looked exhausted. I felt terribly guilty, but I had to know what happened to Fardie.

"And my father?"

"He fell - because they'd dogs, you see. It was the dogs that got him, savaged him the same side he'd been wounded in Anzio, but a great deal worse. I was in the river half up to my waist in the water, clutching onto the bank - waiting. But none of them came ..."

"It's terrible Murray, so, so terrible! But you'd have thought he'd forgive his brother, I mean he *was* his brother, I mean he ..."

"Harold was in no condition to forgive anyone, Charlotte. He was taken back to Bebra in a cattle truck for the operation. Your father had blood poisoning from the bites. He was close to his death for five months."

"But I still don't see. When the war was over, when it was all over ... why couldn't he forgive him?"

Murray sighed. "Maybe, just maybe, he'd more to forgive than we know ..."

"What are you saying?" I asked, rather too loudly.

A nurse had come in with a tea trolley. Two old ladies were looking at me disapprovingly from the other side of the day room. Murray bowed his head and shut his eyes tightly.

"What are you saying?" I asked him again.

His head looked like an over ripe tomato about to split. I could hear the cough lying in wait as his thin chest grappled with his laboured breathing. I was about to call the nurse over when suddenly he looked up and smiled at me.

"I'm saying here comes our tea, Miss Charlotte! Sardine sandwiches, scones, and they've got the Dundee cake out for us. Thank you, Nurse Mackenzie, thank you! This young lady's all the way down from Argyllshire to see me. I was telling her that you take good care of us."

***

On the drive back from Edinburgh I thought about my father returning to a gravely ill young wife and the responsibility of two babies - after all he'd been through. A gentle man Murray had said, a man who cared deeply about the right and wrong of things. Cared, I thought to myself, but misinterpreted. For years he'd subjected himself to inner torment. Loving Ormonde, yet hating him for what he'd done, longing to forgive him, but unable to pardon his betrayal. Why was it Murray could forgive and our father couldn't? That was the agony of it. He'd lived with the memory of that day for over forty years in silence and misplaced shame. 'Sorry Mondy!' he'd said at long last - and, in his confusion, he'd told Iona he wanted to go back for him.

And somehow, with all his caring deeply about the right and wrong of things, he'd got it so wrong about what was right for us: punishments, severity and silence – I ached for Fardie. I ached for his mistakes. He hadn't survived the war at all. It had broken him, just as it broke Ormonde.

I was tired. As I drove I yearned to be back at home with Iona. I knew she'd be waiting up, like a mother. I knew she'd be keeping something hot for me under the big, chafing dish cover. She's the one who has made a success of her life. She's accumulated things about her: a proper husband, children, a linen cupboard with warm, neatly folded sheets and a pantry with bottled fruit on the shelves. She's lovelier than ever - rounder, but just as lovely. Her skin is still like peaches. Her arms are warm. I need her. I couldn't go through this alone.

But I knew I would have to be careful. Little things affect her deeply - like the hare we once saw in a gin trap - after all these years she still won't walk down the gully. I decided I'd only tell her the good parts, about Fardie and Murray lifting Ormonde between them on the march, and how our father and Blair fought the German ferret with their bare hands.

By the time I got back it was late and Vivian had arrived. She was sleeping in Fardie's room on the sofa. Iona told me that she'd had a terrible scare in the morning when she'd thought Fardie was dead. She cross-questioned me about Murray's revelations. I ended up telling her everything.

"Poor, poor Fardie - and poor Ormonde," she said in a low voice. "The wickedness of it all."

"Ormonde wasn't to blame," I said. "He was ill ... he would have been a conscientious objector if he'd had the chance. His father made him fight, remember? Grandmother Eva once told me that in Ireland."

"You don't have to defend him to me."

"He must have suffered terribly."

"They both must."

We went up to bed, undressed and turned off the light. "I wonder what Murray meant," I said, half to myself. I was on the point of dropping off, but Murray's last sentence stuck in my head.

"When? What do you mean?"

"When he said, 'Maybe Fardie had more to forgive than we know?'"

Iona switched on the light between us and sat up in bed. She was flushed and a little breathless.

"It could be we'll find out tomorrow, Char. Something happened today. I was going to tell you about it at breakfast."

"What happened? Tell me now!"

"I was talking to Vivian. She says there's a trunk in the attic with Ormonde's things in it. There are letters, Charlotte, love letters to Ormonde - and a copy of one he sent. She said it was time we had a look. She told me she had tried to read one once, but felt it wasn't fair play ..."

"But why will that change things?"

"The letter she started to read, addressed to Ormonde when he was in Africa ..."

"Yes?"

"You mustn't get upset, Char."

"Go on!"

"Promise you won't?"

"I promise."

"It was from our mother."

***

"Hurry! Hurry! He wants you... I can't make out what he's saying. He's been trying to speak."

Vivian was shaking me. The room was filled with moonlight. I could just make out the dependable elephant armoire settled in its corner and the outline of our chairs, cloaked and formal in the dark.

"Hurry!" Vivian repeated. "I think this is it ..."

Iona was putting on her dressing-gown and bedroom slippers. I wrapped my quilt around my shoulders and ran. When I got to Fardie's room he was asleep. Puff curled up in a chair, still clutching her hot water bottle. We sat there for an hour or more as the stars paled into pinheads and were gradually swallowed into a curds and whey sky.

"Iona ... ? Charlotte ... ?" Our names released like slow bubbles into the quiet room.

"We're here, Fardie. We're both here."

"Both?"

"Yes, Fardie dear," Iona said, stroking his hand, "both of us."

"eeez," he said, faintly.

We looked at each other, mystified.

"eeeass!"

"Peas? Niece? We can't hear you, Fardie," I said. "Try again."

"eeese ... "

"Please?" Iona said, helplessly.

Then suddenly I got it! I put my arm around his shoulders and my mouth close to his ear.

"It's peace. Isn't that it Fardie, dear? Peace, at long last."

His pyjama jacket had somehow come undone. For the first time in our lives we saw the teeth marks ...   raised welts bumping over his narrow chest like a cart track.

He nodded, opening his eyes. Then slowly he turned his head and looked from Iona to me, and back again to her, seeing us both, understanding it was us. Not Olivia, not Ormonde - us.

"The peace which passeth ..." I began.

"Passeth ..." he repeated, his face was tranquil now, as though a hand was ironing smooth the years of agitation.

"The peace which passeth all understanding." I enunciated each syllable clearly, holding him tightly, refusing to cry.

He nodded again. His eyes remained open, as blue and unruffled as the loch on a midsummer evening. We watched them flicker once, as though a fish jumped beside the boat, then gradually the life died out of them.

Neither of us moved. As the room lightened I saw Vivian sitting by the door and realized she must have been there all along. Iona went up to Fardie and buttoned his pyjama jacket so that Vivi wouldn't have to see the teeth marks. She straightened the sheet and retreated awkwardly.

"Aren't you supposed to shut a person's eyes ... ?" I whispered. Now that it was over I couldn't stop trembling.

"I think so ..."

"You do it, Puff."

"I'm not sure that I can."

Vivian came up then. "Goodbye Harry!" she said, sliding the lid over his nearest eye with her forefinger. "Bless you, old dear." She gently lowered the other. "Open the window wider, Iona ... that's right." The early morning chorus of blackbirds, willow-warblers and thrushes came bursting into the room. Fishing boats were rocking their way in with the night's haul. "Go back to bed you two." she said. "Breakfast at eight, and then we can ring the family." We left the room like obedient children.

***

"Mark, he's dead!" Iona burst into tears.

I wasn't deliberately listening in, but I wanted to talk to Missy.

"I don't know if it was very bad," she was saying. "I've never been through anything like it. We've been finding things out, bit by bit. It's been ... shocking. Although the very end wasn't so dreadful, Mark. I mean, for the first time he was at peace. Charlotte knew what to say to him. She just knew - I didn't."

Then I heard her telling him the funeral was on Saturday, but not to bring the kids up before Friday. She told him about the letters and wandered on in an unhinged way about not being able to look at them because Fardie's body was still in the house. I was getting more and more exasperated. I couldn't possibly wait four more days to see Missy. I needed to talk to her. I overheard her asking Mark if all was well at home. Then there was a pause, an awful pause - I grabbed the telephone out of her hand.

"What's wrong, Mark? For Christ's sake! Is she alright?"

"Don't panic," he said. "Missy's fine. It's under control now."

"What's under control? What's happened? I should never have left her, never! None of you have any idea of what she's been through ..."

He told me all had gone well for the first few days, then June had found a stash of marijuana and some uppers in a pair of Missy's socks. She'd tried to deal with it herself. I could just imagine how June would have gone about it in her tactless way: 'Look kid, you're crazy. What did you think you were doing bringing this stuff into the country? The customs guys could have had you in the slammer!' Apparently Missy had stood up for herself and explained she'd brought it as a present for Finn and Hughie - 'so I'd have something to give them, so that they'd like me ...' and June had said, 'That was a bad idea, kid. A very bad idea!' At the word *bad* Missy had flipped. She'd started crying and throwing things around her bedroom, shouting 'I'm not bad! All I've had is bad, bad, *bad* ever since my Dad died. Charlotte doesn't think I'm bad ... fuck off!"

Mark had come home in the middle of all this and found June downstairs with the younger children, mortified, and Finn pacing despairingly up and down outside Missy's bedroom door. I agonized for Missy, abandoned by me, miles from anyone who understood her.

"Put her on, Mark. I need to talk to her now!"

"Calm down, Charlotte. I've told you it's all over. She's having a jumping lesson at the moment."

"How did you sort it out?" I asked.

"I took her to the stables. Stables have a soothing effect on little girls," Mark replied, "we've discovered that with Olivia. After we'd mucked out Jesse's stall and were grooming her together I said what a sweet idea it was - wanting to bring a present to the boys. Then I explained Finn didn't take drugs and suggested that it might be a bit much for Hughie at the moment, since he's so excitable."

"How did she react?"

"Oh, by that time she'd lost interest in the whole thing. She just said 'I guess!' Then I offered to hang onto the stuff till she had time to talk it over with you. She said 'I guess' again - and that was that."

"Well done," I said, grudgingly. "But please bring the children up here right away."

"You were rude to Mark, Char!" Iona said when I'd hung up. "Think of all he's done. Think of how patient he's been ... and what about the letters? Have you forgotten about them?"

"I'm sorry, Puff. You're right. Mark's been a saint. But the letters will have to wait."

Now Fardie's absence is omnipresent. The curtains are drawn and the house is soulful. 'What about the letters,' I wonder to myself. Am I procrastinating? Why is it I think about them with such trepidation?

Chapter 16

1985

IONA

Body, corpse! I hate the words. There were people in the house all afternoon, two women in black clothes laying him out, doing whatever it is they do to a dead person. He wasn't taken away until Wednesday afternoon. Not that that made a difference. His presence was everywhere, even after he'd gone. His chair, his pipe ... at one point we came across his stick.

"What'll we do with it?" Charlotte asked.

"Do with it?"

"Well, it couldn't be sold, could it? Or given away?"

"... or thumped by somebody else," I added, touching the ash handle.

"Leave it! Leave it where it is, Iona. Don't touch it!"

At breakfast it was odd not laying out his silver napkin ring with an 'H' on it, not even putting it on a tray. I couldn't get used to the fact that he wasn't going to eat porridge ever again - or kippers, or poached salmon with mayonnaise. Childish, I know. But I'd never come face to face with death before.

Then Vivian asked us to look up appropriate passages in the Bible for the funeral service.

"The Bible ... you mean his Bible?" I said.

"Of course I mean his Bible. Are you going to help me or not?"

She was busy registering his death, putting notices in the Glasgow Herald and the Scotsman, organizing the tea for after the funeral, making an appointment with Mr. Crichton, the lawyer who was to read us Fardie's will.

The Bible, we discovered, was not an inanimate object but brought back mornings bleak with boredom for me and full of argument and passionate discourse for Char. It also brought back mutual dread of our father's displeasure - and confusion. Just as I was thinking about the confusion, Charlotte said:

"Remember the Holy Ghost morning, Puff?"

I did. I had started all the trouble by saying:

'I forget which one he is, Fardie. Which picture? He isn't in our book.'

'Can't be in a picture, Iona. Think! He's a spirit ... everywhere... God's spirit on earth.'

'You mean a ghost, then,' Charlotte had said, 'like Great-Grandmother Sybil?'

'No, Charlotte, not like Sybil ...'

'Prettier than Sybil?' I'd offered up, ever interested in the superficial.

'Elsie says she's a spook if ever she saw one,' Charlotte had said, excitedly. 'Elsie says we'll not catch her walking past her picture on a dark night.'

Our father got steadily more frustrated.

'Why won't you listen? The Holy Ghost is the word of God, its meaning, its joy on earth ... its comfort' he'd bellowed out in a discomfiting way.

'I don't want him anyway, watching everything we do,' Charlotte had shouted back. 'I just want Jesus!'

'No!'

We both remembered the sequence of events and laughed, but nervously. Our father's wrath had been frightening at the time. We couldn't remember what the Holy Ghost punishment had been - ten verses of Genesis? No pudding for a week? Yet only hours ago my sister had held our dying father in her arms. *The peace,* they'd said together, *the peace which passeth all understanding.* I felt upset and confused. I still do.

***

"Why do we have to walk?" Hughie asked.

We were walking to church by the moor road. The birches and rowan-trees thin out, then there's three miles of rough track with nothing but rock, bracken and tiny wild flowers which glint in the dull green like enamel shirt studs. We passed some overgrown lambs butting their mothers, knocking them sideways. Two buzzards circled above our heads. Twice showers fell, sudden and vehement, like the spasmodic rushes of grief I feel inside my chest. Fardie's customary answer to Hughie's question popped into my head. 'To give you time to digest the sermon on the way home.' But Charlotte answered directly:

"Because we we're made to!" she said. "And it's *his* funeral and we are going to do everything he'd like us to do all day."

Hughie was disappointed. He's attached to Fardie's old Daimler. Vivian, Mark and Finn were well ahead of us. Missy was running to and fro like a spaniel and I was giving Livla a piggyback. I knew what Char was thinking. We'd had to walk to church by the moor road from the age of three. It was never explained. When we lagged behind or sat down in the heather for a rest Fardie waited, but we were not picked up.

"It was to do with good and evil," Charlotte said, interrupting my thoughts.

"I don't think there was anything particularly good about making us walk," I replied. "It made us resentful."

"I know, but it was his idea of good and he wanted it for us, desperately. Like making us kneel on the cold floor to say prayers ... no sugar on porridge - all that. He believed there was no chance of salvation from an armchair, you know."

I do know. I realize that it was his idea of good. Charlotte's been preaching at me constantly since her day with Murray. I loved him too, for God's sake! And I know how noble he was. But it was silly walking, when we could have gone in the car.

You come to a chimney-shaped rock called Dougal's Lum - then it's downhill all the way. As we approached I thought I must be dreaming. We'd anticipated a quiet service with our family and a few neighbours but, from half a mile away, we could hear the skirl of a lone piper. Then, as we got closer, we saw at least thirty men standing outside the church, proud old fellows with bandy legs, dressed in regimental kilts with heavy leather sporrans. I caught sight of Murray amongst them and realized they must be officers and men who'd fought with Fardie. They would have read about his death and the funeral in the newspaper. There were women I didn't recognize too, the soldiers' wives and widows, I imagined. They shook our hands. It was difficult not to cry - with the music, and those men who'd known Fardie loyally giving us their support.

We crushed into the small church.

The opening address was from the minister himself. He managed to work the usual warnings of hellfire and damnation into his eulogy.

"I mind well the day the Major came back from the wars! He'd the portraiture of a scrunt man, ill-thriven and weary, wi'oot his left airm and wi' a gammy leg. He came back alaine. Wi'oot his brither, young Ormonde, that perished by his side. And what did he come hame to? To find his faither deid and his mither hadden doon wi' grieving. And still he'd more to bear ... for his guidwife was afflickit and 'afore long she was deid too. Aye, it was terrible! But there was one thing yon forrin bullets couldna touch and that was his speerit, for in the past forty years I doubt there's been a Sabeth he's not come tae this very kirk to worship the Lord. And I say to you, here's a lesson fur us all ..."

Just the word lesson did it for me. I turned off and started thinking about the letters. We hadn't had a moment to look at them. I thought of them hidden away in our house all these years, letters written in proper ink, the kind you need a real nib for - words from Olivia to Ormonde ... then

Suddenly it was Hughie's moment. He had begged to read *The Charge of the Light Brigade*. We'd been against it as he's a bit of a drama queen, but he'd persuaded us it was just the thing.

Half a league, half a league,
Half a league onward,
All in the valley of Death
Rode the six hundred.

Hughie looked handsome in his passed-down MacIntyre kilt. Fardie would no doubt have grunted 'Wrong war, boy!' but he read it beautifully. He shouted out: *Forward the Light Brigade!* with bloodthirsty enthusiasm and when he recited

When can their glory fade?
O the wild charge they made!
All the world wonder'd.

I saw some of the old boys reaching for their handkerchiefs.

"Old soldiers never die, as the ballad goes," the brigadier of his regiment began, *"they just fade away.* You might think that Harold MacIntyre was such a man. He had a hard war and, after it was over, chose to live very much as a recluse. Yet, to those of us who fought by

his side in Africa and Italy and the men who were with him after his capture in Germany, MacIntyre did not fade away. Not one among us can forget the courage and goodness of the man. I am proud to be here today to honour ..."

My children aren't used to churches but none of them stirred. Despite Missy's dubious record at funerals, she too was paying rapt attention. When Finn's turn came my heart was in my mouth. He's so shy, but he'd asked if he could speak.

"My grandfather told me once ... when we were fly-fishing ... to stick to what I believed was right. He said it wasn't easy. He said that he thought he'd been wrong about some things with Mum and Charlotte. That day he taught me how to put my thumb down a fish's throat and jerk it back so it died quickly. Most people leave them - thrashing."

There was a long pause, while Finn remained at the altar swallowing and looking ahead.

"I've been thinking about that," he went on at last, "and about how terrible it must have been for him, having to kill ... real people. I loved him," he added shyly, and walked back to our pew, looking at his feet.

"Moving stuff." Mark whispered.
"Decent send off!" Vivian hissed.

***

Running feet, bare feet, muddy footprints in the hall, a sea of water beside the bath, tangled piles of dirty clothes and wet bathing towels. The house blooms, opens itself for the children. Finn's been helping with the sheep. Hughie is teaching Missy how to row - she's fallen into the loch twice but doesn't seem to mind.

In two days Mark is taking the children for a trip around the Western Isles, then we'll be alone, at last.

After they come back it will all be over. I mean Craigmannoch will be over for us. Fardie, our childhood, all over. It's hard to take it in. The house has to be sold. I feel a sudden affection for the things we can't take with us: the Esse where the three-legged cat used to sleep by the hen pail, the fat banister we slid down scorching our knickers, the bath with pipes like an organ which takes twenty-five minutes to fill.

Char will live at Loch Cottage with Missy and manage the farm, but the house and garden have to go.

When Crichton read the will we had a few surprises. Firstly, there wasn't much to bequeath. The farm has been losing money hand-over-fist so the 'everything else goes to my beloved daughters' part involved mostly broken down walls and leaking byres. In fact, Fardie had been touchingly imaginative when it came to the children. Finn is to have his fishing tackle, Hughie his medals and he suggested that Olivia will inherit our mother's portrait when we die. Then came an unexpected codicil.

"The testator of the said will, Harold Gordon Boyd MacIntyre, called me to his bedside on the second of July in this year of our Lord nineteen hundred and eighty-five, precisely eighteen days before his death. It was his wish to add a codicil. I consider it my duty ... choose to contest ... due to the fact ... testator ... circumstances ... debatably ... right mind ..."

"Oh, do go on!" Charlotte said impatiently. At last he read it out.

"The small island belonging to the Craigmannoch estate is not to be sold with the house and garden. I leave it to my adopted grand-daughter Melissa Vane."

"Sounds quite clearheaded to me!" Charlotte said, flushing with pleasure. "Any objections, Puff?"

"Of course not."

***

This morning we decided we would have a picnic on the island. Char and I went ahead with the baskets of food: baps spread with farm butter and filled with ham and lettuce, hard-boiled eggs with a paper twist of salt for each person, warm yellow tomatoes from the greenhouse, gingerbread, bottles of beer and orange squash for the children in a battered Thermos.

We pulled the light dinghy over the logs. I held the struggling little boat, my bare feet squelching in the mud, while Char heaved the baskets into the stern, settled herself on the middle plank and began putting the oars into the rowlocks. "Ready!" she shouted, and I leapt in at the last minute - funny how it comes back.

"Why didn't you come home before?" I asked her, remembering her despair after Toby died. "I wanted to help. I missed you dreadfully."

"I missed you too but I was cut off ... I'd lost the sound of His voice, you see.

"Sound?"

"Well, not the sound exactly. I'd lost the listening ... the sense of Him listening to me. It was utter isolation ..."

"Mmm!"

The rowlocks made a soft glucking sound, the oars cut into the sea with brash, even strokes. The whiskery heads of two gleaming seals appeared and disappeared behind us, following the boat. I tried to compare the ephemeral *voice* that comforts Charlotte, with the earthly ones that console me: Mark, Charlotte herself and Gareth - in a probing sort of way.

"What changed then?"

"Isn't it obvious? At the end of the day He came through."

"I suppose you mean God?"

"Yes I do, actually."

"How did He come through?"

"Sometimes, Puff, you are excessively dim."

"I don't see."

"Missy, of course. My child!"

Charlotte threw her head back. Her long fingers grasped the oars firmly. She curved her body back with each pull, abandoning herself to the rhythm. At any moment I thought she'd start singing.

"A screwed up, pot-smoking, thirteen year old is not everyone's idea of a gift from God!"

"Well, she is mine! She's all I want. I never wanted a baby, Puff. I hate washing their bottoms and hanging around waiting for them to do things properly."

"What about the other problems - drugs for a start?"

"I've touched on that already."

"What do you mean?"

"Well, yesterday evening we were up on the hill with Finn. He was showing Missy how the collies work. He's clever at it ... doesn't rush them. He speaks softly, like the shepherds: 'come bye,' 'come bye,' 'awa tae me,' 'g'back, g'back,' 'that'll do...' and Nell helped him by behaving perfectly. She's a brilliant old dog. It was heaven watching her stream up the hill, curving around the gimmers in a perfect arc, then flopping down dead still, while they bustled through the gate, like housewives pushing their way into a Sauchiehall Street sale. When one took off she was after it like an arrow, black ears flat against her head ..."

"So what's that got to do with drugs?"

"Everything! On the way home we were running down the path, pushing each other into the bracken. Below us the loch was bright with feisty, slapping waves. Missy shouted out, 'This is a high alright, Charlotte. I never had one before, just pretended!' I agreed it was about as high as you can get. Then we talked it over and decided chemicals were for the birds and she said, 'Know what? They mess with people's brains - like nerve gas in wars.' I get the feeling she's been talking to Finn."

"Since you mention Finn," I said, "Mark had an odd experience yesterday. He went to the island to watch the kittiwakes. He had to take the heavy boat because the dinghy wasn't there. Anyway, after a lot of hauling he got it in and moored it on the island. He clambered up the path to our old lookout place, planning to lie on the turf with his binoculars ..."

"Well?"

"The first thing he saw was, as he put it, Missy's tight little rear end in those tiny cut-offs she wears. She was leaning over Finn!"

"Don't tell me! They weren't ...?"

"No, it was all very innocent. She was just tickling him and Finn was laughing."

"Oh! D'you mind?"

"Char, it was a relief - I've been worried about him lately."

***

We were alone at last. Mark had left with the children on a MacBrane steamer to visit the Outer Hebrides. Vivian had tactfully taken herself off for the day, leaving us with a key to Ormonde's trunk. There was nothing to stop us.

"Today?" I said at breakfast.

"Definitely!"

"This morning?"

"It could be this morning."

"Why are we afraid, Char?"

"It's because we aren't sure we want to know."

"But I do, really ..."

"So do I."

We finished our coffee and cleared the table.

"Besides, she doesn't have to be perfect any more," Charlotte said as we were washing the dishes.

"No, she doesn't."

"We won't mind, whatever it is."

"Of course not - we aren't children ..."

The metal trunk had the initials OJBM on the lid. We dragged it out of its corner onto the sunlit wooden floor and sat down in the dust. There were quite a lot of clothes, his uniform, riding breeches, two racquets and a pair of binoculars in a leather case. We found a silk scarf wrapped around a signet ring with our family's crest on it and a gold cigarette holder. Beneath all this was a slim leather writing case with some bills and three letters in it.

"I've been thinking," Char said. "It's going to be easier if we do this in turns. Just take a letter and read it out loud, then I'll take the next one."

"You go first!"

She took the top letter and began ... sometimes she faltered, then she recovered and read on in her deep, engaging voice:

25th June, 1942

Darling,

Stolen hours, you wrote - under the cover of darkness. If you say so, but such infinitely precious hours! If we never steal again I can't regret having stolen. If I am discovered, lined up (as you describe being lined up), questioned, tortured with a beastly electric poker I still shan't regret them. Those winy lips of yours, your closeness to me, the way you tell me what we are doing ... that trick of yours of talking about it! Yesterday I thought of something you whispered in my ear - after the second time - I think you remember? I was at a bus stop, about to get onto a number 9, but I couldn't get onto the bus, just couldn't! I had to walk briskly through the park. I still feel you now, Ormonde, like silk against my skin.

If you feel guilty we will lose these hours. I'm the one who ought to and I won't. I can't! It was manna from heaven, whatever manna is. Those fluffy bits of trees that filter down in spring, perhaps, or? or something with a taste - like yours?

I should never have married. I should have waited, read the stars, and divined your existence.

But how was I to know?

I understand it's not safe to write. I promise I won't again, but just this once ... my darling Mr O, I know you love Harry. I do too, in a way. But not this way, not our way.

You ask me to promise to be good to him. I will, I swear. It will be the price I pay. And you must promise to come and stay at your frigid old house every so often, so at least I can fill your bedroom with flowers from my garden, and look at you across the table and say 'would you like some more wine, Ormonde?'

Please be safe! That's all that matters. You said 'The enemy was not only the Germans.' You said I could never understand. I think I know what you meant. The brutality? Being made to be brutal? Oh, Ormonde.

Darling Ormonde, all I can think of is our hours together, The evening in Ireland at Drumtorragh and the six and a half hours in London after H. had left, before the telephone rang.

My love,

     Livla

"Whew!" I said ...

"Good Lord! It's pretty clear ..."

"What's the date on that letter?" I asked suddenly.

"Let's see, the 25th of June, 1942. It's the summer they were both on leave."

"Nine months! It's about nine months before we were born!" I exclaimed.

"So Ormonde could have been our father," Charlotte said slowly.

"Could have ..."

"She can't have known she was pregnant when she wrote that letter."

"It was just after he'd gone back."

"For the last time ..."

I looked at the letter. It was written in a gust of passion. The slanting letters tore along the page, falling over each other.

"I don't think I mind, either way," I said after a pause. "Ormonde was so ... glamorous."

"Weak, you mean," Charlotte said.

"Yes, weak, I suppose. Although hating war isn't precisely weak."

"I meant weak from the point of view of making love to his brother's ... our father's ... wife, for God's sake!"

"Our father? Do you realize what you just said, Char? We can't be sure! Ormonde might have been our father."

"I don't think so."

"Why don't you think so?"

"Because Fardie feels - felt - absolutely feels like our father. You can't suddenly switch."

"I'm not swi ..."

"Hold on a minute," she interrupted, rifling through the case. "Here's another one. "This one is later - 28th April, 1943 - a month after we were born. Listen!"

28th April, 1943

Darling one,

You must have heard the news in the telegram we sent to Harry. Well, in case you didn't, they are here! You said to let you know if they were yours but have you ever looked at a baby, dearest Mr O? They are squiggly little furrowed creatures, not in the least like either of you ... or me! They make mewing noises and catch at the air with imitation fingers. They are girls, by the way, and thank God for that! At least they won't have to fight in a beastly war. So you see I still don't know and does it matter, really? They'll always have each other. I looked to see if one of them was carrying a miniature cigarette holder by way of identification, but no such luck!

I've given them the noblest names. Charlotte, as in Charlemagne, and Iona because it is the prettiest of all the islands. Let me know if you approve.

It was agony having them, utter hell. Like being in a vice and it went on for ages. It's hard to imagine why anyone does it willingly. They were born a month ago and bits and pieces of me still hurt. The archaic doctor wanted me to feed them, but I thought I'd done my bit. Wouldn't you agree, my sweet? Anyway, that's your preserve.

I have to say your mother's a stuffy old brute. She made me drag myself downstairs for tea to meet some neighbours and then suggested it would be better if I were wearing a dress as slacks (my black Parisian ones) were not right for Argyllshire. She's always trying to force me into decisions about the little creatures, and they've got a perfectly good nanny.

I know I promised I wouldn't write again. I know you're with Harry. But, Ormonde, I'm desperately worried. There's been no word from either of you for two months. All I know is that you are somewhere in Africa and Africa is so vast. I shut my eyes and try to imagine you trundling through the desert in a tank, or on a camel? A camel would be nicer. I think of all the glorious birds but I suppose frightful Messerschmitts and things petrify the life out of them. At night it must be beautiful? Are you lying with the flap of your tent open? Are you reading this letter in lustrous, starry, desert light? Oh, do be safe, Ormonde. Oh, do promise me you will.

I've found a photograph of us! Remember the day I was shelling peas in the garden and you came out and made me laugh? It was right at the beginning, before we knew. But there's a dazzle in the air - an invisible telephone wire between your eyes and my laugh.

Darling O, I'm listening to our Fred Astaire record; 'Must you dance, every dance ...' I'm sitting up in bed in the blue silk dressing-gown you gave me. Oh, my love, it's all taking so long, so very very long.

I dream of you. I think of you, sweet, sweet Ormonde. I hold you in my heart for ever,

Livla

For some time neither of us spoke.

"You see, Puff," Charlotte said, her voice charged with the hurt I was feeling myself, "you've got to stop sanctifying her."

"What?"

"Olivia."

"I don't sanctify Olivia."

"I'm afraid you do. You've always seen her as a nurturing young mother, wanting us, suckling us, dangling us on her Chinese silk dressing-gowned knee ... we were a wartime mistake, for God's sake!"

"I haven't felt like that for some time, actually ... I happen to know she didn't even want to breast feed."

"Squiggly little furrowed creatures - there you have it! Lucky for her she didn't have to worry about us as we had a perfectly good nanny. Lucky for her we didn't distract her from her Fred Astaire records."

Charlotte is bad at sarcasm. Her voice was breaking all over the place.

"Well, I still love her!" I said, "And I don't blame her, I would have had a love affair with Ormonde myself. Fardie was probably hopeless in bed ..."

"That's hardly the point."

"You're so tough on her - think how young she was. It happens, you know, falling in love with someone else ..."

"Actually, I love her, too." Charlotte shouted. "But, don't you see, she doesn't *have* to be perfect."

"I do see she doesn't have to be perfect. I'm the one who is saying I understand her. You're a judgemental maniac - like Fardie."

"Don't dare criticize Fardie! Think of all he went through ..."

I couldn't believe we were fighting. I couldn't believe we were sitting on the floor of the attic bawling at each other. We were just about to shut the case when I remembered there was another letter. It was in a different handwriting. There were three almost identical copies of the same letter in one envelope.

"We might as well read this while we're at it," I said, picking it up. "It won't make any difference now." I read it aloud.

2nd July, 1942

Dear Harry,

I'm dreadfully sorry, Harry, I'm sorry you had to find out and I'm terribly sorry it happened.

I quite understand if you never want to see my face again. The hell of it is that Pa won't hear of my not going back, even though I think I could get out of it, medically speaking.

This is the hardest letter I've ever had to write. The fact is I've always jolly well looked up to you, Harry. I've admired you all my life. You've been father and brother to me - got me out of terrible scrapes. I wish I had an iota of your sense and bravery. It's the damndest thing. The first time I saw her I fell in love with her, when we went to stay at Clairy, before your wedding. It wasn't her fault. It was all mine.

Nothing happened, I swear it, until this leave when you went up to see Father and left us in London. I suppose it had to do with all this ... terror. I'm not brave, Harry. I'm a bloody coward. I can't take it much longer. I suppose it was the desperation of it all - and dreading going back that broke things down between us. It's hard for a beautiful young girl like Olivia, too. Being alone and having to live at Craigmannoch most of the time with Father and Mother. A fate a hell of a lot worse than death, I'd say! But seriously, it's been too much for her, thinking you might be dead and minding about me, too. It wasn't her fault, Harry. Blame me. It was rotten of me. I'm deeply ashamed.

I love her, Harry. But when the war's over, if I make it, I swear neither of you will have to see me again. I'll go to Australia or wherever you say. Forgive me, old boy, please. I'll never see her again. You have my word.

> *Your loving brother,*
>
> *Mondy*

"Poor devil!"

"I'm thinking about that remark of Murray's," Charlotte said, "when he suggested that Fardie might have more to forgive than we knew ..."

"It all fits in."

"And remember when Fardie said 'One of us had to live, for Livla?' It was only the other day, when he was out of it, when he thought he was talking to Ormonde ..."

"You can see that apology was an agonizing letter for Ormonde to write. And think ... poor Fardie. He must have known all along."

"Known what? He knew that they'd had an affair. But did he know if we were his? Or did he spend his whole life thinking we might be Ormonde's?"

"Were we? Are we? Does anyone know?"

Tossing in waves, swept in a high tide ... I felt like a dinghy that had broken her rope, taking in water, the rudder banging uselessly. Char had her frosted look, stiff and intent. She was packing up the trunk, smoothing Ormonde's clothes with her long thin fingers. Smoothing them unnecessarily. I knew how she felt. She wanted to do something for him. He had been rotten alright. He'd got two men killed and almost a third, almost his own brother. Even the German had called him a coward - *Ferdammt feigling!* He'd died with those words in his ears. But we needed to mourn him, whether we were or weren't his daughters.

At that point they caught my eye, only a few feet from where we were sitting, rusted piles of mouths with bared teeth jumbled on top of each other. They were like Fardie's Kraut dogs, savage, designed to kill or maim - only temporarily out of use.

"Look!" I whispered.

"Gin traps!" Charlotte said, shrinking back.

We pushed the trunk back into the cupboard. We ran from the room, slamming the door behind us, clambering and skidding down the narrow steps.

Late that night, in the dark space between half-sleeping and fear of waking, a single evening came back to me - the time when Vivian got drunk and the blue knitting fell from her lap. She'd begun to tell me a story about our mother ...

I looked across at Charlotte. Her quilt was humped over part of her but an elbow stuck out and one cold foot dangled over the floor.

"I think there's more," I whispered, on the off chance that she was awake.

"Just what I was thinking," came back loud and clear from under the slipping quilt.

"Let's talk to Vivi in the morning."

"Yes, let's."

* * *

The rain fell in a silent green sheath. We sat having breakfast with Vivian. It was unusually quiet. The grandfather clock had stopped when Fardie took to his bed and none of us knew how to wind it. It's hard to gauge yourself at Craigmannoch without the familiar chimes.

"We've read the letters," Charlotte said abruptly, cutting into the silence. "Vivi, you've got to tell us who our father was. You've got to tell us now."

Vivian looked at us, nonplussed for once.

"I don't know." she said. "I knew about the affair ... I've realized for years that Ormonde *could* be your father. It is a possibility. But I don't actually know, kiddos - take it or leave it."

"Didn't you ever talk about it with Fardie? All the time we were growing up?"

"I broached it once - tried to get it out of him. But all he would say was that it didn't matter ... he told me he thought of the word father in the biblical sense. Personally, my bet is on Harry," she went on more cheerfully, as if we were talking about a steeplechase. "You're the spitting image of him, Charlotte - same frown, same temper. Ormonde didn't have a temper. He was the gentlest boy, hated Father's shouting, wept when Harry got a beating. He abhorred violence of all kinds, shooting, snares ... traps."

"My bet is on him too!" Charlotte said.

"And mine," I said after a while. It came to me slowly - like drops from an IV filtering into my veins. I felt more related to Fardie than I ever had before.

"Got to feed the nanny goat," Vivian said, getting up.

"What goat?"

"I thought it would be nice for Missy to have a goat."

"But I'll be looking after nine hundred sheep!" Char said. "The last thing she needs ..."

"Of course she needs a goat!" Vivian snapped. You're as bad as Morgan thinking Oran doesn't need goslings."

***

"Wait, Vivi! Wait - please!" I said. "You started to tell me once, that time we were up here together ... about when Olivia summoned you? Called you up to her room?"

"That's true, Puff dear," Vivian said more kindly, sitting down again and reaching for her cigarettes, "although it makes me ashamed to have to tell you what happened."

"We'll understand," Charlotte said. "It can't be any worse," she added doubtfully.

I wanted to go and sit beside her, to hold onto her while we listened to what Vivian had to say - but neither of us moved.

"The fact is, by the time you were about twenty months old, you were pretty darned sweet," Vivian said, "running around picking up lambs twice your size. Then one day you escaped, absolutely vanished. Elsie was distraught and roped me in to look for you. We searched in all your favourite places - then suddenly we heard sounds from Olivia's room. We were amazed."

"Why were you amazed?"

"You never went there. It was forbidden. I don't think you really knew she was your mother. Besides, she was very ill by then - she only had weeks to go.'"

"So tell us! What happened?"

"We rushed in and there you both were on her bed, clambering all over her. She'd given you her hats to play with and fastened her pearls round your fat little neck, Iona. She was lying back on her pillows with an odd blueish pallor, but laughing ... laughing again, like she used to."

" 'Come away ye wee devils,' Elsie said scooping you up. 'I'm right sorry, Mrs. Harry, I'll put the pretty things back ...' "

" 'Oh, let them keep the hats. Oh, please let them keep everything ... ' "

I didn't need to look at Char - I could feel her smile, like sun on my arms.

"After that she asked for you when she wasn't in too much pain. Then she sent for me. I remember it clearly. 'Viv, darling,' she said, 'hold my hand, please!' She told me she had something important to ask me. I must have said I'd do whatever I could. That was when she ..."

"Go on, please!"

"That was when ..."

"Please!" we almost shouted.

" 'I know all about your baby, Viv dearest,' she said to me. 'It's the saddest thing in the world, but I want to ask you to try ... try to love mine.' I must have flinched. I was frightened, you see. You reminded me ... it was only five years since I'd lost my own baby. Anyway, then she gave me instructions."

"Instructions?"

" 'All you have to do is lie on the floor,' she said. 'It's easy, just lie down and let them sit on you. Then, you see, it happens ... they put their hands on your cheeks. It happens by itself. And it's heaven. It's utter heaven.' She was crying. She told me she'd wasted months of getting to know you. She begged me to try."

"I told her I would. But I couldn't do it - just couldn't."

"Of course not - after all you'd been through with Morgan," I said quickly. "So was that all? Was that the end of it?"

"No! Several days later Elsie came running up to me when I was feeding the geese. 'Mrs. Harry's in a dither, Miss Vivian, greetin' her heart out. She's been asking for you, she'll no take no for an answer.' "

"When I got to her room she was sitting up in bed - terribly thin - terribly white. Her skin was almost transparent ... she was fading, like a flower that's dropped out of a basket, trodden under a boot."

" 'Did you do it, Vivi? Did you lie on the floor?' she asked me. Her beautiful voice came out in hoarse gasps. I've never felt more ashamed in my life."

"Oh, God ..."

" 'I'm sorry!' I told her. 'I'm terribly sorry, Livla, but I couldn't. Harry will take care of them. I'm hopeless at that kind of thing. I'm another knotted-up Scottish disaster. You once told me so yourself.'"

"'Harry won't be good at it. He's too ... destroyed,' she said, 'I love you, Viv. They'll love you too, if only you'll let them. Help me, help me, I'm dying ...' "

"It was horrifying!" Vivian's voice shook, but she plunged on. "I must have told her that I'd do my best."

"'Promise?' she whispered, as I left the room. 'Promise?'"

"So I went straight up to your nursery and lay down on the floor."

"What did we do?"

"I don't remember. I expect you were sick on me."

"You mean it wasn't a sudden, glorious, womb-tugging, bonding event?" Charlotte asked.

"No! But you know how it is? She was right. You started trailing around after me, hugging my legs, picking the heads off flowers for me and, well, the fact of the matter is that it did work - both ways. It wasn't such a tall order after all."

I held my breath. "Did you tell her, Vivian? Did you tell her it had worked?"

"I did, Puff, just in time. Then, at the very end, she got Harry to bring you to her one by one - to say goodbye."

"One by one," Charlotte repeated. She said the words with reverence, as if she were memorizing them for a play, as if they were part of a very long prayer.

As for me, I couldn't think clearly. A cherry tree was shaking in the wind, a whole orchard was shaking. Olivia had said goodbye to us, one by one. The light white flowers went on and on coming.

Printed in the United Kingdom
by Lightning Source UK Ltd.
106225UKS00001B/289-432